The Rose Without a Thorn

The Rose Without a Thorn

JEAN PLAIDY

Harper Weekend

The Rose Without a Thorn
Copyright © 1993 by Mark Hamilton as Literary Executor
for the Estate of the Late E. A. B. Hibbert.
All rights reserved.

Published by Harper Weekend, an imprint of HarperCollins Publishers Ltd

Originally published in the United Kingdom by Robert Hale Limited in 1993

Published in Canada by HarperCollins Publishers Ltd in this
Harper Weekend trade paperback edition: 2012

HarperCollins books may be purchased for educational, business,
or sales promotional use through our Special Markets Department.

HarperCollins Publishers Ltd
2 Bloor Street East, 20th Floor
Toronto, Ontario, Canada
M4W 1A8

www.harpercollins.ca

Library and Archives Canada Cataloguing in Publication information is available
upon request

ISBN 978-1-44341-260-5

Printed in the United States

RRD 9 8 7 6 5 4 3 2 1

Contents

The Scribe

She is young, beautiful and very frightened.

She said to me: "It is coming nearer. I feel it all about me. There will be no way out. It will be as it was with my cousin Anne. Why did I not see it? Tell me."

I answered: "Your Majesty must not distress yourself. The King loves you as he loved none other . . . not even your cousin."

The long-lashed hazel eyes regarded me intently.

She answered: "He loved her much in the beginning. He defied the Church for her sake. He sent good men to their deaths because of her. And then he ordered her to be killed. The same fate awaits me. I can already see the executioner's axe ready for me."

"There is no need . . ." I began.

"There is every need," she replied. "I know you love

me. I know you speak out of regard for my feelings. You would give me cheer. But it remains, and there is one thing I would ask of you. The desire has come to me to set it all down, to see it all in clarity, just as it happened. Mayhap it could have been different. I could have been happy with Thomas. He is waiting for me . . . even now. If I had never gone to Court . . . if only the King had never looked my way . . . if only I could go back to the time when it had all begun. No, right to the beginning, those first days—that day when I left my father's home at Lambeth, before I went to my grandmother in Horsham . . . yes, right to the very beginning, mayhap I could then discover where I might have saved myself. But I am not good with the pen. I was never tutored as I should have been."

"Your Majesty would indeed find such writing an arduous task."

"Yes. And you are my good friend. That is why I ask you to help me in this."

"I? How so?"

"You are a good scribe. It would be an easy task for you. I have a conviction that there will be some time for us to be together in the weeks to come. It will turn my thoughts from what awaits me. I shall tell you how it happened—scene by scene—and you shall write it down as it should be written, for you will know well how to do that. Then you will read to me what I have said, and I shall say, 'Yes, that was how it was.' And I shall say to myself, 'This . . . or that . . . is the way I should have gone.'"

"I think Your Majesty will tire of this ere long."

She shook her head. "I shall not tire, my good friend, for I want so much to see it as it was. Mayhap Thomas will see it. It will help him to understand that, whatever happened before, he was the one I loved."

Her lips trembled and she hesitated for a while before she said with emotion: "And I shall do so as long as there is breath in my body."

I bowed my head and said: "I shall be ready to start as soon as Your Majesty commands."

The Duchess Calls

I see now that it began when I went to my grand-mother's house in Horsham. That was a long time ago but, without doubt, that was the move which set me on the path which led me to where I stand today. There was nothing I could have done about it. I was a child and such decisions were not made by me. If I had possessed a different nature, if I had not been so ready to love and trust, I might have been wise enough to avoid the pitfalls; but we are as God made us, and what was irresistible temptation to me could have been thrust aside with ease by some. The road is laid before us and we must pass along it, and, through ourselves, come to salvation—or damnation.

Before that significant event, my carefree days were passed in the midst of my large family. There were eight of us children. I was the fifth in order of age, having three brothers and one sister older than myself, and, in time, three sisters younger.

Looking back, it seems that those days were made up of unalloyed pleasure. The fact that we were very poor did not worry us. We lived in a once grand house in Lambeth, by the river, and our overgrown garden ran down to the water's edge.

What did we care that the house was in need of repair, that there were not enough servants to look after us, and that those who were there were either faithful retainers or stayed because they needed a roof over their heads? Our clothes were torn or patched. Indeed, it was often difficult to know which was patch and which original garment.

Sometimes there was not enough food to go round and we must eat sparingly. We had no tutors, no governesses. We ran wild and we were free. We played our games: often hide-and-seek which was played in an ancient house, fast falling into ruin, and was very exciting; we danced and sang, which I particularly enjoyed; and we were very happy.

The family fortunes had declined with the coming of the Tudors. My great-grandfather, the first Duke of Norfolk in the Howard family, had supported Richard III and had died with the King on the field of Bosworth. The inevitable outcome was that, when Henry VII came to the throne, he confiscated the family's estates and titles.

However, my grandfather distinguished himself at Flodden Field, where he secured a great victory over the Scots, and his titles and estates were then restored to him by Henry VIII.

My father also fought in the battle at Flodden and, as a reward for his share in the victory, he was awarded the Controllership of Calais. This helped to relieve his poverty to some extent, but he needed more than his remuneration for this post to keep his family and to settle the enormous debts he had accumulated.

He was away from home often, which was a blessing, for it helped him to escape from the creditors who were constantly pursuing him.

So we remained poor but happy. Perhaps it was my nature to be happy. I know I was during those years when I was rushing towards disaster. I certainly had hours of great pleasure, and that is surely happiness. It is one of the reasons why I find it so hard to face this terrible fate which has come upon me.

In those days, I saw little of my father, for he was often in Calais. My mother sometimes accompanied him; and when she was home, she seemed either about to have a child or had just had one. She was loving and kind when I did see her, but I think she found the hardships she had to endure in the Lambeth house not to her liking; and I guessed this was due to the fact that it was very different to the house in which she had been brought up. She was the daughter of Sir Richard Culpepper of Hollingbourne in Kent. There were occasions when some members of her father's household travelled to London, and naturally they must visit us, and I knew then that my mother was ashamed of the squalor in which we lived.

I remember one occasion very well because, with the visitors from Hollingbourne, came Thomas Culpepper. He was a sort of cousin, a little older than I. I thought him wondrously handsome in a rather angelic way. He had the clear features portrayed in a Greek sculpture and such graceful manners. I knew at once that he came from a well-ordered home, quite different from ours; perhaps that was why he seemed to enjoy our free-and-easy manners so much.

We played games. Hide-and-seek was a favourite for, as I said, the large, untidy house and the neglected gardens provided wonderful places in which to hide.

Thomas and I went off to hide together. I showed him the shrubbery, which was especially overgrown, even compared with the rest of the place, and we had to force our way through the shrubs.

"Why do your gardeners not take better care of it?" asked Thomas.

"Nobody looks after anything here," I replied. "We are too poor to pay for it."

Thomas looked at me in dismay and, seeing a fallen tree trunk, I sat down on it, and prepared to enjoy the company of my exciting young kinsman.

I said: "This is as good a place as any to hide. We should hear anyone approaching." And I signed to him to sit beside me.

"I thought the Howards were a very important family," he said. "The Duke of Norfolk is at Court and close to the King."

"That does not mean we are not poor. You can see that, can you not?"

"I can indeed," said Thomas.

"I heard one of the serving men say some beggars in the streets have more than we have."

"Poor Katherine," he said. "And you are so pretty."

That pleased me, and I wanted more compliments. I looked down at my dress, and I said: "My dress is threadbare. Soon it will be impossible to patch it. All our clothes are patched, and they say that my father goes to Calais to escape his creditors."

"It's a shame," replied Thomas. "So your father goes away . . . and your mother?"

"There are times when she goes with him."

"I know that she is too ill to go now."

"Yes, she stays in her chamber most of the time."

"It is the reason for our being here. They thought we should come to see her before we had word summoning us."

I must have looked bewildered, for he turned to me and, putting his hands on my shoulders, looked intently at me.

"Yes," he said, "you are very pretty, Katherine Howard."

Then suddenly he kissed me.

I was very pleased, so I returned his kiss.

My sister Margaret said that I showed affection too readily. It was not the way in which a Howard should behave. I did not agree with Margaret. What was wrong with showing people that you liked them, if you did? For one thing, they usually liked you in return, which was surely good.

Thomas looked somewhat embarrassed and drew away from me.

"Do you think we shall be found here?" he asked.

"It is not easy to find people in the gardens."

I wanted to know more about him, so I went on: "My brothers are always talking about going to Court. Do you want to go to Court?"

"I think I shall go," he answered. "They are trying to find a place for me, but it is not easy."

"You would see the King."

"That would be most exciting . . . particularly now."

"Why now?"

"There is all this talk about the 'secret matter.'"

"Tell me about it," I said, nestling up to him.

"It is said the King wants to divorce the Queen."

"Divorce her?"

"Yes. Send her back to Spain so that he can marry the Lady Anne Boleyn."

"Why doesn't he?"

"The Church won't let him."

"I thought the King could do anything he wanted to."

"That is what he reminds them. The Cardinal is involved. They say it augurs no good for him. There are such comings and goings. It must be very exciting to be there."

"Tell me all about it."

He smiled at me and I thought he was going to kiss me again. I waited, smiling and hopeful. But his mood seemed to change suddenly.

He stood up. He said: "Come. They must have given us up by now." And though I must have shown my disappointment, he was determined. He started to run.

"I'll race you to the house," he said.

A few days later, he left with his family; and it was shortly after that when my mother died.

∼

We were a house of mourning. My father came home from Calais and stayed for a long time. Life did not change very much. I was sure my father deplored the fact that his children did not live as gentlefolk should, but there was nothing he could do about it and he was still in fear that those from whom he had borrowed money would descend upon him, demanding payment.

Then he married again. Her name was Dorothy Troyes and it may be she brought him some dowry, but we still continued to live as before. The new wife must have tried to bring a little order into the establishment, but, with so many children and the house in such ill repair, she found it a hopeless task.

However, change was about to come for me.

My grandfather, the second Duke of Norfolk and hero of Flodden, had died some time before but that had made no difference to our financial position. He had had eight sons by his first wife, and three by his second, one of whom was my father, and there were also daughters, so very little came my father's way.

Then one day the Dowager Duchess of Norfolk, my grandmother, decided to visit her son, probably to inspect the new wife.

There were some rather futile attempts to clean up the place for the Duchess's arrival, accompanied by an unusual amount of activity in the kitchens. We children watched from a hidden vantage-point, over-awed by the coming of this very important lady.

She sat in state in the hall, which had once been magnificent, with its vaulted ceiling and the weapons hanging on the walls. I noticed with certain relief that she was sitting on one of the few chairs which were not broken in any way. It had an engraved back, and arms on either side. She looked very regal.

She inspected all the children who stood before her, inarticulate and fearful lest we should give the wrong answers when she addressed us. Her eyes lingered on me and I was greatly alarmed, fearing there must be something particularly wrong with me which had displeased her. Therefore it was with trepidation that I later received a summons to appear before her in the hall.

My father was with her, and he smiled at me encouragingly. He had always a kindly smile for us whenever he saw us, but I never failed to feel that he was rather vague about us. He knew we were his children, but I doubted whether he could put a name to most of us.

Now he said: "Katherine, Her Grace would speak with you."

I curtsied in her direction and waited with apprehension.

"Come here, child," she commanded.

I approached. Although aging, she was quite handsome, and clearly took pains with her appearance, for she was most elegantly dressed. There were several rings on her fingers, and she was holding a stick, the handle of which was set with stones which looked like emeralds.

"Come closer," she said.

I obeyed and she went on: "Hmm. Pretty child. And knows it, I doubt not. Do you, child?"

I did not know what to say to that, so said nothing.

"Do you? Do you?" she went on with a hoarse chuckle.

"Yes, Your Grace," I answered meekly.

That made her laugh. "Truthful, eh? That is good. But what a state you live in, Edmund. No way to bring up children. I hope the child remembers she's a Howard. Do you?" she demanded of me.

"Yes, Your Grace," I said again.

"Come closer."

I obeyed.

"Sit on the stool where I can see you."

Then she addressed my father.

"This matter will have its effect on the family."

"Do you think it will come to pass?"

"Of a surety it will. The King has set his heart on it, and none will dare gainsay him."

"And Anne?"

The Duchess smiled complacently. "I have spoken with her." Her eyes shone. "I am proud of her. She will have her way. He is dancing to her tune. We shall have the coronation soon. Think of it, Edmund. My granddaughter, Queen of England. She is a girl in a million. They knew that well enough at the French Court. I've heard Francis himself had an eye on her. But she knew how to deal with that. I tell you, she is a clever girl. That affair with Northumberland, that would have been a good match in itself. But this . . . this is beyond all our hopes."

My father said: "There are many against it."

"Edmund! That's the trouble with you and always

has been. You are timid. That is why you are here . . . in this place. Controller of Calais!" She gave a short, derisive laugh. "This will change everything. You will see."

"Shall you go back to Horsham?"

"For the time. Then, when it is all signed and sealed, my plans will doubtless change."

I was wondering why she had sent for me that I might sit on a stool and listen to this conversation between her and my father, of which I had no understanding, when she said: "This little Katherine reminds me of her in some degree."

"What?" cried my father. "She is not highly educated . . . unaccustomed to Court manners, I am afraid."

"That is indeed so, but there is something. I shall not forget little Katherine. Come here," she added to me.

I rose and stood before her. She touched my cheek lightly with her finger.

"Yes," she said. "There is that certain quality with the Howard women. I saw it at once here in this one."

I was so bewildered that I had no idea what was expected of me when my father intervened suddenly, saying: "You may go now, Katherine. Her Grace is tired and will wish to rest."

I curtsied and, as I turned to go, I noticed that the Duchess was watching me, smiling and looking rather pleased.

It was all very strange and, although I felt it meant something, I could not be sure what; and, as I was apt to think only of the moment's pleasure, I very soon ceased to think about the visit of the Dowager Duchess of Norfolk.

~

My stepmother sent for me. She wished to talk to me. She was smiling and looking rather pleased. I felt she was almost a stranger to us. She had been with my father in Calais for much of the time since her marriage and only now was she getting to know the family into which she had married.

"You are very fortunate, Katherine," she said. "Indeed, I would say you are a very lucky little girl."

I waited expectantly.

"Your grandmother, the Duchess of Norfolk, has taken a liking to you. She feels that it is not good for you to stay here." She lifted her shoulders and looked disparagingly round the room. "So . . . she is offering you a home with her."

"With my grandmother!" I cried in dismay, remembering the autocratic old lady, sitting upright in her chair, addressing me.

My stepmother nodded. "It is a great opportunity. You will find Horsham very different from here." Again there came that disparaging look.

"You mean, I am going away . . . from home?"

It had suddenly become very dear to me, with all its squalor and deprivations—and its comforting freedom.

"You will look back on this place and wonder how you could have endured it."

I was surprised that she could talk thus of her new home and the family which she had willingly accepted as her own; or was it willingly? Had the Troyes thought it good for their daughter to marry into the Howard family? Even to such an impoverished member of it?

"I would rather stay here," I said.

"My dear child, you speak with folly! The Duchess has a fine establishment in Horsham. She also has a mansion in Lambeth, but it is to Horsham you will go."

"Oh, no . . . please . . ."

"It is your father's wish. He has long been anxious about you children, and hoped that one of the illustrious members of your family would help in this way."

"But why me?"

"Because Her Grace took a liking to you. Come. You must not be foolish. You must rejoice in your good fortune."

"I like being here with my brothers and sisters."

"There is not one of them who will not envy you."

"Must I go?"

She nodded. Then she laughed.

"Oh, you are indeed foolish, to be the smallest bit downcast. This is great good luck for you. You will grow up as a Howard should. I know it is great distress to your father that he could not give his family what by right of birth should be theirs. You must never forget that you belong to the Howard family, which is one of the foremost in England. The Howards have been close friends of kings and would have remained in favour if they had not been true to the House of York. They have always been loyal upholders of the Crown, and if York had not been defeated by Tudor, they would have continued in their glory. It was a Duke of Norfolk who carried Richard III's sword of state at his coronation."

"I know," I said. My mother had told me that many times. Were they not always reminding me of the importance of the family?

She was not to be diverted. I expected she had had to listen to such talk when she had been persuaded to marry a man who could offer her, along with a ready-made family and a life of poverty, a famous name.

"Your grandfather was committed to the Tower because he was loyal to a king to whom he had sworn allegiance, and you know he was robbed of his titles and estates because of this. Fortunately for him, King Henry VII was an astute man and recognized his qualities, and after Flodden, he restored him to favour."

It had been told to me many times, I reminded her.

"Your grandmother, the second wife of this illustrious duke, is now offering you a home with her. You cannot be so young and ignorant as not to realize what this means. The Duchess would be received at Court. Who knows, there might be a time when you could go there. Imagine that—especially now, when your cousin might be very highly placed. So you are a foolish child indeed if you do not rejoice in this great good fortune which is to come to you."

"When am I to go?"

"The Duchess is already sending those who will conduct you to her house. You will not take much with you." She smiled ruefully. "What have you to take? Not those patched gowns of yours, certainly. Oh, you will find it very different in the household of the Duchess! She is sending grooms and there will be a woman to look after you. It is all settled and soon you will have said goodbye to all this." She waved her hand disparagingly. "You will be living the life which will be right and proper for a young girl of such a family as that to which you belong."

～

My brothers and sisters were clearly envious. "Our grandmother of Norfolk," they said. "Why, this could mean you have one foot in the Court."

I tried to imagine what it would be like at Court. Dancing, singing, fine clothes and a glimpse of the

King who, so I had heard, was big, strong and handsome. There was talk about a "secret matter," which must be very exciting, particularly because my own cousin Anne was involved in it.

Of course, my grandmother would be there. She had changed in my imagination from the formidable old lady and become young and beautiful, exquisitely gowned, taking me to Court with her. I must make the deepest curtsy I had ever made to the King . . . and the Queen, the lady from Spain, who had been married to the King's brother before he died. I was surprised that I could remember so much of that, for I had listened only vaguely in the past.

So, I forgot my fears and basked in the envy of my siblings, and on that day when the little cortège arrived at Lambeth, prepared to take me on the journey to Horsham, I was in a mood of eager anticipation.

Nights in the Long Room

I was overawed by the grandeur of my new home and, as we approached the great stone edifice, with its battlemented towers and embrasures, I felt a touch of nostalgia for the one I had left.

We passed through the gates and were in a cobbled courtyard. There seemed to be people everywhere, chattering, laughing, and all very interested in our arrival.

One girl cried out: "'Tis Her Grace's granddaughter. She is come."

They clustered round me, laughing, familiar, friendly.

"Her Grace did say that Mistress Katherine Howard should be brought to her as soon as she arrived."

"Marry, she did," said another.

One of the men lifted me down from my horse. I felt tired and a little unsteady after riding far that day; but I was very excited.

They surrounded me as we went into the hall, which was like ours at Lambeth, built in the same style, extending, I imagined, the whole length of the house; but the timbers in the roof here were more elaborately carved. At one end of the hall was a dais on which was a long table; and there were big windows looking out over lawns. The weapons on the walls were highly polished and, as I looked round and compared this hall with the one I had just left, I realized afresh how dingy and neglected ours had become.

There was little time to dwell on comparisons, for I was hustled through a door and, with a girl on either side of me, taken up a staircase, through a gallery and up more stairs until I arrived at what I guessed to be the Duchess's apartments.

She was seated and seemed as regal as she had in the hall at Lambeth. She looked as though she had just awakened from a doze.

One of the girls who had escorted me remained beside me, the other left us.

The girl who was with me curtsied to the Duchess and said: "Your Grace. Mistress Katherine Howard is come."

The Duchess yawned and looked about her as though not quite sure where she was. Then she said: "Ah, Katherine Howard." She seemed as though she were trying to recall who I was. "So, here you are. Pretty child. Tell me, how old are you?"

"I am ten years old, Your Grace."

"Very young. But it was no place for you in your father's house. You'll be better here."

"Thank you, Your Grace."

"Yes, you do have a look of your cousin. It is hard to say what, but it's there. The Howard look. We can hope you do as well as she has." She laughed. "You could not do that, of course, but I see a bright future for you. Too young to go to Court yet."

She laughed again suddenly. "You lack the grace of your cousin. You may see her one day. Then you will understand what I mean by that. But you do have a look of her. The Howard look. I saw that at once. You could have stayed there in your father's house and been passed by. You're too pretty for that."

She yawned again and half closed her eyes. I did not know what I was expected to do, and suddenly I wanted to be back with my brothers and sisters— even with my elder brother, who despised us younger ones, and my domineering sister Margaret, who did everything better than I did. Yes, I was already thinking lovingly of the squalor and dingy hangings, the unpolished furniture, the meals that were never on time and scanty when they did come.

My grandmother seemed to remember why she had sent for me, for she suddenly said to the girl who had brought me to her: "Isabel shall look after her. Go and bring Isabel to me."

The girl disappeared and my grandmother half closed her eyes again, and there was nothing else for me to do but study the room while I awaited the arrival of Isabel.

Through an open door, I saw the bedroom containing a large four-poster bed with bed curtains in elaborately embroidered material. I could glimpse an ornate carved chest. The walls of the room in which I waited were covered in tapestries which depicted battles, in which I presumed members of the family had taken part and scored successes. There was a painting of a very splendid gentleman, whom I guessed to be my grandfather, the second Duke of Norfolk.

I studied him intently, remembering that he was my father's father, who had been a prisoner in the Tower of London until Henry VII, the present King's father, realized he should be working for him instead of being his prisoner, and then he had won the Battle of Flodden Field and worked with the King ever since.

The girl who brought me to the Duchess then came in with another young woman of about seventeen years of age, buxom and lively looking; she had light green eyes, closely set together, and rather thin lips that were not in accord with the rather frivolous nature with which I was to become familiar.

Isabel made a deep curtsy to my grandmother and said: "Your Grace sent for me."

"Ah," said my grandmother, rousing herself from what seemed to have been a delightful dream which she was reluctant to leave. "Isabel, this is my granddaughter, Mistress Katherine Howard. She is come to live with us. You will see that she is looked after as becomes her rank."

"Yes, Your Grace."

"You will show her where she will sleep."

"Your Grace will have given orders."

The Duchess yawned again and nodded. "You will look after her and show her the customs of the household. Now, you may take her away."

"Yes, Your Grace."

Isabel looked at me and smiled, and we both made a deep curtsy to my grandmother. We went out together, followed by the girl who had first taken me to my grandmother's apartment.

As soon as the door shut, Isabel and the other girl laughed silently, and Isabel said: "Mistress Katherine Howard, of the great Howard family, I shall be your guide and I shall make it my pleasure to attend you."

We had moved away from the door as the girls' laughter was no longer silent. I thought this was all rather odd, but it seemed jolly, and I said: "Thank you, Isabel."

"I am going to show you how we live here, Mistress Howard. We have good fun, do we not?" she asked of the other.

There was a nodding of heads and secret smiling.

"We shall have to remember that you are Mistress Katherine Howard, of course."

That made them laugh again, and then they put on rather prim looks, which I understood were not to be taken seriously.

I expected to be taken to my apartment, but Isabel quickly discovered that none had been prepared for me and that I was to sleep in the Long Room.

That seemed to amuse Isabel. In fact, I was discovering that a great deal amused her.

My memories of that day are a little hazy. I ate dinner at a long table in the hall near the kitchens. Isabel sat beside me and there was a great deal of chatter among the young people. Isabel told them that I was the Duchess's granddaughter, Mistress Katherine Howard—one of the family and "please do not forget it," she added, at which they all laughed.

They were friendly enough and some of the men—and one of the girls—told me I was very pretty; and one of the men added that I should find much that was interesting here; and that seemed to amuse most of them. All I had to do, they said, was grow up . . . just a little . . . but not too much.

A good deal of what they said seemed to have a hidden meaning which I could not understand but which to them seemed very funny, and I was so fascinated by all these people that I forgot to be homesick.

By evening time I was very sleepy. Isabel had been my companion all through the day. She showed me the house and the grounds, and introduced me to people always with the words: "Mistress Katherine Howard, the Duchess's granddaughter." And she always added: "Pray, do not forget she is a Howard." Then they would laugh. I could not understand why.

Isabel noticed how tired I was.

"Marry," she said, "'twas a long journey. You need to sleep."

"Thank you," I replied. "Will you be so kind as to show me my bedchamber."

"I have learned," replied Isabel, "that you are to sleep in the Long Room with the rest of us, as no separate apartment has been prepared for you. The Duchess must think you are so young that you need me to be near you in case you should need anything. Did you sleep alone in your home?"

"No. With my sisters."

"So you have sisters. And brothers?"

"Yes."

"Did they sleep in the same bedchamber?"

I saw that look in Isabel's eyes which I already knew meant she was enjoying some secret joke.

"Oh no," I said. "Just my sisters."

"Well, you will not be lonely in the Long Room, I promise you. I will take you now. Then you can fall asleep before the others come to bed."

"What others will there be?"

"The other ladies. All those of us who attend upon Her Grace. We have one large room in which we sleep. The Long Room. I will show you."

She took me up some stairs. The Long Room was almost at the top of the house.

I looked at it in amazement. It was indeed long, and there were two rows of beds in it. On some of them lay garments.

My first thought was one of relief. I had imagined myself sleeping in some ghostly chamber alone. I should have plenty of company here.

I turned and smiled at Isabel and she returned my smile.

"Here you will have some amusement," she said. "And, Mistress Katherine Howard, I believe you are of a kind to enjoy the fun. This will be your bed. Here . . . at the end. I shall draw the curtains about it so that you will not be disturbed when the others come to bed. Then you will quickly recover from your long journey."

"I am sure I shall, and, to tell the truth, I like not to sleep alone."

That amused her again. "No, you are not of that kind, Mistress Howard." She hesitated. "Some of the girls can be very merry. Heed them not. Just sleep tonight, and tomorrow you will feel as fresh and well as you ever did, I'll warrant."

Isabel had drawn the curtains. I was exhausted by the long journey and my new experiences. I soon fell into a deep slumber, completely unaware that the first step towards my ultimate doom had been taken.

～

It is not the following days which live in my memory . . . but the nights; and it was on my second one that I first witnessed some of the strange scenes which occurred in the Long Room after the household had retired.

I had gone early to bed and lay there with the curtains drawn, as Isabel had advised, because, she said, the ladies were apt to forget how late it was when they came to bed and when others, like Mistress Katherine Howard, might be wanting to sleep.

I was not so tired as I had been on the previous night, yet it was my custom to fall asleep as soon as I lay down, and this I did, to be awakened some time later by the sound of low laughter.

I opened my eyes. I could see the light of some candles through a gap in the bed curtains, and I lay there listening.

People were talking in low voices; there was a good deal of giggling and what I imagined to be suppressed laughter. I lay in my bed, wondering what was happening beyond my curtains.

I guessed that several of the girls were awake. Certain sounds made me wonder whether there was some sort of feast. I could contain my curiosity no longer. I must see what was happening out there.

I slipped out of bed, stood close to the bed curtains and, very cautiously, parted them.

It was a strange scene. A number of the girls were sitting up in bed. I could not believe that I saw aright, for the girls were not alone. Young men were there. Some of them were lying on the beds, their arms about the girls.

I had been right. They were eating and drinking. Several held goblets in their hands and it was clear that they were having a very happy time.

I could not understand why the young men were there. They had their own apartments, surely. Some of the men were familiar to me, for I had already seen them about the house. The Duchess had a big retinue of people to serve her, and among these were the young men and women of lesser houses whose parents sought to introduce them into a ducal establishment.

They were whispering together and, young as I was, I was old enough to know that they were doing something which, if it reached the ears of those in authority, would bring dire punishment upon these men and girls. I was stunned, shocked; and I knew they must not catch me spying.

I went silently back to bed and lay there shivering—not with cold, but with fear. I was asking myself what I ought to do about this startling discovery.

~

The next day, Isabel said to me: "I saw you last night. You were peeping through the curtains. What did you see?"

I felt myself flushing.

"Come, Mistress Howard," urged Isabel. "You must tell me."

I stammered: "I saw the women . . . in their beds."

"Yes. What else?"

"I saw the men . . . beside them."

"It was just a little gathering . . . of friends. An entertainment. You understand? It is the sort of party people have when they are grown-up."

"I did not know."

"Of course you did not. You are not grown-up, are you? You did not live in a great house like this one. There is much you do not know, but you will see and learn here. Have you told anyone what you saw?"

"No. No one has asked me."

"If your grandmother should . . ."

"I did not see my grandmother."

"No, but if you did, you must say nothing to her."

"Why? Is it wrong then?"

"Wrong? Who says it is wrong? Did you think it was wrong?"

"I . . . I don't know . . . but as you say not to tell . . ."

"You are too young to understand. It is what people do but do not talk about."

I was bewildered, struggling to understand, and suddenly she put her arms about me.

"Mistress Katherine Howard," she said. "I am growing very fond of you, and you are growing fond of me, I do swear."

"You have been kind to me."

"So you will promise me that you will say nothing of what you saw last night."

I promised.

❦

I had been in Horsham more than a week before my grandmother remembered me, and a summons came for me to present myself to her.

I had changed a little since my arrival. Some new gowns had been provided for me, and, although they were by no means grand, they were a marked improvement on my previous wardrobe. I sat down to regular meals, which I took with the waiting women, and this pleased me because Isabel had now become my closest friend and she was always pleasant to me in a rather conspiratorial way, which I realized was because I shared the secret of what happened in the communal bedchamber on some nights. No governess had been provided for me, and I was left a great deal to myself, for all the waiting women, though not overworked, had certain duties to perform. It was an extraordinary life, largely because of those scenes which I witnessed through the bed curtains. They did not occur every night, and I was never told when they would. I would go to the Long Room before the others and sometimes sleep through the night. On other occasions, I would wake and hear the giggles, the protesting murmurs which, some instinct told me, were more invitations than protests. I would be unable to resist the temptation to slip from my bed and peep through the curtains and look at the girls and men laughing, whispering and fondling each other.

Life was very different here from that in my father's house, but, of course, there had not been all these young men and women in the service of the household, and I had not been able to observe how people behaved when they grew up.

When my grandmother sent for me, I went to her in some trepidation, for I feared she was going to find some fault with me and decide she did not want me to remain in her house.

I had begun to think that she had forgotten all about me, and was hoping that this was so, but now I knew that this could not be the case as she had sent for me. I realized that I did not want to leave. Life here fascinated me, particularly the night scenes I witnessed through the bed curtains. I sometimes wished that I could go out there and join in the fun which they seemed to enjoy so much.

As I approached my grandmother's apartments, I

heard music. I rapped on the door and, as there was no command to enter, timidly I lifted the latch and walked in.

My grandmother was seated on her chair, as she had been on our first encounter in that room. Beside her was a table on which was a tray of sweetmeats. She was eating—presumably one of them—and on a stool nearby her sat a young man playing the lute.

He was beautiful, I thought, with dark hair falling about his face, almost to his shoulders, in graceful curls. He went on strumming and, glancing at me, gave me a very warm smile.

My grandmother said: "'Tis Katherine Howard. Come here, child."

"Your Grace sent for me," I said.

"Did I?"

As she had apparently forgotten, I wondered whether I had been wrong to come.

"Silence, Manox," she said to the musician, who immediately bowed his head and let his hands fall from the lute.

She took a sweetmeat from the bowl and threw it towards him; he caught it with graceful dexterity and put it into his mouth.

He then stood up, and said: "Your Grace would dismiss me?"

She considered for a moment, then she said: "Nay, nay. I would hear you play a tune for me. One that my granddaughter, the Lady Anne, will be listening to at Court. So . . . Manox, stay."

"I thank Your Grace," he said with great respect, but he was looking at me.

"Now, Katherine Howard," she went on. "Your new gown becomes you. You look more as Mistress Katherine Howard should than when you came here. And the women look after you well?"

"Isabel does, Your Grace."

"And behaves to you as she should towards my granddaughter?"

"I . . . I think so, Your Grace."

"You must always remember that you are a Howard. More so now that our star is rising high. You are the Lady Anne's cousin and great things will come to her, and through her to us. Come closer, child, where I can see you better. Yes, there is a faint resemblance. Of course, she is a fine lady. She has been well tutored. All those years in France. There is no gainsaying that there is something about the French. They are our natural enemies, but that does not mean they have not a certain elegance. The Lady Anne likes well the French fashions. Those hanging sleeves. She only has to wear them and others follow. French fashions are everywhere at Court. I shall be leaving for Lambeth soon. I trust it is just a matter of settling this 'secret matter.' Secret no longer. We all know of it. You know of it, Manox, do you not?"

"Oh yes, Your Grace."

"And is not our Katherine Howard a little like the Lady Anne? I thought I detected a resemblance when I saw her. Have you seen the Lady Anne, Manox?"

"I glimpsed the lady when she called upon Your Grace recently."

"And did you see what I mean? Cousins of the blood, they are."

"Yes, indeed, Your Grace. There is a shared excellence. They both are blessed with beauty of a distinctive kind."

"Beauty. Bah! Many girls have beauty. There is that extra . . . the Howard look. Do you see what I mean?"

"I do, Your Grace. It is a rare . . . quality."

My grandmother threw another sweetmeat to the musician and took one herself.

"You may offer the dish to Mistress Katherine Howard," said my grandmother.

He rose from his stool, took the dish and proffered it to me with a deep bow.

I smiled and took one of them. He replaced the dish and sat down on the stool, smiling at me.

I felt elated. The sweetmeat was delicious.

"It will be well, Manox," went on my grandmother, "that you do not fail to treat Mistress Howard with respect at all times. She is a Howard and my grand-daughter. Please inform those around you of this."

"I serve Your Grace with all my heart," he said. "And in all ways I will give the utmost respect to Mistress Howard."

"Manox is as good a courtier as he is a musician," said the Duchess to me. "Do you like music?"

"Oh yes, Your Grace."

"And were you taught to play an instrument in your father's house?"

"No, Your Grace."

"Well, it is different here, is it not?"

I said it was, and I found myself thinking mainly of the nights in the Long Room. I was feeling a certain relief, because I had feared my grandmother would ask about those nights and I should not know what to say, since Isabel had warned me not to speak of them.

The Duchess was saying: "The King loves music, and the Lady Anne is very musical. But, of course, she is gifted in many ways. I think you should have some music lessons here, and Henry Manox is on the spot to give them to you. What say you, and you too, Manox? My servants are lazy. So, Manox, here is a new task for you. Instead of sitting strumming your lute to please yourself, you shall instruct Mistress Katherine Howard on the virginals."

"Your Grace could offer me nothing I should like better."

"'Tis agreed then. Henry Manox, you will begin without delay to teach Mistress Katherine Howard to play the virginals."

He was smiling at me. "It will be my great pleasure," he said.

The Duchess was regarding him intently. "And, Manox, you will remember that the young lady is my granddaughter, that she is a member of the illustrious Howard family, cousin to one who will soon . . ."

She stopped abruptly, smiling to herself, and Henry Manox said: "I understand, Your Grace."

"And, Manox," went on my grandmother, "make sure that the others understand this too."

"I shall always remember Your Grace's words," replied Manox. "What I desire above all things is to serve well Your Grace and her noble family."

The Duchess sat back in her chair, smiling with self-gratification.

I understood enough to realize that she was feeling a little conscience-stricken for forgetting me until now, but she had made up for that by arranging music lessons for me.

~

I had a new interest in life. I was enjoying my music lessons. I learned quite quickly and without a great deal of effort; and I looked forward to my daily sessions with my tutor.

He was always helpful and kind. He said I was the

perfect pupil. I learned more quickly than anyone else, he told me, and he was sure my grandmother would be delighted with my progress.

Apparently she made no enquiries about it; nor did she summon me to her presence again. I had quickly come to the conclusion that she felt no great interest in me except when she fancied she saw a resemblance to my cousin Anne; but, as she rarely saw me, she was not often reminded even of that. There were so many young people in her establishment—those who had posts in the household and impecunious relatives and dependants of the Howards—that she could not remember who they all were. I believed that I came into that category, and it was only that faint resemblance which singled me out.

I began to understand that she had taken me into her household on the whim of a moment because of that resemblance, and once there I had become one of a crowd.

I must adjust myself and make my own friends. This I was enjoying doing. I had Isabel and some of the other women, and now my music teacher.

Henry Manox was a good musician. The instruments

in his hand seemed to speak to me. I would sit listening entranced while he played, letting the music carry
me along.

He had a very pleasant tenor voice too; he would
play the lute for me—he was teaching me that instrument as well as the virginals—and suddenly he would
break into song.

One morning, he was playing the lute and singing a
sad song about a man who had died because his mistress no longer loved him. I sat listening, my eyes closed,
when suddenly I felt his hand on my cheek stroking it.

I opened my eyes quickly and saw his face close
to my own. I noticed his bright, dark eyes, with their
long eyelashes.

"You would not have been so unkind, sweet
Katherine," he said.

I blushed. "Oh . . . you mean the song."

"He died of love," he said softly. "Fancy! He died
because the lady he loved was cruel to him."

"She was not cruel," I replied. "She could not help
that she did not love him in return."

"His heart was broken."

"But that was not her fault."

"What do you know of love, Mistress Katherine?"

"Very little, I suppose."

"But you would learn very quickly."

"How do you know?"

"Because I see that in you. There is much that you know and do not realize you know. I saw it the first moment we met."

I managed to say: "'Tis a strange way to talk, Henry Manox, and in a way which is not connected with music."

"It is connected with music, and everything else around us. The world would stop, dear Katherine, if it were not for love."

He laid his hand over mine and suddenly lifted it to his lips and kissed it.

I did not know what I should say, and at that moment Isabel came in.

She said: "The music lesson has been long this morning."

"Mistress Katherine amazes me so much with her talent that I am apt to forget the time."

Isabel laughed. "Come, Mistress Katherine Howard," she said. "You must tear yourself from the lute, the virginals and the musician, I fear. It is time to eat."

Henry Manox stood up and bowed, and Isabel, smiling to herself, took my arm and drew me away.

～

That night, I was awakened by revelry in the Long Room, and, peeping through the curtains, I saw Isabel and, sitting on her bed was a young man whom I had never seen before. He was kissing her and she was looking very happy.

It was the usual scene—the laughter, the giggling, the banter. Isabel knew that I watched them through the bed curtains. Some of the others did, also.

I knew this because I had heard Isabel tell Dorothy Barwike, a young woman who had come from a village nearby, and who had joined the household only recently.

Dorothy had said: "You take great risks. Katherine Howard knows. I have seen her looking out through her bed curtains. What if she were to tell the Duchess?"

"Katherine will not tell," Isabel had replied. "She has promised not to. She doesn't altogether understand.

She is only a child really. Young for her years in some ways. I know she has that air, in a way. I don't know what it is. She is so little and slender, but there *is* something. In spite of her youth, she is almost a woman in some ways, if you know what I mean. She may not have the book learning, but she's got something else. She likes to watch, so she's part of it in a way. She would not tell."

"Well, don't forget, she's a Howard."

They had laughed.

"Great ladies!" Dorothy had said. "They can be as bad as the rest of us. Often worse."

That was all I had heard of that conversation. I wished I had heard more, but eavesdropping is often unsatisfactory. Conversations are cut off when they become the most interesting.

I talked to her about the young man I had seen with her.

"He was kissing you, and you seemed very closely entwined with each other. I was surprised."

"People who spy often get surprises!"

"Spy!" I cried. "I am no spy."

"What else? Let me tell you this, Mistress Howard.

The young man who was with me that night had every right to be there. He is my affianced husband."

"You are going to marry him!"

"Soon now."

"I did not know him."

"He is not of the household. He is a farmer. When I marry, I shall leave this household."

"You mean go away from here?"

"Of course."

"But who will be my friend?"

"There are many here who will be friends to you if you will with them. The Duchess has said that Dorothy Barwike will take my place when I go."

"And the man you are going to marry is allowed to come here at night to be with you?"

"Hush, Mistress Howard. You are but a child. You do not understand these matters."

I was mildly irritated that, when I asked people to explain something to me, they often began by telling me I was a child so could not understand.

She sighed and went on: "He comes at night because I arranged that he shall. We are to be married, so it is best that he should be with me."

"And no other," I said.

She looked at me sharply, and I thought she was going to say again that I was too young to understand, but she changed her mind and gave me a little push.

"You must tell no one," she said. "You understand?"

"Yes, I understand."

I was really too worried to learn that she was going away to think of much else.

Later I heard another scrap of conversation between Isabel and Dorothy.

Dorothy said: "Katherine Howard is growing up. It may be that she knows a little more of what is going on than she admits. I declare you should be careful. If the Duchess knew, she would have to bestir herself, much as she would like to forget all about it."

That was all I heard, but I thought about it a great deal.

~

One day Isabel said to me: "You are getting on very well with your music."

I smiled, gratified. "I can play the virginals well,

Master Manox says. And if I am not quite as good with the lute, he says I shall be in time."

"You are very happy with your music teacher, I believe," went on Isabel.

"Oh yes. He is a good teacher."

"So I understand. But what does he teach you beside the virginals and the lute?"

"What should he? Perhaps to sing a little?"

She laughed and shrugged her shoulders. "Oh, take no heed of what I say. I think he is very handsome."

"Oh yes, is he not? He looks very graceful when he plays the lute. He is like a statue I have seen somewhere."

"He admires you very much."

"He says I am a good pupil."

"Oh, it is more than that."

"What do you mean?"

"He thinks you are beautiful. I wonder . . . but perhaps, you would not want to . . . it would be an opportunity . . ."

"What are you talking about, Isabel?"

"About you and Henry Manox. Would you not like to talk to each other . . . not always at the music lesson?"

"Well, yes, I would. I always enjoy talking to Henry Manox."

"Then why do you not? I have an idea."

"What is it?"

"Well, for you and Henry to see more of each other, to improve your acquaintance apart from music lessons, I mean. Why don't you ask him to one of the evenings . . . ?"

"You mean . . ."

"Why should you not? You are growing up. You have a good friend. You could ask him to come one evening . . . when the others do. Why not?"

She was looking at me eagerly, and I knew she was urging me to agree to this.

"How . . . ?" I began.

"It is simple. You write to Henry Manox, asking him to come to the Long Room when the household has retired."

It was surprising that the first difficulty that presented itself to me was the writing of this invitation.

I said: "I am not good with the pen."

"I will help you," said Isabel. "We shall do it together."

So we did, and the note was sent to Henry Manox.

They had drawn back the bed curtains. They were all very pleased to see this and they clustered round my bed laughing and all talking at once.

"Well, I feel no surprise."

"She is so pretty."

"Too pretty to spend her nights looking out through her bed curtains."

"And Henry Manox is coming."

"He is very handsome."

"And skilled in music."

"And in more besides, I'll warrant."

When he arrived, every one of them welcomed him, but he was not interested in any of them—only in me.

I sat in my bed, dressed in flimsy night attire which Isabel had found for me, and Henry Manox sat with me.

"They said I must ask you here," I told him. "Before, I watched through the bed curtains."

"How happy I am to be here," he said. "I never thought to attain such happiness."

His hands were on my shoulders. He kissed my cheek, then my forehead, and my lips. Pleasurable sensations crept over me. I fancied some of the others were watching us with amusement, although they pretended not to be.

I was excited. At last I was one of them.

Henry Manox had an arm round me and was holding me closely. We talked, first of music. He told me how he dreamed of being something more than just a teacher of the virginals and lute, as well as the harpsichord, to people who would never understand the magic of music. They were unlike myself, of course, who was a natural musician. He wanted to have a house of his own and to live his life with a companion who, like him, was devoted to the art.

I told him of my father's house, of my brothers and sisters and how poor we were. He listened intently. Then he said: "But now you have come to the Duchess, and fate has brought us together."

I thought that sounded wonderful, and I laughed gleefully, at which he bent his head and kissed my bare shoulder.

Isabel called from her bed, where she was snuggling against her farmer: "Not so fast, Manox. Do you want to get us all sent to the Tower?"

There was a great deal of laughter, and Manox said: "You can trust me to play this right."

"It is not the virginals now, Manox," said someone else.

And everyone was laughing. I laughed with them. It was so exciting and amusing.

I shall never forget that first night, when I became one of them and not merely an onlooker, sitting up in bed with my own good friend who, I thought, was more handsome than any of the others, as well as being such a fine musician.

~

There was a certain tension throughout the house. People were whispering and looking wise.

I heard scraps of conversation.

"They say the King is tired of waiting."

"He is not a patient man, our noble King."

"They say that he is determined to marry her and

that he cares for none . . . not even the Church or the Pope himself."

"What then?"

"Some say he is already married to her."

"How can that be?"

"They say with kings all things are possible, and with our King Henry, what he desires will most certainly be."

"And the Lady Anne?"

"She lives as the Queen already."

"Some say she is with child."

"Then we can be sure she will be his queen."

"What of the Queen herself?"

"Poor lady. I fear she suffers."

"Hush, be careful what you say!"

"Foolish one, what matters it here?"

"It matters wherever such words are spoken if they are overheard by some bent on mischief. The King likes not those who even hint that he is in the wrong."

"I did not. I just said 'poor lady.' And what am I? Waiting woman to the Duchess!"

"It matters not who, so have a care what you say."

It was all very exciting, and a little sinister, and it was particularly interesting to me, for one of the main people at the heart of the drama was my own cousin.

During the nights, when we were gathered in the Long Room after the household had retired, they still talked of the King's divorce and how the Pope would not agree, and that Thomas Cranmer, the Archbishop of Canterbury, had brought forth the theory that there was no need for a divorce after all, because the King had never really been married to Queen Catherine. Had she not been married to his brother Arthur previously, and if that marriage had been consummated then the ceremony of marriage to Arthur's younger brother, Henry, was no true marriage at all.

It was one of those laws which were set out in the Bible. And there was a great deal of speculation over this. It was an ideal solution. Had the marriage been consummated or not? That was the theme of conversation in the Long Room. Prince Arthur had been only a boy at the time of the marriage, and he had died very soon after. Of course, it was very possible that they had never truly been husband and wife, but hardly conclusive.

It was all very amusing to the young people, and

meanwhile I sat with Henry Manox's arms about me and each night we progressed a little further with our love making.

The Duchess sent for me one day. This time she was not seated in her chair and I was told to enter her bedroom where she was reclining on the four-poster bed. There were two maids with her. They were bringing clothes from her wardrobe and she was nodding and saying: "Not that, you addle-pate. Take that to Lambeth! Only the finest, I said, did I not?"

In another room, seamstresses were working on new garments and there was bustle everywhere.

"Ah, Katherine Howard," she said when she saw me. She looked at me, nodding. She seemed rather pleased with me.

"Growing up fast," she said. "You will have to look to your manners, girl. We are going to Lambeth. Oh, don't look alarmed. Not to your father's house. We shall be closer to the Court." She smirked with satisfaction. "I shall be there, I doubt not. My granddaughter will not let me be passed by. And, as for you . . . you must prepare yourself. I am having a few gowns made for you. She is your cousin, after all . . . and we must be prepared. Who knows, there may be a place for you at Court!"

I was alarmed. It sounded frightening, and I was enjoying life at Horsham, especially the nights shared with Henry Manox and the rest of them.

"Don't gape, girl. Oh, if you but had the grace of your cousin! How I long to see her Queen of England, which she will be ere long. So now you know that we are going to my residence at Lambeth."

"To see my cousin, Your Grace?"

"To see her crowned Queen of England. Yes, we are going to see the coronation of Queen Anne. Now . . . I have little time to see to these matters. I want you to be able to curtsy gracefully. Manox tells me you play both lute and virginals well and are a good pupil. I want to make sure that, if the Queen does decide to honour you, you are ready for it. You must have some knowledge of the art of dancing and learn not to flush and stammer when you are spoken to, and to answer brightly and wittily, as your cousin has always done."

I was uncertain as to what was expected of me, but

as no one was sent to instruct me, I need not have worried. I had realized by now that my grandmother would have sudden reminders of what she should be doing and then quickly forget all about them. I had seen that happen more than once in my case. In the first place, she had brought me here because it had occurred to her that my father's house was an unfit place in which to bring up a child, and that child a member of the Howard family; and she had chosen me because of the resemblance she had thought she had detected to my cousin, Anne Boleyn. Then she had forgotten me. Later, something would bring me to her mind and she bestirred herself. If the memories persisted, she took some action—as in the case of my music lessons.

Meanwhile, preparations went on apace and there was talk of little else in the Long Room, for everyone was excited about going to London, and at Lambeth we would be very close to the Court.

Isabel's happiness in her coming marriage was a little dulled by the fact that she would not be coming to London. I was seeing more of Dorothy Barwike who would take Isabel's place with me.

It was spring of the year 1533 when we set out for Lambeth. We should be in time for the coronation of Queen Anne, for, in spite of all the opposition and the long fight to attain his desires, the King had decided to accept the case as set out by Archbishop Cranmer, to defy the Pope and declare that he had never been married to Queen Catherine of Aragon and therefore could no longer live in sin with her. So he had married Anne Boleyn at the beginning of the year.

She was already pregnant and on the coming Whit Sunday was to be crowned Queen of England.

A Silk Flower

Lambeth was beautiful in the late spring when we arrived at the Duchess's mansion. It was built very much on the same lines as my father's house at Lambeth, but this was well preserved and comfortable. There were numerous retainers and quantities of food. The gardens ran right down to the river and it was thrilling to be so close to the Court, especially at such a time.

Queen Catherine had been discarded and Queen Anne was in her place. There were many who disapproved of this, and we had to be very careful in what we said. We heard rumours concerning those who had spoken rashly and were now languishing in the Tower.

Sometimes we rode past that sinister building. Mysterious and evil happenings had taken place there.

People had been sent into that grim fortress and never been heard of again. I often thought of those two little princes who were said to have been murdered there. There had been a great deal of talk about them at one time. People said they had been murdered by wicked King Richard, who had been turned from the throne by our King Henry's father—another Henry.

But in some respects life went on in the same way as it had in Horsham. The architecture of the house being very like that other, we had a similar Long Room in which the nightly revels still took place.

Henry Manox accompanied us to Lambeth with the Duchess's musicians; he and I had become the greatest of friends by this time and I looked forward to his company both at the virginals and in the Long Room. He told me that I was the most gifted pupil he had ever had and that he loved me dearly—but not only for that.

I missed Isabel and often wondered whether she regretted leaving the Duchess's household. But I think she was very eager to be married.

Dorothy Barwike watched over me, and in Lambeth I met Mary Lassells. She came to the house soon after we arrived and she told me she had been nursemaid in the house of my uncle, Lord William Howard; and when Lady Howard died, the Duchess took Mary Lassells into her household as one of her waiting women.

This meant that Mary Lassells was now sleeping with the rest of us in the Long Room.

Shortly after we arrived, I suffered a disappointment, for Henry Manox left the Duchess's service for that of Lord Beaumont. But this was soon proved to be not so bad as I had first feared, for Lord Beaumont was a close neighbour of the Duchess, and Henry could easily slip across the gardens in order to join me in the Long Room.

There was less supervision than there would be normally, because everyone was completely occupied with the coming coronation. The Duchess's ambitions had been realized, and she left Lambeth for Court in a state of bliss. She was to hold the new Queen's train at the ceremony of the coronation.

The weather was beautiful. Everyone said it was the best time of the year, and even before the event there were days of rejoicing, with spectacles and processions in the streets. I went out with Mary Lassells, Dorothy Barwike and some of the others who took part in the nightly revels. I was delighted that Henry Manox joined us.

It was the day before the coronation—a time when the celebrations were at their height. I had already decided that there was nothing the people like more than such occasions, and they would be overcome with love for the King because he gave them such opportunities for merry holidays.

On the river were craft of all descriptions, and from many came the sound of sweet music. As was the custom, the Queen had been staying at the Tower with the King and was now preparing for the great tomorrow.

It was the last day of May and, the weather being so perfect, people were saying that Heaven itself was showing its approval of the marriage.

Rails had been set up in the streets so that the horses, who would play such a big part in the procession, could not harm the spectators. There would be crowds of them, of course, and the streets were elaborately decorated; cloth of gold and velvet hung in the Chepe, and Gracechurch Street was brilliant in crimson velvet. I was pressed against the rail and Manox's arm was about me while we watched the procession. There were the Archbishops of York and Canterbury with several ambassadors, and I glowed with pride when my uncle, Lord William Howard, appeared among them.

Henry Manox glanced at me and said: "You are indeed one of a noble family, are you not, sweet-heart?"

I giggled, and thought of my grandmother, who was to hold the Queen's train.

"Lord William is not the marshal," said Mary Lassells disparagingly, as though she did not like this reference to the Howards.

"No," retorted Manox, "but he is standing in for his brother, who, as ambassador in France, cannot be here for this great occasion. And is not that brother, the great Duke of Norfolk, yet another uncle of our noble little companion."

Mary looked sullen, but could not remain so for long, and she was soon exclaiming in delight, for the moment for which we had all been waiting had arrived. Here was the Queen herself.

There was a gasp through the crowd. She was in an open litter so that we could all see her clearly. It was a beautiful litter, covered with cloth of gold, drawn by two white palfreys which were led by gentlemen of the Queen's household.

I glowed with pride when I saw my fascinating cousin, for I thought I had never seen anyone so beautiful. Her surcoat was of silver tissue lined with ermine; she wore her long dark hair loose about her shoulders, and round her head was a circlet of rubies. Four tall knights held a canopy of cloth of gold over the litter.

I felt deeply moved and wished her happiness with all my heart. Her litter had passed on and then came her attendants in their litters, and in the first of these sat my grandmother with the Duchess of Dorset.

Henry Manox threw a sly glance at Mary Lassells and squeezed me closer to him. "Marry," he said, "our noble companion's family is very well represented here today. 'Tis so, is it not, Mistress Lassells?"

What a happy day that was! We revelled in the pageants, liking best the fountain of Helicon from which Rhenish wine spurted in jets and fell into cups, one of which Henry Manox brought to me, and we drank together, as he said, from our loving cup.

We were all too weary at the end of the day to indulge in our usual revelries and slept soundly.

The next day was the glorious first of June; and the Queen, her train held by my grandmother, went from Westminster Hall to the Abbey, attended by a great company, including my Uncle William Howard as deputy for that other, even more illustrious uncle, the Duke of Norfolk; and there she was crowned Queen of England.

Days of rejoicing followed. There were banquets and ceremonies and jousting in the tilt-yard where the King and his new Queen sat side by side watching the display.

There would be further rejoicing to come in September when the Queen gave birth to the child she carried. It would be a boy—everyone was determined on that; and then the King's happiness would be complete. And so would that of us all.

But it was not quite so peaceful as it had seemed. Everyone was not rejoicing, and there would always be some to make their views known, however dangerous that was.

Friar Peto was exceptionally bold. He was a man of strong religious beliefs, a man completely without fear. The sermon he preached at Greenwich was not couched in parables as some were; it was not merely hinting at the dire punishment which might befall a man who put away his wife for the sole reason that he was tired of her and lusted after another woman. Friar Peto spoke fiercely against both the King and the Queen. Rome had refused the divorce, and the King had snapped his fingers at the Holy Pope and acted without his approval. He preferred the advice of his obliging Archbishop. The King and the woman he called his Queen were sinners. Friar Peto even went so far as to liken King Henry to Ahab, whose sins were not forgiven and at whose death had his blood drunk by dogs. He said Anne was a sorceress, and, still in biblical mood, likened her to Jezebel.

The King must have been in a somewhat tolerant mood, for Peto was not immediately sent to the Tower, though he was there some months later, where he stayed for two or three years; and at the end of that time, not being so enamoured of his Queen, the King might have felt that the Friar was perhaps not so wrong as he had appeared to be at the time of the coronation.

The Duchess remained at Court and the household was more relaxed than it had been, even in Horsham. Meals were regular and household matters attended to, but there was little supervision of the servants.

I could not understand Mary Lassells. There had been times when it occurred to me that there was something behind Isabel's words, but this seemed doubly so in the case of Mary. Her attitude towards Manox was a little mysterious. Sometimes she seemed to hate him, at others quite the contrary. I often saw her watching him, and she seemed very pleased when he paid attention to her. She was not easy to understand. Sometimes she almost sneered at my family; at others seemed to show great respect for it.

"You come of a *very* grand family," she said to me once. "The Queen's coronation brought that home to us, did it not? The Queen herself . . . your cousin! And Lord William Howard, your uncle. And the Duchess, your grandmother, holding the Queen's train and now in the Queen's household!"

"I believe my cousin to be a very kind and generous lady," I said.

"Oh, it is well for families when some of its members creep into high places."

"Creep into high places?"

"Oh, I mean when they are favoured by royalty."

She smirked a little. Then she went on: "I wonder that you are on such terms with a musician of low birth."

I flushed. Henry Manox and I had become even closer than we had been before. But there was a certain restraint in him. There was so much of which I was ignorant. Our love making excited me. It was like making new discoveries, but I did have the notion that there was more to learn and that Henry Manox wanted to teach me, and had the power to, but, for some reason, was not altogether sure whether he should proceed.

Henry had once said: "My little Katherine, you were born to love, but you are so young as yet. That will change though. One day, it will be even better between us two."

I had snuggled up to him and he had said: "You are a temptress."

I heard Dorothy Barwike say to Mary Lassells:

"Henry Manox says he loves Katherine Howard to madness."

I was enthralled, and thought: "Dear Henry, I know he truly loves me."

Dorothy went on: "He believes he is troth-plighted to her and so contracted."

What was Dorothy saying? That Manox thought to marry me! I was eleven years old. Some princesses married at that age. This was rather disconcerting. I had not thought of marriage.

Then something alarming happened. Mary Lassells came to me one morning, looking as though she wanted to talk to me and did not know how to begin. I asked her if anything was wrong, to which she replied hesitatingly: "I know not what I must do. But do something I know I must."

"What has happened?" I persisted. "Pray tell me, Mary."

"Mayhap I have failed to understand. Mayhap I should not speak of it, but you do not always remember that you belong to a noble house. I know that your father is not rich . . . but the Duchess would be most disturbed if she knew . . ."

"Knew what?"

"Your . . . er . . . being of such a noble house . . ." She could not prevent the little smirk appearing—the one which was always there when my family was mentioned. " . . . and I being here to serve the Duchess . . ."

"What are you trying to tell me, Mary?"

"I have been bold. I said to Manox, 'You play the fool in a most dangerous fashion.' 'How so?' he asked. And I said, and this is true enough, 'And if my Lady Duchess knew of this . . . love . . . between you and Katherine Howard, she would seek to undo you . . . this talk of troth-plight . . . . What think you Her Grace would do an she heard you have planned to marry this noble-born young lady?'"

"You said that to him? How could you?"

"'Twas my duty as I saw it. Consider, I pray you. If the Duchess were to hear of this . . . what would happen to Manox, or to you? Give a thought to it. I did, and I thought it was right to speak to Manox rather than to Her Grace."

"But in the Long Room . . ."

"Yes, in the Long Room. You and Manox sporting with the rest. But let me tell you his reply. It is not pleasing to hear. He said: 'Fear not. My intentions are not of the nature you believe. They are what is called of a dishonourable nature, and from the freedom I have so far enjoyed with the lady, I doubt not that I shall be able to attain my purpose without taking the steps you suggest.'"

I felt dizzy, and a sudden rage possessed me—not against Mary Lassells but against Henry Manox. How could he speak thus of me? Was it true that Mary Lassells was jealous of his devotion to me? I could not believe that he had said such words. But something told me that they could be true.

"Fie on him!" I cried, stamping my foot, and Mary put an arm round me.

"I understand," she said soothingly. "You are so young, you have not yet experienced the perfidy of men. This is how they speak of their mistresses when out of hearing, yet when they are with them it is all honeyed words and vows of eternal faithfulness."

"I cannot believe he spoke thus of me."

"Ask him."

"I shall . . . and now. I cannot wait."

"He will lie. All men lie."

"Henry Manox has always told me how much he loved me and would die for me. I shall go to him now and you shall come with me."

She looked aghast, and then she smiled secretly.

"You could see him tonight and there tell him."

"No," I said firmly. "I shall not wait, and shall speak to him now."

"But how?"

"We shall go to Lord Beaumont's house . . . through the gardens, and I shall ask someone to bring him to me. And you will be with me, Mary. We shall confront him . . . face to face."

Mary was uneasy, but I did notice a certain relish in her eyes, as though she would enjoy confronting this traitor and, of course, prove that she was telling the truth because she could see that this was the only way she could make me believe it.

I had never known I could be so angry. I felt degraded. I kept thinking of Uncle William Howard, marshal at the coronation, and my grandmother, holding the Queen's train and riding in the carriage near her. I was indeed of a noble family, and this low-born servant had dared speak of me as though I were a common slut!

I think Mary Lassells was surprised by this determined girl, who had hitherto seemed so young and helpless. I strode over the lawns to the Beaumont gardens, Mary walking meekly beside me.

I saw one of the servants and I called to him. I said in a voice which might have belonged to my grandmother: "I would speak with the musician Henry Manox. Pray tell him that Mistress Howard sends for him, and bring him to me here."

The servant bowed and hurried off, and it was not long before Manox appeared.

He looked startled, and I said immediately: "Henry Manox. I have heard what you have said of me."

He stammered, and I saw the look of hatred which he gave to Mary, and I knew then without a doubt that she had told the truth. My heart sank, and I felt wretched. The love I had imagined was a fantasy. It was not real love. What a fool I had been to indulge in childish dreams. I might have known that, if he had loved me, he would have had more care for me. He would never have spoken of me as he had to Mary Lassells. I was overcome by many emotions, but the greatest of these was a bitter humiliation.

I repeated to him what Mary had said, and I cried: "Will you tell me that you did not say those words?"

He wanted to deny them, but Mary burst in: "I have told you what he said, because I think you should know how he thinks of you."

"It was a mistake," was all Manox could say.

"I have only repeated what you said to me," persisted Mary. "I warned you that you could be in trouble, and that was your reply."

"It was a misunderstanding," said Manox.

"You have said enough," retorted Mary.

I added: "Yes, such words need no explanation. They are enough."

And I turned and left him.

~

I had fallen out of love at that moment while he stood stammering there. I saw him for what he was—low-born and cunning, eager to rise in society through his musical talent. He was handsome in a way, with his dark curling hair and rather soulful eyes which could hide the calculation of his scheming mind. I had been so innocent, wanting to be liked, wanting to be as one of the others in the Long Room at night. I knew that now, for I had grown up a little in the last hours. What I wanted was to be loved. It was not love I was witnessing and sharing in the Long Room. It was a lustful playing at it.

I sent a note to Manox telling him not to come to the Long Room at nightfall.

A few days passed, then I received a note from him. He must see me. There was so much to explain. It had been a terrible misunderstanding.

I hesitated for a while and then I agreed to meet him at the spot where the Duchess's garden adjoined that of Lord Beaumont.

He was there, looking unlike the man I had known; he was sad and solemn.

"Katherine, Katherine," he cried, "my heart is broken."

Oh yes. I had grown up. Previously I would have relented immediately, I should have wept with him and we would have resumed our old relationship. But, as I said, I was not so easily deceived now.

"I love you, Katherine," he said. "With all my heart, I love you."

"I believe that those who love do not speak of their loved one as you did of me."

"I did not . . ." he began, but I cut him short.

"You could not deny it before Mary Lassells. You may do so now, but I do not believe you."

"My passion for you transports all reason. I knew not what I said."

"But, Henry Manox, I no longer believe you."

"It is that sly creature," he said angrily.

"She may be sly, and doubtless is, but she has revealed much to me which before I could not see. You cannot deny you said those words. I doubt not you could have done so if you had not been taken by surprise and confronted with her. I saw at once that she spoke the truth. It is over, Henry Manox."

"Oh come, sweet Katherine. You have taken her words to heart. I tell you, I did not mean them. They were said in a moment when I knew she was trying to take you from me. Remember how you enjoyed our love play?"

"Love play!" I retorted. "It was a pretense of love. That is not for me, Henry Manox. I want no pretense."

"If you but knew how restrained I have been. How careful of you. You are so young . . . so innocent."

"And you feared my family's wrath if they discovered."

There was just a brief hesitation, and I knew I was right in that; and I knew without a doubt that I had fallen out of love with him forever. In fact, when I looked at him now, I wondered how I could ever have thought I had been in love at all.

I turned and ran away from him.

That night I lay in my bed, my curtains drawn. I had no wish to be with the others. Love play! Yes, that described it for what it was. Playing at love. It was not true love. It was not for me. I could not deny that I had wanted to be loved. Manox had awakened certain instincts in me. He had directed me into this pretense, this searching for sensation, this playing at love.

So I was content to lie there, the curtains tightly drawn, no longer taking part in the merriment of the Long Room.

~

It was in the September of that year that the Queen's child was born. There had been a great deal of anticipation throughout the whole of London, for the celebrations which would accompany that great event would be as splendid as those for the coronation with dancing, pageants and wine flowing in the streets.

Preparations were already being made to welcome the heir to the throne. It was universally accepted that the child would be of the desired sex—a boy, of course.

That was why the joy in a healthy child was slightly tempered with disappointment when she turned out to be a girl. However, the bright side was that there was nothing wrong with this child—except her sex. She was healthy; she had all the right parts which any child should bring into the world. She was an indication that Queen Catherine's many failures were due to no fault in the King, and although the Queen this time had produced a girl, there was hope that the next child would be a boy. We could look confidently to the future. Although, of course, there were some to remind us that Queen Catherine had produced a girl child who had survived. Poor sad Lady Mary, now broken-hearted because of the cruel treatment meted out to her mother, and embittered because she had lost her inheritance and was branded as nothing more than the King's bastard.

How sad that the glory of our Queen Anne had had to be bought at such a high cost to her predecessor. Little did I know then that, at a not far distant day, Anne herself would have to pay a greater price for the elevation of her successor.

It was only to be expected that the birth of the child should set the Howard family even higher in the social hierarchy.

The Duchess spoke of the occasion in her usual somewhat disjointed way when I saw her soon afterwards. She was still at Court, but she had visited the house briefly for some reason, and she could not resist telling me of the glorious turn her life had taken.

"Well, my child, I shall not stay here long. I shall, of course, be returning to Court. The Queen has need of me. She does not forget her grandmother. I was with the Court at Greenwich at the birth of the Princess Elizabeth. Marry, and we were so sure it would be a boy . . . right up to the last moment. The King was deeply disappointed. He had set his heart on a boy." She sighed. "Do not they all? How he would have doted on a son. But the Princess is a bonny child. We must be thankful that nothing went wrong, as it did so often with poor Queen Catherine. Poor lady." She made the sign of the cross. She was uneasy, I supposed, about the trouble with the Pope, who had uttered some rather unpleasant words about the King and Queen. But facts were facts, and we were not in Rome, but here, where our King was supreme—more now than ever, now that he had snapped his fingers at the Pope and made himself Head of the Church.

"Oh, if only the baby had been a boy!" went on the Duchess. "But alas, one cannot always have what one wants in this life. There is plenty of time. There will be others. The Queen is young and strong, and there is great love between her and the King. Oh, how he

adores her! There is to be a Te Deum sung in honour of the child. She will be called Elizabeth after the
King's mother. And, here is the greatest news of all.
I shall carry the little Princess. Yes, well, am I not her
great-grandmother? And who else should have that
honour? George Boleyn, Lord Rochford now, with
your uncles Thomas and William and Lord Hussey
are going to carry the canopy which they will hold
over me and the baby. Oh, it will be a grand occasion!
I trust you are all behaving well during my absence?"

I thought of those nights in the Long Room, but
then, they had been the same when she was there. I
sometimes wondered if she had been half aware of it.
She certainly would not have time to think of that now.

My uncle, the Duke of Norfolk, kept in his household what were called his pensioners. In the past, it
had been the custom of great houses to do this. It
was a custom which was dying out now, but my uncle
still had a number in his service.

I suppose it was worthwhile for, in the event of
trouble, these people—young, for the most part, for
they were biding their time until they should marry
or inherit titles and land—were pledged to serve their

benefactor in any way he needed while they were pensioners under his roof. Most were of good birth, and several of them had some connection with the families with whom they lived.

At this time, there were a number of these young people in our household which, although I had always thought of it as my grandmother's house, did, in fact, belong to the Duke. These young people were fed, housed and even granted some pay; they had little to do unless called upon, and then they must spring to immediate action. They spent their time riding, jousting and generally indulging in manly sports and pastimes.

I was sitting in the gardens with Dorothy Barwike and one of Dorothy's friends called Joan, and was trying to make myself one of the silk flowers, of the kind which were very fashionable at this time. Living near the Court, we could see the elegantly dressed members of it now and then, either on the river or walking, and some even visiting the house when my grandmother was there. It was different to Horsham. That was how I knew of this fashion for silk flowers.

I was not good with my needle, and was showing my work to Joan and Dorothy as a young man strolled by. I had seen him before and I guessed that he was one of the Duke's pensioners.

He had one of the most pleasant faces I had ever seen, though he was not striking like Manox with his dark curls and flashing eyes. This young man was, I guessed, in his mid-teens . . . eighteen perhaps, with soft brown hair about a gentle face which was by no means lacking in manliness. He was tall and slender, and had an unmistakable air of good breeding.

He paused, bowed to us and said: "What a pleasant afternoon. You young ladies are very intent on your work."

I laughed. "Work?" I said, and the others joined in my laughter. I liked him and did not want him to move away.

I went on: "My work, as you call it, is trying to make a silk flower."

"And are you succeeding?" he asked.

I held up the piece of silk.

"If this bears some resemblance to a red rose . . . yes," I said.

"It is red," he said, and we all laughed again.

"I trust you did not object to my speaking to you."

"We certainly did not," replied Joan.

We were sitting on a bench, of which there were several dotted round the garden. He looked at it and went on: "If I might be seated . . . ?"

Joan waved her hand, and he sat down next to me.

"I have seen you young ladies before," he said. "I know you have duties with Her Grace. I'll swear her absence leaves you with time on your hands."

Joan and Dorothy admitted that this was so.

"I am Francis Derham," he told us, "in the train of the Duke of Norfolk."

"We guessed that was so," said Dorothy. "There are many of you here."

"And you, Mistress?" he asked me.

"Katherine Howard, granddaughter of the Duchess. The Duke is my uncle."

"Well met," he said. "I am of the family . . . of some remote branch, naturally. But still, I am of Howard blood, which is why I am here. I dare swear you and I are of the same kin." He was studying me intently and smiling.

"Then well met," I said.

We talked awhile, and then he told me that he had recently come from Ireland and should shortly be returning to that country.

"But I shall be back," he added, "when I trust I shall once more be allowed to enjoy the Duke's hospitality." He smiled on us all, but I was sure the smile lingered on me. "And, mayhap I shall be privileged to meet you all again."

"That," I assured him, "will be a great pleasure." I turned to the others. "Will it not?"

Both Dorothy and Joan agreed that it would.

When he had gone, we discussed him. We all agreed that he had great charm, and we said it was a pity he was going away as soon as we had met him.

I did see him before he went. I was in the garden, alone this time, when he came.

"Mistress Howard," he said. "I had been hoping to see you. I know you come this way. I confess, I have watched you on one or two occasions. I wanted to say goodbye to you before I went away."

"Mayhap we shall not meet again."

"We shall," he said. "I shall hope for that. There is

something I wish to show you. Will you wait for me here until I bring it to you?"

"How long should I wait?" I asked.

"Five minutes. A little more perhaps, but not much. Rest assured I shall be with you as soon as it is possible."

I stood under the shelter of the oak tree, waiting for him with anticipation. I liked him. How different he was from Henry Manox! I wondered how I could ever have thought I loved that musician.

When my new friend returned, he was carrying a small box tied up with red ribands.

"It is for you," he said. "Open it when you are alone, and when you look at it, always say, 'Francis Derham will return.' Will you do that?"

I promised readily. And he was gone.

Excited, and very curious, I looked down at the box in my hands. I could not wait to open it. I untied the ribands and, nestling in the box, was a red silk rose.

Dangerous Games

I did not forget Francis Derham. There was the red rose to remind me. I often wore it. Dorothy and Joan smiled when I told them Francis Derham had given it to me. They often commented on it and afterwards I wished I had not told them whence it came. So then I did not wear it as much as I should have liked to; and it seemed they forgot him. But I did not need the red rose to remind me of him.

Something was happening, and we were aware of it. This was due to living near the Court and not in Horsham. Moreover, my grandmother and the Duke of Norfolk appeared to be concerned in it.

I saw little of my uncle, but my grandmother often left the Court and returned to the house. The Court was constantly travelling round the country and my grandmother did not like the journeys. She said she was feeling her age, and Court life could be exhausting.

Her limbs were stiff, she complained. She had procured some soothing lotions from her physician which had to be rubbed into her swollen legs, and she summoned me, as a member of the family, to perform this intimate task.

This, although somewhat distasteful to me, had its compensations, for, as I massaged, she would slip into a dreamy state and talk almost as though to herself, which meant she often forgot discretion and said more than she intended. Thus I began to understand much of what would otherwise have been a mystery to me.

It quickly became clear to me that all was not well with Queen Anne. The euphoria was fast evaporating, and the King was less devoted than he had been.

"It began with the birth of the child," mused the Duchess. "If only she had been a boy. That would have bound them together. He had set his heart on a son. All the documents announcing the birth . . . they had all been prepared for a boy. And then comes the Princess Elizabeth . . . a beautiful child . . . no weakness there . . . but a girl. He had thought my granddaughter perfect. He had thought she could give him all he wanted. But it is the good God who decides the sex of a child, and he chose to give them a girl! And there are those to say that this is a sign of divine disapproval. That Peto. Oh, he is not the only one. They should have been silenced. Well, there it is. If it had been a boy, all would have gone well, all would have been saved."

"Saved!" I gasped. It was a mistake. I should have kept silent.

"What's that, eh? What are you doing, child? Get on with the rubbing."

You must not interrupt her, I admonished myself. She must forget that you are here. No talking then from me. Let her do it all.

I rubbed, gently, soothingly, and she was soon continuing.

"Poor child. So beautiful. There is no one to rival her. What if it is he who can not get the boys? There is the Lady Mary and now the Princess Elizabeth . . . and all the boys Catherine had were born sickly and did not live. There is Richmond, of course, the King's son. Did he not admit to it? Did he not rejoice in the boy? But a bastard. He can get bastards, but no heirs.

It is as though God is against him. Can it be? That is what they say. Some of them are so bold . . . they risk their lives. They are like the saints. They do not care for the axe—and they are lucky if they get that. That's for the nobility, but it's hanging, drawing and quartering for some . . . and still they do not care. They will say what they believe to be the truth. The people don't like it. They don't like *her*. They are all envious of my beautiful granddaughter. Oh, what a lovely creature! When she came back from France, there was no one to touch her. And now . . . she is Queen indeed . . . but he begins to wander, they say. The Duke is worried . . ."

I wanted to ask if the Queen were worried too, but I stopped myself in time. It was an unnecessary question. Of course she must be worried. And my uncle was disturbed. There would be reason for that. The family had been greatly honoured since one of its members had become the Queen.

My poor cousin Anne! I remembered the glimpse I had had of her at her coronation. So proud, so beautiful, the most powerful woman in the country; but even she had to remember that her power came through the King, and everything depended on her pleasing him.

The months passed. Often I thought of Francis Derham, and I wondered whether he would ever come back.

I saw Henry Manox now and then. He was still at Lord Beaumont's. Whenever we met, he looked at me pleadingly, but I was not in the least tempted—perhaps because I carried the image of Francis Derham in my mind. He was so different.

I learned more of what was happening. It was well known now that all was not well between the King and the Queen, and throughout the house there was an air of impending doom.

On the rare occasions when I saw my uncle, the Duke, he was clearly disturbed; as for my grandmother, she was very obviously affected. Not so long ago, she could not have spoken of our kinswoman, the Queen, without glowing with pride; now she did so with apprehension.

Where would it end? He was married to her, but some said it was no true marriage. Had he not been married to Queen Catherine? But he had thrust her aside; and she was related to the great Emperor Charles, which was why the Pope could not accept a bribe from the King to agree to the divorce. And Anne . . . who was she? Who would defend her? The family of Howard? A great family, yes, but insignificant compared with such as the Emperor Charles, the most powerful ruler in Europe. And who were the Howards to set themselves against the King? A previous king had shown them how easily he could humble them.

I was indeed growing up, and learning something of the world, and I was deeply sorry for my brilliant cousin.

And well I might be! I often thought later what she must have suffered during those months, and then I understood it so well.

Everyone knows that story.

There was a time when I was aware of the lightening of my grandmother's spirits. There was a definite new optimism. The Queen was pregnant.

The Duchess talked of it while I rubbed her legs.

"This could save everything. It is God's answer to our prayers. True, it will not be the same . . . he is not a man to stay constant. His fancies stray and many are standing ready." She laughed mirthlessly. "I think of those Seymour brothers . . . a fine pair they are. Mischief makers, both of them. Edward is a rogue, and so is Thomas. They have always been enemies of the Howards. They are seeking advancement through this . . ."

It was all rather vague, and I dared not ask for clarification since this would be the quickest way to silence her. But there was a good deal of gossip going on, and I was able to glean something of the situation, so I soon learned that the King was enamoured of one of the Queen's ladies-in-waiting. Mistress Jane Seymour was not of significantly high birth, but she had those two ambitious brothers. Anne Boleyn, lady-in-waiting to Queen Catherine, had ensnared the King. Now it seemed it was the turn of Jane Seymour, lady-in-waiting to Anne, to do the same.

My grandmother had gone back to Court to be near her granddaughter when she gave birth.

Oh, for a son, we prayed. Only God could give Anne that.

Alas, he did not listen to our prayers, or only partly.

It was very dramatic, I understood. The Queen had burst in on her maid, Jane Seymour, and the King. They were in each other's arms and certain familiarities were taking place. How Anne must have hated that woman and longed to be rid of her, but naturally, she could do nothing about the matter, for the King would not allow her to be dismissed; and Queen Anne, who once could have demanded anything from him, must now stand by and suffer the humiliation of seeing another preparing to take the place which had been hers—just as Queen Catherine had had to do before her.

Queen Anne was so angry that she gave vent to her rage and the King shouted at her that she must perforce endure what others had before her. Poor Anne, she must have seen the end in sight, and the only way she could avert the fate which had fallen to Queen Catherine was to have a son. And that was not in her power, except by prayer, which was not always reliable.

It was certainly not in her case. There was not even a daughter like the Princess Elizabeth. The shock of that encounter between herself, the King and Jane Seymour brought on a miscarriage. It was the end.

The Duchess returned to us, sad-hearted and

defeated. She could no longer delude herself into thinking that all would come right. There was no son. The King was tired of her whom he had once desired sufficiently to defy the Pope and break with Rome; and now she was no more to him than poor, sick, tired Catherine of Aragon.

The Duchess had been with Anne when she lay in her bed, sick and frantic with worry, and during one of those sessions when I was rubbing her legs, she talked of the occasion.

"She was in need of comfort. She had lost her child . . . a sadness for a mother at any time, but when so much depends on it . . . Oh, he was cruel. The anger in his little eyes . . . his tight, straight mouth. And it was worse, because the child had been a boy. Oh, if only she had not come upon them . . . if only she had not lost what she so needed. But how could she help it, poor soul? She knew how he had behaved with Queen Catherine—and, alas, she had helped him in that, one could say. But he was cruel. He may be the King, but I will say it. He said, 'You shall have no more boys by me.' And there she lay, sick, deserted, my poor, poor child."

Through the spring the gloom persisted. It was exactly three years since those glorious days when we were preparing for Anne's coronation. I remembered my grandmother's pride and joy because of our connection with the new Queen. The atmosphere had changed a great deal. It would have been better now if we were not related to the Queen. The Duke was very gloomy. He came to the house more frequently. I gathered that he was not as popular at Court as he had been, for the King no longer had the same welcome for members of the Howard family.

My grandmother was frantic with anxiety. She shut herself in her room. Lord William was often at the house, and there were earnest conversations between him and the Duke. I saw them walking in the gardens, and I believed that they did not want what they said to be overheard.

Greatly daring, I went to the Duchess and asked if she needed me, for during one of these sessions of ours I thought I might hear something important from her ramblings; but she sharply told me to be off and not bother her.

Then came that terrible day when our hopes that

the storm would blow over were foundered forever.

It was the topic of conversation everywhere. There were several versions of it, but most were hearsay. The King and Queen had been together at the May Day joust, seated side by side in the royal box. The King did not speak to the Queen, and it was clear to everyone that all was not well between them. The King was glum, while the Queen put on an air of false gaiety in an effort to maintain the pretense of harmony.

Lord Rochford, the Queen's brother, had challenged Henry Norris; and, with their followers, they began the mock battle.

Perhaps the Queen acted unwisely, but I supposed that, if the occasion had not arisen then, it would very soon afterwards, for there were many bent on her destruction—first and foremost among them being the Seymour brothers.

What happened was that, in the heat of the contest between Rochford and Norris, Norris came near to the royal balcony and at that moment the Queen dropped her handkerchief. Norris picked it up and wiped his brow with it. It was certainly an act of familiarity. Perhaps when the Queen was in favour, she might have acted so with Norris, but now such conduct gave the King an excuse for a fresh grievance.

The King rose and left his seat. The Queen was naturally nonplussed and shortly afterwards followed him. As for Norris, he was arrested a little later when he was leaving the joust. Francis Weston was also arrested.

The storm which had been brewing for months had now broken in its full fury. The King was an impatient man. He would wait no longer. His passion for our poor cousin was at an end, and he was as determined to marry Jane Seymour as he had been to marry Anne Boleyn.

The tragedy of Anne, three years a queen, was now nearing to its end. She was sent to the Tower on a charge of adultery which, of course, was treason. I was horrified to learn that my Uncle Norfolk was a member of the Council which condemned her. I never liked him after that. In truth, perhaps I had never liked him, but I had always thought of him as a great man, for he was the head of our family, and my grandmother always spoke of him with awe. How could he, I asked myself, he, who had always been so eager to stress his connection with her, desert her so cruelly when she needed his help? Perhaps it is so with those who put family pride above all else, for what was their professed affection worth?

It was not so with the Duchess, my grandmother. She was deeply grieved for her granddaughter, and it was not entirely because the once-cherished Queen had placed our family in jeopardy. She would murmur to herself: "My poor child," and her eyes were red from weeping. Then her face would grow dark with anger, and she would murmur against that cruel monster—the King, of course. But that was only rarely and when I was alone with her.

What happened is known to all. Anne was brought to the block.

For a long time I could not pass the Tower. Nothing would induce me to, and when eventually I did, I was filled with a sudden anger against fate which had sent my clever cousin to Tower Green and cut off her beautiful head. By fate, I meant the King—but it was wise not even to think such thoughts. It would be treason.

Others died with her. Norris, Weston, Brereton swore to the innocence of the Queen, even under torture. Poor delicate Mark Smeaton, the musician, gave way and admitted to his and the Queen's guilt. He was not entirely believed, even by the Queen's enemies. Poor Mark Smeaton, who had sworn his innocence before entering that grim fortress, where he had been prevailed upon to change his mind.

Thomas Wyatt was lucky. He escaped death and went abroad. I was glad of that, but deeply shocked when my cousin George Boleyn, Lord Rochford, was accused of being his sister's lover. That was monstrous, and I think even my Uncle Norfolk would have questioned its plausibility if he had not feared to offend the King by doing so. He should have shown more courage, but who can be courageous when one word could betray one and result in suffering to equal that of the victim?

What was particularly shocking in the case of Anne and her brother was that it was due to Lady Rochford's evidence that the case against her husband and sister-in-law was brought.

My grandmother gave way to her grief. "The vixen,"

she cried. "How could she? It is lies . . . lies . . . all lies. But that creature was very jealous of those two. They were so brilliant. George loved his sister and she loved him. But it was a pure love. I would swear that on my life . . . the love between a clever brother and sister. Oh, the wicked creature! She will live to regret it."

My grandmother might be lazy, comfort-loving, greedy, obsessed by grandeur, overweeningly proud of her noble family, intent on preserving its greatness and seeking more, but beneath all that there was kindness in her. She had loved my cousin and I believed she had some regard for me. There was a softness in her that was unlike the flinty nature of my uncle, the Duke.

Everyone knows now how bravely Anne went to her death on Tower Green and how, the moment she was dead, the King set off to Wolf Hall to become betrothed to Jane Seymour.

I was growing up. I was now fifteen years old.

~

Sometimes I looked at the silk rose which Francis Derham had given me. I did not wear it. If I had, my grandmother would have wanted to know whence it came, and I was wise enough to know that she would not be pleased to hear it had come from a young man.

She had changed a little since the death of my cousin. It had been a great shock to her, from which I felt she would never quite recover. She had set such hopes on her and she had been so proud. Now it seemed that the Howards wanted to forget they had ever known such a person as Anne Boleyn.

The King had married almost immediately, and the Seymour brothers were now in high favour, while the Howards, though not exactly in decline, were naturally not enjoying the honours they once did. The Seymours saw to that.

It appeared that Jane Seymour was all that the King desired in a wife, for very soon after the marriage we heard that she was with child.

The King was delighted. This was divine approval. Any lingering doubts people might have had that Anne had been cruelly treated would be dismissed. Obviously the King had been right in his action. She had been an adulteress and Heaven had frowned on the union, for there was only Elizabeth, a mere girl—and out of favour now on account of her mother. One girl and a stillborn boy. Proof enough! And here was Jane, his wife of a short duration, docile and sweet—who would not be, with the memory of what had happened to her predecessor hanging over her?—pregnant in the shortest possible time.

I suppose I did not give a great deal of thought to these matters then. Remember, I was only fifteen, and a giddy fifteen at that, with my head full of things like silk flowers for my gown and admiring looks from the young men of the household. I was untutored for, with all the excitement of life at this time, who could spare a thought for my education? I could read a little, write with some difficulty, and picked up knowledge where I could. I was not of a serious enough nature to seek to educate myself. I liked to sing and dance and be merry, so was not concerned with my academic shortcomings.

I think my grandmother might have noticed the deficiencies if she had been more aware of me. But how could she have been expected to, with one other granddaughter taking up so much of her thoughts?

We eagerly awaited the birth of Jane Seymour's child. The question everyone was asking was, will it be a boy? Would there be another disappointment? People talked of little else. Some whispered, and if not, how long will it be before Queen Jane follows Queen Anne? That scene on Tower Hill was too recent to be forgotten easily.

It seemed all was well. Oh joy! Oh jubilation! The child was a boy and the King's dearest wish had been granted. At last, he had a son—a legitimate heir to the throne!

There must be rejoicing throughout the land. Alas, the Queen was in a sorry state. The doctors shook their heads in dismay, but even so the King could not hide his delight, for it was believed that the boy would live, if not his mother.

The child must be baptized at once, even though the doctors assured the King that he would survive. No chances must be taken. Poor Jane, how ill she must have been, exhausted, craving rest, too tired to enjoy her triumph in succeeding where her predecessors had failed.

The boy was to be named Edward. I heard accounts of his baptism: how he was taken from his nursery in Hampton Court to his mother's chamber, accompanied by the sound of trumpets, while poor Jane lay there, pale, wan, desperately trying to take part in the ceremonial ritual. It lasted for three hours and at the end of it Jane was in no condition to understand what was happening.

The King, however, insisted on her presence. They said he could not take his eyes from the baby Prince, who behaved with impeccable good manners throughout the proceedings and gave only the occasional whimper.

Poor Jane! She never recovered from the ceremony. So died the perfect wife. Not only had she produced the longed-for son, but she had had the good grace to die before the King had tired of her.

He could now ask himself where he could find a new wife?

~

Queen Jane was taken from Hampton Court to Windsor for her burial.

It was a day of mourning. The people were in the streets, and we must be among them. There were masses to be said and hymns to be sung in St. Paul's Cathedral, where, a day or so before, there had been rejoicing over the birth of an heir.

There would be no revelry, of course, which was a pity, and even the rejoicing on the baby's birth had to be subdued because of his mother's death; but nevertheless it was an occasion for an outing.

So, with Joan, Dorothy and Mary Lassells, and some of the others from the band of Norfolk pensioners, I boarded the barge at the privy stairs and we sailed down the river to the City.

There were crowds in the streets and, after leaving the barge at Westminster stairs, we walked through the press of people to St. Paul's.

The cathedral was overflowing and we remained among the crowds outside, and it was there that I saw him.

He was standing before me, staring in undisguised

delight. Then he took off his hat and bowed low. I was tingling with excitement.

"Mistress Katherine Howard!" he cried. "Oh fie! Do you not know me?"

I was never subtle. I cried out: "Of a surety I know you. You are Francis Derham. You gave me the silk rose."

"Well met."

I could think of nothing to say but: "So . . . you are back."

"Yesterday noon. I have been seeking you ever since."

"You remembered. It is long."

"Did I not say I would never forget?"

"You said you would come back."

"That is what I meant. What do you here? Come to sing hymns of sadness for the Queen?"

I nodded.

"I am on the same mission. But chiefly to look for you."

Joan and Dorothy were listening with some curiosity.

"You remember them?" I asked.

"Well met, Mistresses," he said, bowing first to Joan and then to Dorothy. But I knew he had not remembered them, and I was rather pleased about that.

"You came with a party?" asked Dorothy.

"Yes. But I am begging to be allowed to join yours."

Joan and Dorothy laughed. I could see they liked him. He was so handsome and charming that it would have been difficult not to like him.

He walked along with us and slipped an arm through mine. He told me how often he had thought of me during those long absences when he was far away.

"Where?" I asked.

"Too far from you," was the answer, which made me laugh happily.

"And now that you are back, shall you stay?"

He looked at me soulfully and, pressing my arm, said: "I could stay with you forever."

We were seeing each other often, and it was very soon after that meeting at St. Paul's that he told me he loved me and had done so from the moment he had seen me making the silk rose in the gardens.

"You were such a little girl then," he said. "You are still a little girl, but methinks you have grown up somewhat since then."

"I am much older," I assured him.

"You will always be young to me. My little girl."

We progressed quickly from there. He told me he would love me until the day he died. It was a time of enchantment, and he sought to please me in every way.

Naturally I wanted to look my best, and it was no easy task for I had very little money. It was only now and then that my grandmother would remember my existence; then she gave me little more than a coin or two to buy something I fancied.

She had changed since the death of Anne. She was more serious. Sometimes she would look at me sharply, as though considering me; but that was rare; more often, she lapsed into the old style of ignoring me.

The Court ladies, whom I glimpsed now and then, were now wearing silk flowers again. The favourite was the French fennel—a sort of love-in-the-mist— most beautiful, and worked in various colours. It was the very ornament to enhance the beauty of a gown and bring out the colour of a lady's eyes and soften her face.

I longed for a French fennel and was saving up my money to buy one.

When Francis discovered this, he said: "Once it was a red rose, now it is a fennel. I know a woman . . . a little hunchback in London. She is said to make the most exquisite flowers in the world. What if I asked her to make one for you?"

"Is she very expensive?"

"She knows her worth, and the ladies of the Court acclaim her."

"Alas, I could not afford it."

"Then I shall buy it for you."

"And when I have some money, I shall insist on paying you back."

"Insist if you must, but in the meantime, you shall have your French fennel."

I was delighted when he brought it to me. It was blue and the feathery leaves were very attractive. I put it on, and was even more enchanted. Then I thought of what my grandmother's reaction would be, for she could not fail to notice it. She would ask questions. She would know I could not afford to buy a flower like that, and she would discover how it was between

Francis and me, and I knew there would be disapproval. She might even tell my father, or perhaps the Duke. They would remember that I was a member of the Howard family and, after what had happened to Anne, they would be especially careful.

I looked at my beautiful French fennel and wept. It must not be known that I was in love with Francis Derham.

Lady Brereton came to visit us; she was worldly and friendly, but rather sad at this time, for a relative of hers had been accused of being one of my cousin's lovers and had been executed with her. She noticed the friendship between Francis and me and told me what an attractive young man she thought him. She was sure he would do well at Court. She was the kind of person with whom one could share confidences, and I was soon telling her about the French fennel.

"Wear your flower," she said. "And if Her Grace asks, tell her I gave it to you."

"Oh, thank you, Lady Brereton," I cried. "That is kind of you."

And so I was able to wear my French fennel.

The flower was a beginning. There were other things I coveted—silks . . . velvets, which could be made into gowns. Francis liked me to look well. He told me he had earned money when he was away from the country and could buy these things for me.

I said: "Only on the understanding that, when I have some money, I shall pay you back."

I studiously made an account of all he spent on me and called it my debt to him.

Oh, they were happy days! I wondered how I had existed without Francis.

One day he said: "We shall plight our troth, for in time we shall be married. What say you?"

I replied: "There is nothing I want more!"

"Then 'tis done. You are my wife, I your husband. So, wife, you must call me husband."

"But we are not that yet."

"We are now troth-plighted, and that means that I am yours and you are mine."

"If my grandmother knew . . . if she told my father . . . the Duke . . . perhaps they might seek to harm you."

"Am I not a Howard? Am I not of that illustrious family? The only thing I lack is fortune. I shall make my fortune and then, sweet Katherine, all will be well. But in the meantime, you and I are man and wife."

He kissed me with a yearning passion. I returned his kisses. I told myself that this was the most wonderful thing that had ever happened to me.

Dorothy appeared suddenly, as some of the women had a habit of doing. I wondered how much she had overheard.

"You are very familiar with Mistress Howard, Master Derham," she said with a touch of severity which astonished me, for they all knew what went on in the Long Room and were indeed part of it.

Francis replied: "Who should hinder a man from kissing his wife?"

"Is that so then?" asked Dorothy.

"We have plighted our troth."

"So, you are determined to have Mistress Howard?"

"By the saints!" retorted Francis. "You could guess twice and guess worse."

Dorothy smirked. "Well, 'tis no great surprise, I grant you."

Then she left us and went off—I am sure to tell her friends what she had seen and heard.

~

So they knew now. Francis used to come at night. He would bring strawberries and apples and wine—anything which he thought I might fancy. We would spread it out on my bed and we would feast. After that we would lie in the bed together.

This was different from the time with Manox. I wished I could remove all memory of that man from my mind. What I had experienced with him was distasteful now, and I deeply wished it had never happened. But what was the use in trying to change something which is already there? The only resort is to force oneself to forget.

So now I thought of Francis only. I need have no qualms. I was free to indulge in any exciting experience. Were we not troth-plighted?

Francis said: "Forget not, you are my wife."

So I remembered.

Very occasionally, I saw Manox. He would look at me, half-pleading, half-angry. Sometimes I thought he hated me because I would not look at him. The fact was that I saw him as I never had before. He was conceited; he believed himself irresistible; that was why he could not forgive me for rejecting him.

I know now that he was the one who betrayed us to the Duchess, for surely none of the girls or the young men who came to the Long Room on those nights would have done so.

However, my grandmother received a note suggesting that, if she knew what took place in the Long Room on many nights, she would not approve of it.

As a result, one of the older women received a summons to attend the Duchess. Her name was Baskerville, I think.

She came back with a wry face.

"Someone has betrayed us," she said. "The doors to the Long Room are to be locked at night, and the keys taken to Her Grace's apartments where they will remain during the night, and at daybreak one of her attendants will come and unlock the doors."

We were all alarmed to realize that the Duchess must have an inkling of what was happening.

For about a week we were disconcerted. Also, we missed our merry evenings. There was silence throughout the Long Room, broken only by complaints about how dull it had become.

And then one night, after we were all in bed, the

door was opened suddenly and one of the Duchess's waiting women was there. She stood very still, holding up the keys and shaking them. Then she tiptoed into the room in a mocking manner.

She said: "I liked not to think of you naughty girls missing your fun. Listen. Tell your gallants that they may return, but they must be very careful. I have unlocked the door and shall take the key back to Her Grace's apartments. In the morning, I shall come again with the key, but there will be no unlocking of the door because the door will have remained unlocked throughout the night. You must make sure that before I come your friends have left for where they should rightly be."

Then she sat on one of the beds and we all clustered round her and there was much merriment.

After that it was as it had been before—except that now we knew that the Duchess had been aware of what was happening, and it might have occurred to her that we could find a way of deceiving her—which, of course, we had.

∾

Francis loved to give me presents. He was very anxious to make a fortune. He wanted to take me away with him. He often talked of sailing the seas, and I guessed that that was what he did during his absences. He had returned with money—far more than he could have earned as a pensioner in the Duke's household, but still not the fortune he must have.

He was impatient. He wanted to marry me in truth. He knew that the Duke would never accept him as a suitor for his niece as he was; but if he were a rich man, his remote connection with the Howard family might carry him through.

So he would go away. It should only be for a short trip. He would earn money and come back. I did not want him to go—nor did he want to, but he was convinced that he must.

The Duchess was becoming wary. Neither of us could imagine what would happen if she knew how it was between us. We were troth-plighted and that was sacred to us, for no one could say we were not man and wife.

The Duke would doubtless have Francis removed. Who could say how? Taken to the Tower on some pretext, there to disappear, as so many had who had offended the great? And if we were caught by the Duchess and betrayed to the Duke, it would be the end of our hopes. And what would happen to me? Sent into a nunnery? Married to someone I should hate? It could be one of many things. However, once Francis was a man of great fortune, they would be ready to welcome him as a member of the great Howard family . . . which he undoubtedly was.

So, much as I disliked the idea of his going, he had made me see the necessity of it.

I was desolate, but he said I must not be, for he would be back ere long with the fortune which would make the way clear for us.

He already had one hundred pounds, and he would leave the money with me. I should keep it safe, for it was the foundation of our fortune. And if he did not return, that money should be mine.

Then he went away.

The days seemed long and the nights wearisome without him. I put the hundred pounds in a bag which I determined should always be with me. I kept it under my pillow at night and attached it to my waistband in the day, but it was too bulky for that, and I had to find another place for it. I had little privacy; but I did have a drawer in which I could put some of my clothes. I sewed the money up in the pocket of a petticoat and every day I took it out to make sure it was there.

At times I was tempted to spend a little on some ornament to which I took a fancy, some piece of silk or velvet which one of the women could make into a gown for me. I tried to persuade myself that Francis would have given it to me if he had been there. But I never did. It was a sacred trust. It was to be the foundation of our life together. Perhaps I guessed that, if I took a little at first, I should go on doing it again . . . and again. But I knew that one day Francis would come back. When he did, the hundred pounds must be his, just as he had left it with me.

One day, when I was sitting in the garden, I looked up and there was Francis. I leaped to my feet and we ran to meet each other. We could only laugh and cling together for some minutes, too moved for speech.

"Am I dreaming?" I cried at last. "Holy Mother, let me not be dreaming."

"My own Katherine," he murmured. "My sweet

Katherine." And I knew in truth that he was there.

It transpired that he had come back without the fortune he had hoped for, but what did that matter? All I cared for was that he was back. And how happy he was to be with me.

He asked earnestly, had there been someone else of whom I had grown fond?

No, no, no, I assured him. No one. I had spent my lonely days and nights thinking of him, longing for his return.

He was reassured. He confessed he had been afraid. And himself? Had he been faithful?

"As I shall be all my life. Once I had seen sweet Katherine, there could be no one else for me."

We talked as lovers do, and then he told me that he was going to ask the Duchess for a place in her household.

"So that I may see more of you," he said. "All through the day I shall be so much nearer than I am as the Duke's retainer."

"What post would you have?" I asked.

"Oh . . . gentleman usher . . . or page. I would do anything if I might be near you."

The Duchess liked to have handsome young men about her, and she agreed to make him one of her gentlemen ushers. That was what we wanted, for it did mean we could see each other far more frequently than before.

I gave him the hundred pounds and told him how carefully I had preserved it, and how glad I was that I had not been tempted to spend any of it!

Francis was delighted. The fortune would come, and in the meantime we would give ourselves up to the pleasure of being together. We had much time to make up.

~

It was true that the Duchess had changed. She was watchful, and especially of me. I had grown up. I was fifteen years old. I was a little alarmed, for I guessed she was thinking of the future, and, now that the once dazzling Anne was someone she did not wish to think of, her thoughts seemed to turn more and more to her humble little granddaughter.

The Maids' Chamber was a room put to the use of

the women. There we did tapestry . . . embroidery and listened to the music one of us would play while the others worked.

It was a duty to go there and perforce I must do my stint, but I was never any good at tapestry, and embroidery bored me. Sometimes I would play the virginals, at which I was more skilled than at needlework; but I was not so happy as I might have been doing that, because occasionally it reminded me of Henry Manox, whom I would rather have forgotten.

I was seated there with Joan one day. There were only the two of us in the large chamber, and I was reluctantly working on a piece of embroidery when Francis came in. He stood by the door, smiling at me.

"Two industrious ladies, I see," he said mockingly. "What great work is this?"

He came close to me and laid his hand on my shoulder.

"Oh, I see. Very fine. Very beautiful." Now he had his hands about my waist and was nibbling my ear.

"I am working," I cried. "And, Master Derham, what are you doing in the Maids' Chamber, pray?"

"Oh, I just came in to make sure you were working."

"And should you be here, sir?"

"Mistress Howard, why so stern?"

He looked at me in mock menace, and I leaped up and drew away from him. He came as though to seize me, and I ran round the table with him in pursuit. Joan was watching us, smiling that secret smile which I knew so well.

I dashed round the room; he was close behind me. I tripped, he caught me and we fell together; we lay on the floor, rolling over and over; he was on top of me when the door opened and my grandmother came in. She stood still, staring at us; her face was white, then scarlet. She was nearest to Joan and she turned to her and slapped her across the face.

Joan looked startled and my grandmother repeated the action.

"And you sit there and watch with that grin on your face! What do you think you are about, girl?"

Joan started to stammer something, but my grandmother had turned to Francis and me. We stood up. Francis looked sheepish; as for myself, I was too bewildered to do anything but wait for the storm to burst.

My grandmother stepped towards Francis and slapped him across the face in the same way as she had slapped Joan. Then she did the same to me and said: "Get out, Derham."

He bowed and muttered some apology; she looked as though she were going to strike him again and he hurriedly left us.

Then she turned to me. She seized me by the ear and pulled me close to her. I saw the fury in her eyes. She started to shake me, then she pushed me away from her.

"Go to my bedchamber," she said. "I will deal with you there."

I heard her say to Joan: "As for you, girl. You deserve a beating. That you do. You sit there and watch *that*. What next, I wonder?"

I went to her room, trembling and fearful. What would happen to us now? Francis and I were troth-plighted. We might play as we did. We were doing no harm.

It was not long before my grandmother came. She was seething with anger.

"You foolish girl!" she cried. "What do you think you were doing with Derham?"

"It was naught but play," I began.

"Rolling on the floor . . . his arms about you . . . pressing down on you. Do you know nothing, girl?"

I was very afraid of what could happen to Francis if she told the Duke how she had found us together. They would not listen to explanations. Besides, Francis would be sent away. He had not made his fortune yet and, until then, we must not talk of marriage.

She gave me a look of contempt and I was afraid she was going to strike me; but she looked tired, exhausted by her emotion.

"You are young, I know," she murmured, "and you were never very clever, Katherine Howard." A sadness came into her eyes. She was thinking of that brilliant one, who had been brought to her sorry end—one might say through that very brilliance. Even she had not been clever enough. And there was I, now fifteen years old, playing childish games with a young man of the household. No . . . dangerous games . . . when I was too young, or stupid, to know they could lead to disaster.

I may not have been brilliant in book learning like my cousin, sophisticated, with the gracious manners learned in the French Court, but there were certain things I knew about and one was the way of the sexes. It may be that there are some of us born with the knowledge. I had in any case been a ready pupil . . . responsive, eager. She decided however to talk to me.

"Katherine Howard," she said. "You should know something of the ways of men. Some of them . . . in particular the young . . . think of little but what they can get from unsuspecting women. It is the nature of them. Derham is a handsome young fellow. He will swagger round boasting of his conquests, like as not."

Oh no, I thought. Not Francis Derham. He was faithful to me, as I was to him. It might not have been so with Manox. Oh, do not think of Manox . . . that is unhealthy and uneasy thinking. Francis is a good man; he loves me and he is faithful. He swore it, and I believe him; and we are troth-plighted.

But I must not tell the Duchess this. I must not betray anything. I must be wary.

I hung my head and played the young girl, innocent of the world, too stupid to know the danger she was in. That was what my grandmother wanted. What she had seen was a romp, entered into on the impulse of the moment.

I should not plead for Francis Derham or myself. I should stand there, my eyes downcast, while she sat in her chair and rambled on about the dangers that could beset young girls, and the need to keep themselves untouched; and how this applied especially to those who belonged to noble families.

"It will not be long now," she was saying, "before it will be time for you to look to the future. There might be a place at Court. Of course, it would have been different . . ." Her lips trembled. If only her once brilliant granddaughter had kept her place instead of losing her head, what glory might have been in store for little Katherine Howard.

I did not tell her that I did not want such glories. All I wanted was to marry Francis Derham, to whom I was troth-plighted.

Her wrath had subsided a little. The Duchess was a lady who would make herself believe what she wanted to—particularly if the alternative was too unpleasant to contemplate—so she sat in her chair, talking of the pitfalls which could befall a young girl—particularly one of a great family. She was deluding herself into believing that I was an innocent child who knew nothing of the urgent desires of young men and the readiness of young women to yield to them.

I was dismissed and, bruised and very frightened, I left the Duchess and tried to forget my stinging cheek by telling myself I had had a lucky escape. But I could not stop worrying about Francis.

She might think that I was an innocent, but could she apply the same judgement to him? If what we had done was due to my ignorance, youth and general stupidity, what had such a romp indicated about him?

A few days passed. I saw Francis surreptitiously in the garden. We clung together, dreading we might be seen.

"Has anything been said to you?" I asked.

"Nothing," he replied.

"Have you seen the Duchess?"

"*En passant*. She did not look my way."

"Do you think they will send you away?"

He was silent, and I knew he did. We clung more closely together in desperation.

He was not sent away. Until this happened, he had, I believe, been a favourite of the Duchess. She did have a liking for handsome young men. I think she decided to forgive us, for a week or so passed and nothing happened. We were beginning to think that the escapade had been dismissed as a matter of little importance.

~

As time passed, we were lulled more and more into a sense of security; we slipped back into the old ways, and at night Francis would come up to the Long Room; but everyone knew that we had been caught rolling on the floor together in a compromising situation, and there was a certain uneasiness.

"What if Her Grace should discover that the room is left unlocked through the night?" asked Dorothy. "We shall have to be very careful. If she found Derham in Katherine Howard's bed . . ." Dorothy suppressed a giggle. "Well, that would not be so easy to explain as a romp on the floor."

"We should hear her coming," I said. "She would be using her stick to mount the stairs. Then Francis could slip into the little gallery. She would not know he was here then."

I could not bear that we should be deprived of those meetings. It was not long since he had returned from that long absence.

Fewer people were coming to the Long Room. Many of them had decided that it was too dangerous.

The Duchess, however, did not come to the Long Room, nor did she discover for herself about the matter of the key. It happened in a different way.

One of the maids, terrified, I suppose, that we were in danger of being discovered, went to her and confessed what was happening. I was sure that that was the last thing the Duchess wanted, and she was more angry than ever.

It might have been Dorothy, Joan or Mary Lassells—she was a sly one whom I had never understood—or someone quite different. I never knew. All I was aware of was that one of the maids went to the Duchess and told her how the men came to the room, how the door had remained unlocked throughout the night; and chiefly how Francis Derham called Katherine Howard his wife, kissed and caressed her and spent the night with her under the sheets in her bed.

My grandmother was horrified, and this was too important a matter to be set aside.

She sent for me and, as soon as I arrived in her room, she seized me, slapped my face, tore off my gown, pushed me on to her bed and with her stick beat my bare buttocks until I screamed with pain. I think she might not have stopped until she killed me if she had not exhausted herself. Her hair was falling about her face, her eyes were wild; she looked like a witch intent on evil, and that evil was directed at me.

Then the stick slipped from her hand; she fell into her chair and she sat looking at me lying across her bed. I rose and tried to pull my clothes about me.

"Do not attempt to show modesty to me, slut," she cried. "Do not simper and play the child, you little harlot. I know of your lechery with Francis Derham."

I cried out: "It is not fair to talk thus. I am his wife . . . may not a wife caress her husband?"

"You are what! Oh, what pain you cause me! What have I done, I ask God and all His saints, what have I done to deserve this?"

"There is nothing wrong, Your Grace," I began.

"Be silent, you little whore! How long has this been going on? Under the sheets . . ." she moaned. "After midnight . . . with Derham. Are you with child?"

"Your Grace, you do not understand."

"I understand. I understand too well. Do not deny this . . . harlotry. Derham has been your lover, has he not? He will die for this. When the Duke hears . . ."

"Oh, I pray, do not tell the Duke." I thought of that cold-eyed man who had condemned Anne Boleyn. We should have been better without such a kinsman. And now his anger would be turned on Francis and on me. What would become of us? And there had been nothing wrong. We were husband and wife. How often had we said that?

"Stop muttering to yourself, girl. You cannot tell me they have lied. If that were so . . ." She was almost pleading to me. She wanted me to say that what they had told her was a lie. She wanted to continue to delude herself into believing that. But she knew it was true. Had she not seen us in the Maids' Chamber, and that was a clear indication of how it was between us.

I said nothing. I knew it would be no good.

"How could you?" she cried. "Have you no regard for your virtue . . . for your family?"

I persisted: "Your Grace does not understand. Francis Derham and I love each other."

"Love!" she sneered. "Rolling about under the sheets. You could not even wait for nightfall to hide your shame. You must try it on the floor."

"It was not so."

"I saw it with my own eyes."

"It was just . . . fun . . . as you say . . . a little romp."

"Romp! Fun! Is that what you call it when the name of a noble house is desecrated! Holy Mother of God, this is too much to be borne."

"I will explain. Francis and I are troth-plighted. That is enough. We are married. We did nothing wrong."

"You are even more stupid than I thought you. I had hopes for you. A place at Court. It might well be. The King will marry again. There is no doubt of that. The new Queen will need ladies-in-waiting. There was a chance there might be a place for you. What do you think will become of you, you stupid child? What hopes have you if it is known what you have been about? These girls know . . . the men too. By all the saints, it will go ill with them if they whisper it abroad. And you, addle-pate, talk of troth-plight. Derham will suffer for this. As for you . . . you deserve to be turned out of this household."

I said nothing. I could only think of what might happen to Francis.

She tired of railing against me at last, and when I begged leave to go, she granted it.

My body was sore and bruised, but my heart more so. This was what we had always feared. What would they do to Francis? That was the fear which dominated my mind. If only he had made that fortune! If only we could have been married.

It would not be so now. That was clear. My grandmother might well tell the Duke, and then what would they do to poor Francis?

≈

The women were all subdued. They had been discovered. One of them had betrayed, not only me, but all of them. There would be no more deception about the unlocked door, no more nightly revels. And who knew what other secrets would be revealed?

One of the pages, whom I knew to be a friend of Francis, sought me out. He looked frightened and afraid to speak. I fervently hoped he had brought me news of Francis.

He said: "Mistress, I have a message for you. Will you go to a spot you know well in the gardens?"

I understood that what was meant was that spot secluded by bushes and trees not far from the water's edge which Francis and I had called our own little garden. So I knew, of course, that this was a message from Francis. I hurried to the spot and within a few seconds he appeared. He was dressed as for a journey.

He held me tightly in his arms and we both wept.

Then he said: "I must go, Katherine. They will kill me if I stay. They will say that I have brought disgrace on the Howard name. Oh, my love, how can I leave you?"

"I have been beaten and reviled," I said. "I do not think more will be done to me. They will not want it known."

"I thank God for that," he said. "But I must go . . . or they will find some way of killing me."

"Then you must go quickly . . ."

"Some day I shall come back," he said.

"Where shall you go?"

"I shall go to Ireland. There I shall make that fortune and return."

"You will come back to me . . . ?"

"I swear it. And you, Katherine . . . ?"

I said fervently: "You shall never live to say to me, you have swerved."

We clung together. I wanted to beg him not to go, but I knew he must. He wanted to beg me to go with him, but we knew that would be the final ruin of us both. This bitter parting had to be. But in my heart I knew that one day he would return.

The Fourth Queen

Life was very dull after that. I missed Francis sadly, but I knew I must be grateful that he had escaped with his life. When I considered that, I realized the importance of what I had done.

There was strict surveillance throughout the household. One of the Duchess's attendants—nearly as old as herself, on whom she could entirely rely—had the duty of locking and unlocking the door of the Long Room. The nights of revelry were at an end. We were given tasks to do and long hours were spent at needlework of some kind. A musical instrument might be played while we worked, or one of us would read aloud. While this was in progress, one of the Duchess's older ladies would inspect us at any moment to make sure orders were being carried out.

The Duchess had had a shock which had aroused her to action, and she was determined to put an end to the careless manner in which her household had previously been conducted.

The new way of life had its effect on me. I listened to the music and surprised myself by becoming interested in the readings. My longing for Francis faded a little. I was thinking of other things than what I called to myself "romping." That was a pleasant, comfortable word, suggesting innocence.

One letter was smuggled into me from Francis. Dorothy Barwike brought it to me with a sly smile, so I knew she was aware whence it came.

"How did you get it?" I asked.

Dorothy could only say that it had been given to her by someone to whom it had in turn been given. It was not possible to say how it had arrived in Lambeth.

It was full of protestations of undying love. He was in Ireland and would soon be sailing off on a great adventure which he knew would be profitable, and when he returned, he would come to claim his wife. None should gainsay him then. He lived for that day.

I read it through again and again and thought of his coming home. Then we would marry.

My grandmother, who, immediately after that scene when she had beaten me so severely, had treated me with coldness and disgust, now relented a little.

She said to me one day: "My child, we will not talk of what happened. 'Tis best forgot." Then she immediately began to talk of it. "It must be hushed up. Your uncle, the Duke, must never hear of it. No one must know."

I thought of all those who did know. All those women who slept in the Long Room . . . and doubtless others.

"It would disturb the family," she went on. "Your father would be distressed. It could prevent your sisters making good marriages. Your uncle would never forgive you."

I tried to explain again that Francis and I were as husband and wife, and we only did what married people were entitled to do.

"Be silent," she snapped. "You do not know what you say. You are a child. You know nothing of these matters. It was but child's play."

"Your Grace, Francis was my husband in very truth."

I saw exasperation and fear in her expression. I was sure that, if I had been near enough, she would have struck me.

"Did I not say that we were not to speak of the matter?"

I nodded, not reminding her that it was she who had brought up the topic. But I knew how very deeply alarmed she was, for I too was understanding that what I had fallen into in a lighthearted way was, after all, a serious matter.

This was continually brought home to me in my conversations with my grandmother. I was once more rubbing her legs, and at such times she would continually stress the importance of the Howard family.

It was the old theme. "Oh, it is a wondrous thing to belong to a family such as ours. We have always been so close to the King, except on one or two occasions in our history, for we are by no means fools . . . except on those occasions when we seek to gratify our foolish desires and plunge near to disaster." A significant look at me followed this remark. "But that is when we are young and too stupid to know better. And remember this, Katherine Howard, it behooves us all not to demean ourselves with those of low standing. We must always remember that we owe the utmost respect to the noble family to which we belong."

I did not speak, but bent low over her leg, rubbing soothingly. I had always thought Francis so courtly, so handsome, comparable with the highest in the land, but all this insistence on the family's greatness was making me think, well, he is, after all, only a pensioner of the Duke. I remembered him cringing before the Duchess when she slapped his face.

"I could see a good life for you, Katherine Howard," went on my grandmother. "That is, if you are sensible. There might be a place at Court. Would you like that?"

I thought of the Court. Dancing, music, grand balls, beautiful gowns and money with which to buy them—not having to rely on a friend, or a lover. Mercy me! How much did I owe Francis Derham? How many ells of velvet and fine silks had he brought to me? That beautiful French fennel from the crooked old woman who made flowers for the Court ladies could not have been cheap, for she knew her worth. There had been other ornaments which Francis had delighted in giving me, and I had always said, "I will pay you when I have some money." And he would laugh and kiss me and tell me how this or that became me. I should not have allowed it. A proud Howard should not have taken money from anyone—especially someone so far below her.

Almost immediately, I chided myself for thinking so of Francis, but the fact remained that he was not considered to be one of us although he claimed to have some remote connection with the family.

My grandmother was saying: "Eh, eh? Do you hear me? How would you like to go to Court?"

"It would be very interesting."

"Very interesting! Is that all you have to say? Listen to me. I tell you this, Mistress Howard, it would be something for which you would bless your family. Marry, and so it would. There could be a great marriage for you."

"I am married to . . ."

"Don't dare let me hear such nonsense, or I shall beat you till you scream for mercy." She reached for her stick and shook it at me. "Are you mad? Never let me hear you talk such nonsense. You would bring down the wrath of your uncle the Duke . . . and that would mean more than a slap or two from me, I can tell you. Much, much more. You may have been taken advantage of by a stupid young man as careless as yourself, but I was at hand to protect you and put an end to your folly before it was too late. Did you hear that? Before it was too late."

"Yes . . . yes, Your Grace," I murmured.

"Well, rub a little harder. Oh . . . that's a relief. You have good hands, child. Well, of a surety the King will marry again . . . soon." She laughed. "He is a man who cannot do without a wife. There are some like that."

I thought, he must be getting old now. I had thought he was old when I saw him beside my cousin. She had looked so dazzlingly beautiful. But I did not say this, as any mention of Anne always depressed the Duchess.

"I hear he is making enquiries on the Continent," went on the Duchess. "And he is deeply desirous of making Marie of Lorraine his wife. She is said to be of unsurpassed beauty, but she is betrothed to the King of Scotland. But His Majesty would thrust that aside. What is the King of Scots compared with the King of England? Yet, I do not think the lady is so eager to take our King. Some are saying that it is unlucky to be the wife of the King of England. One wife put from him after years of marriage, the next . . ." Her voice broke. " . . . sent to the block . . . the third dying in childbirth. It might indeed seem that Heaven is set against a happy marriage for him. That is what they say."

"And it is indeed the truth," I put in.

"Do not dare say such things!" reproved the Duchess, seemingly unaware that she was the one who had just said it.

"The French King mocks him," she went on. "Those French. Would you trust them? They have their graces and prancing manners, I grant you . . . and beneath all that, they are wily. No friends of ours, they cover their wicked actions with graceful words. Do you know, the French King sent word to His Majesty condoling with him on his unfortunate explorations into matrimony and to wish him success with his fourth choice. And when His Majesty said that he would be delighted to take a lady from the French Court, King Francis replied that any lady of any degree should be at his disposal. French manners, of course, are not to be taken seriously, and when the King sent a message to King Francis to the effect that he would come without delay to inspect the ladies, the French King pretended to be shocked that his gracious politeness had been misunderstood and he replied that the King of England would understand that noble ladies could not be taken to market like horses at a fair."

I began to laugh.

"It is not for laughing, child," she reproved me. "Whom His Majesty marries is important to us . . . to the family. Remember the Seymours. What airs they give themselves. They think they are above us all because they are uncles to the young Edward. It is not a laughing matter. We must trust that the King's new wife will favour the Howard family. That is why your uncle would like to have a hand in the choice."

"Doubtless the King will choose his own queen."

The Duchess nodded gloomily. "Of a surety he will."

She was thoughtful for a while, then she said: "Enough of this, child. Put away the unguents." She brightened a little. "There will be a new queen . . . and soon, I trow. You are growing up and you have the Howard good looks. Who knows, with the coming of a new queen, there may be an opening for *you* at Court."

I was becoming more interested in what was going on around me than I had ever been before. Perhaps it was because I was getting older, but more likely because the Duchess's household was no longer a forcing ground for latent sensuality. Restrictions set by the Duchess had to be adhered to, and there was stern punishment for any who diverged from the new laws now laid down. There was a subdued atmosphere throughout the house and certainly not the same familiarity between the sexes there had been previously. Everyone was careful not to attract suspicion.

I suppose some of the bolder spirits continued their associations, but, as Francis was gone, I was not tempted. I read a little and even wrote the occasional letter when necessary. I found that there were other interests than kissing and thinking of a lover all the time.

So I learned something of what was going on. I now knew a little about the powerful people at Court—men like Thomas Cromwell, who had taken Wolsey's place. Poor Wolsey! It was said that he had died of a broken heart which saved him from the axe. He had done all he could to prevent the King's marriage to my cousin Anne but, brilliant as he was, he was no match for the King in the heat of his desire, and he had died because he had lost the King's favour.

There was Thomas More, who had refused to sign the Act of Supremacy. The King was, at that time, seeking to rid himself of my cousin and blamed her for that good man's death.

How lightly all heads seemed to rest on shoulders! I began to realize more fully how alarmed my grandmother had been when she discovered what had happened between Francis Derham and me. Not that I was of any importance, except in a very minor way as a Howard.

I thought once more of my poor cousin. They had

said she had lovers, and that was treason towards the King. Yet he had broken his marriage vows to her. There was Jane Seymour to bear witness to that. But that did not seem important. And Anne had died for her transgression.

It was all very difficult to understand, but that in itself made it more dangerous. I began to wish there had not been that passion between Francis and myself almost as much as I had wished I had never known Henry Manox.

I felt I wanted to go on living this restricted life, becoming interested in what was going on around me, being the young, innocent girl I could have been if I had never known those nights in the Long Room.

How different it was now. We all slept behind locked doors and talked together sometimes of what was going on in the country. Would the King marry? And whom? It all seemed of the greatest interest.

Some of the leading spirits of the Long Room had disappeared. Joan was one of them. She was going to be married, I believe. I was rather relieved when she went, because she often reminded me of that occasion when the Duchess surprised us in the Maids' Chamber and had seen Derham and me rolling on the floor.

Throughout the country, for some time, there had been a conflict between Catholics and Protestants. The Howards were firm Catholics and Stephen Gardiner, the Bishop of Winchester, stood with my uncle; the Seymours, with Thomas Cromwell, were in the opposite camp. I had never before realized how important such men were, and how they worked in a devious manner to attain their ends and influence the King's actions without appearing to do so.

It was for this reason, of course, that my uncle and his brothers had been so delighted when the King was attracted by my cousin. They must have temporarily forgotten how fickle royal favour could be.

Perhaps I am running ahead. I cannot believe that the frivolous girl I was at that time suddenly began to take an intelligent interest in her surroundings and to understand something of their meaning; but certainly I began to change then.

We were all excited when it seemed that the King was making his choice of a wife. One of the likely candidates was a lady known as Anne of Cleves, the Lutheran daughter of John, Duke of Cleves. My uncle was naturally against the match, Thomas Cromwell for it.

We heard her name mentioned often, and I learned a little about her. She was said to be beautiful, but were not all royal ladies beautiful? Especially those who were seeking—or being sought in—marriage with a highly desirable consort.

She had an elder sister who had been married for ten years to the Duke of Saxony, the leader of the Protestants in Germany. Her name was Sybilla and not only was she reputed to be of outstanding beauty, but she was known for her wisdom and the happiness she had brought to her successful marriage. In fact, she was reckoned to be one of the most distinguished and admirable of ladies.

The sister of such a lady must surely herself possess some excellent qualities? She was twenty-one years old.

"Why," I said, "she is very old." It was a remark which provoked some laughter.

"Mistress Katherine Howard," said Dorothy Barwike mockingly, "having seen all of fifteen years, finds twenty-one . . . old."

I blushed. I stammered: "No . . . I suppose it is not in truth . . . old. But for a queen . . ."

"The King is not exactly a young man."

That was true enough. When I had seen him with my cousin I had thought he was old—and now he was even older, so it did not matter that Anne of Cleves was twenty-one.

I daresay the King would have liked to see her for himself but, after the snub he had received from the King of France, he might have felt wary of suggesting this.

The next best thing was to have a portrait of her, but portraits, of course, did not always tell the truth.

The Duchess told me that the Duke did not like the proposed marriage. He thought it was most unsuitable. Then "that knave, Cromwell," as my uncle called him, had the idea that he would send our finest painter, Hans Holbein, to make a picture of the prospective bride, and he was sure that when the King saw it he would be in favour of the match.

This is what Hans Holbein did, and he painted a beautiful picture. It came in an ivory box, shaped like a rose, I heard, and when it was opened, the portrait was disclosed, lying at the bottom of the box. The King was enchanted. He was not interested in the lady's religion. What he cared about were her personal attractions and, according to the exquisite miniature, they were completely desirable. So the King would marry Anne of Cleves.

There was gloom throughout the house. Anne of Cleves, with her Protestant upbringing, was certainly not what the Howards were looking for.

By the end of the year it seemed certain that she would be the new queen. I gathered, through the gossip, that my uncle blamed Thomas Cromwell for this.

It really was a very short time since Jane Seymour had died, but the King was clearly not greatly grieved by that sad event. Jane had served her purpose. She had given him what her two predecessors had failed to, but he could be only moderately pleased with his heir, for the child was not very robust and was therefore a constant source of anxiety. It seemed hardly likely that such a weakling as Jane would have produced healthy children had she lived, and, as the King was no longer young, it was as well to get himself a new wife as quickly as possible.

We were getting excited. There would be a coronation and that meant revelry in the streets, and if, at the appropriate interval, little Edward should have a strong and healthy half-brother, that would ease the tension which had always existed about the fragile heir.

There were delays. In the first place, the future queen's father died. Then we heard rumours that Sybilla's husband, John Frederick of Saxony, had expressed doubts as to the wisdom of the marriage. He was uneasy that the bridegroom had already experienced three unsatisfactory marriages—the first to a wife who was said to have been no wife and whom he had put from him; the second to one whose life ended on the scaffold; and the third to a wife who had died in childbirth almost immediately.

Everyone was asking the question, would there be no marriage with Anne of Cleves? Would the King have to look elsewhere? And despondency settled on us all.

Then there was good news. John Frederick's fears were stifled by the League of Protestants, who declared that the marriage would be good for the

Cause. Had not the King already broken with Rome? That was one step in the right direction. It might be that his wife could persuade him to take more.

At last Anne left Düsseldorf for England. Nothing could delay the King's marriage much longer. We thought she would arrive for Christmas, which would be a most appropriate time; but, alas, it was not to be. The weather was bad; the winds were especially fierce, which perhaps was to be expected at this time of the year.

We heard that the Lady of Cleves would perforce spend Christmas in Calais. Then the winds suddenly subsided and we were delighted when we heard that she was to sail, and she arrived in Deal two days after Christmas.

My grandmother said, as I rubbed her legs: "The Duke is most displeased."

"There is little he can do about that," I replied, having become much bolder during those days. I should soon be sixteen years old and a child no longer. I had changed a great deal, and I tried not to think too much of the foolish, thoughtless girl I had once been, believing everything that was told me. I was now dreaming of going to Court. My grandmother had such ambitions for me.

"With a new queen," she often mused, "though she is not of our choosing, but . . . who knows? The Duke has kept favour, even after . . ." Then she would sigh and be sad, thinking of her favourite granddaughter.

Now she said: "True, we must needs accept that. They say she is very fair. The Duke has seen Master Holbein's portrait and it depresses his spirit."

"She is very beautiful then?"

My grandmother was silent. After a while she said: "Your uncle is among those who will go to Canterbury to greet her. It will not be long before she is crowned Queen, and it seems only yesterday . . ."

She was going to be sad for a while after this. The prospect of a new queen brought back too many memories of that other.

There was great excitement in the Long Room. Someone always managed to get the latest news from a friend who had either heard or actually witnessed it. We had to sort out the truth from fantasy, but there was usually a grain or two of the former involved; and it all made fascinating listening.

Now there were reports of what had happened at the royal meeting.

When the King had his first glimpse of her, he was filled with horror.

"They say she is by no means as fair as he had been led to believe by accounts and, of course, Master Holbein's portrait. She is big and he likes not large women. Master Holbein makes her skin look like velvet, and hers is marked by the pox. She wears the hideous fashions of her country and she is no beauty."

"And what says the King?"

"The King is beside himself with wrath. He stayed for a very short time in her company. Then he made his excuses and left. He was in a fury. Be assured, someone will suffer for this."

"It will go ill with Master Holbein for painting such a false picture."

"Oh, he will not harm the artist. He likes well Holbein's work, and the painter would say that was how he saw her. When he looked at her he was seeing her as she might have been before she caught the pox. That is how artists are. It is Thomas Cromwell who will bear the brunt of this. He wanted the match.

He commanded Holbein to paint the picture . . . and mayhap he commissioned it to be done without the pox marks."

We were all very excited.

"I hope this will not spoil the coronation," said one.

"It has gone too far to retreat," added another.

"Poor King."

"Poor lady, I say. He will find some means of being rid of her, as . . ."

Mary Lassells gave the speaker a push. "Have a care, girl," she said; and there was a brief silence.

Someone knew someone who was a page to Lord Admiral Fitzwilliam, Earl of Southampton, who had brought the Lady of Cleves to England. In his presence, the King was reputed to have said: "Persons of humble station have advantages beyond the reach of princes. They may choose their wives, whereas princes must take those who are brought to them."

Master Cromwell was of the company, and the King berated him for having brought him to this pass. He said he did not like the lady. She seemed to him like a great Flanders mare, and she had none of those virtues which he looked for in a wife. He shouted to

Admiral Fitzwilliam in a great rage and said that the Admiral should have given him notice of the kind of woman he was bringing for his King to marry. The Admiral was very bold. He retorted that he had not known he had such authority. His orders had been to bring the lady to England and that he had done.

Cromwell, it appeared, knowing that the King's fury was directed mainly at himself, pointed out that the Admiral had, in a letter, referred to the lady's beauty, to which the Admiral replied that he had reported what he had been told, and he presumed that, as the lady was to be Queen, she must naturally be beautiful.

"The King was so angry," went on our informant, "that he ordered them to stop their bickering blame of each other. He was surrounded by a pack of fools and they would do well to find a way out of the situation into which they had placed him."

Then one of the women said in dismay: "Then there will be no marriage . . . no coronation!"

"There may be or may not," replied the knowledge-able one. "They are saying now that the lady was once betrothed to the Marquis of Lorraine."

"Then depend upon it," said Dorothy, "there will be no marriage. I'll swear the lady will be sent back to her family."

"That could never be. There would be war. No one would accept such an insult. The Schmalkaldic League would be up in arms. These Protestant communities can be as fierce as the Catholics."

And it did seem that they were too strong for the King. It was proved that any proposed alliance between Anne and the Marquis of Lorraine had merely been a discussion between the parents of the young people and it had been abandoned several years ago.

The King realized that he was caught. We heard he had asked: "Is there no remedy? Then must I needs put my head in this yoke?"

I was more sorry for the poor Lady of Cleves. What a terrible thing for one's bridegroom to say. I thought of Francis Derham and his great tenderness for me, and that it would be pleasant to see him again.

There was speculation everywhere. Would there be a wedding? No one was sure. The King certainly would have welcomed a release. And I was sure the lady would have too. What a sad and humiliating position for her! To leave her home and come to a strange country, only to receive such a cold welcome!

The Duchess was half-jubilant, half-fearful. Nothing would please the Duke more than if the Lady Anne were sent home. But how could that be? Yet, we had had experience of our King's methods. He could act drastically when his desire for some object was strong enough. And now he certainly desired to be free of the Lady of Cleves as ardently as he had of Catherine of Aragon.

"The King is furious," said the Duchess, as I rubbed her legs. "Only God knows where this will end. I would not be in Cromwell's shoes for a kingdom. The King rants against him and all those who had a part in this. He cannot bear the sight of her. He was thinking he would get a beauty, and he has this 'Flanders mare,' as he calls her."

"I wonder how *she* likes *him*." There was a brief disapproving silence, and I stammered. "He is not young."

"Will you never learn?" demanded the Duchess. "Any lady should be glad to marry the King."

I wondered about that. In my heart, I suspected that the Lady of Cleves was probably as eager to go back to her home as he was to send her there. What a pity this could not be done.

The Duchess said: "It is the Duke's opinion that there will be a marriage. There must be. It has gone too far to return her now. It would never be tolerated. Her brother, who is now duke, would be driven into the hands of the Emperor Charles and the King of France. They are hand in glove, those two. Lord have mercy on us, how things change! They are laughing together, praying that the King will send back this girl, and Cleves will be *their* puppet then. It would be disaster for the King to turn back now."

I did glimpse the King and Queen on their wedding day. I, with my party, had sailed down to Greenwich in our barge. How splendid the King looked in his crimson satin coat with its clasp of diamonds. He was smiling, but I guessed he was far from happy. I heard later that he had told Cromwell just before the ceremony that, if it were not to satisfy the world and his realm, he would not have done what he was about to do for any earthly thing. I can imagine Cromwell's misgivings at those words; he must have already felt the axe at his neck.

For the first time I saw the Queen. She was in cloth of gold embroidered with pearls and a gown made in the Dutch fashion, which was not becoming. Her hair she wore loose about her shoulders, and on her head a coronal of gold and precious stones. She looked demure, her eyes downcast; and none could have guessed what she was feeling; but she must have been very unhappy.

My quick glance at her showed me she was not the ugly creature whom I had been led to expect. It was unfair to liken her to a Flanders mare. True, she was not graceful, and the Dutch fashion was far from becoming. She would have looked much better in the English styles which, to a large measure, we had copied from the French, chiefly at the time when my cousin led the Court. Anne of Cleves was certainly not dazzlingly attractive like Anne Boleyn, or pretty like Jane Seymour. But she was not ill-favoured. She had a very high forehead, dark hair and eyes and, if she were not exactly beautiful, she looked clever and interesting.

But whatever the cost to herself and those who had promoted the marriage, and to the intense displeasure of the King, the people were determined to enjoy the occasion.

Betrothal

"When the time comes," said my grandmother, "we shall find a match for you. You should do fairly well. Your uncle will see to that."

I was nearly eighteen years old. I rarely allowed myself to think of Henry Manox now. It was too distasteful. I had been an innocent child and he had done his best to seduce me. I must admit that I had not been exactly reluctant. Fortunately, he had been aware of the dangers of the situation, which had restrained him to some extent. And then there had been Francis Derham. That had been different, but it should never have been allowed to happen. I had kept the red silk rose and the French fennel, but I did not wear either of them now.

I did not blame Derham. There was that in my

nature which was easily aroused to love—I mean physical love. I had been as eager as Derham. I thought of this suitable match which would be arranged for me with some trepidation.

I longed to be safely married—the past behind me, forgotten.

When my uncle visited Lambeth, I used to wonder if I should hear of a proposed match. I wondered what he would do if he knew about Derham. Doubtless have us both sent to the Tower. I laughed at the foolishness of that. It would be a shock, though. My grandmother had called me a harlot in the first flush of her rage when she realized what had happened. Perhaps she blamed herself when she was giving me that vigorous beating. People often vented their rage on those who were the victims of their neglect because they were in truth blaming themselves. But, in spite of the fact that I so often received a sharp slap from her, she was fond of me in her easygoing way—when she remembered me. But not only did I dislike my uncle, I feared him.

I had discovered certain things about him of which hitherto I had been ignorant. My grandmother had let one or two matters slip out during our sessions; and then I listened to the gossip whenever I had the opportunity.

Of course, he was very important. He and Suffolk—the King's brother-in-law—were probably the two most powerful men in the kingdom under the King.

Norfolk had been married twice, I discovered. During the Wars of the Roses, the Duke—or as he had then been the Earl of Surrey—had been a staunch supporter of the House of York, and, so close had he been to the royal family, that he had been betrothed to the Lady Anne, a daughter of Edward IV. Naturally he supported King Richard at Bosworth, where the present King's father overcame Richard; and Norfolk, surviving the battle, was, of course, then out of favour.

The King's father, Henry VII, being a wise man, recognized that he could make better use of Norfolk's skill if he were working for him instead of languishing in prison. So Norfolk was restored to favour and Henry even allowed him to marry the Lady Anne, to whom he had been betrothed before Richard fell.

Henry himself was married to Edward IV's daughter, Elizabeth, so my uncle's first wife and the Queen were sisters. The Earl of Surrey was by this time Duke of Norfolk and gradually became one of the most powerful men in the country.

He had been instrumental in bringing about Wolsey's fall, and he was not a man of whom the wise would want to make an enemy. Not that he would consider me worth a moment's thought, but I did tremble to think of what his reactions would be if he discovered I had abandoned myself to Manox, in all innocence, and later, less innocently, to Francis Derham.

Then I learned something of the Duke's own private life which I found comforting as well as revealing. I realized, though, that he would apply different rules to his own conduct than to mine. In fact, I had noticed that often those who might have something disgraceful to hide, could be quite censorious of fellow sinners.

The Duke, it appeared, was not a man of such rigorous virtue.

His first wife, Anne—the daughter of Edward IV—had died of consumption at an early age, and very shortly afterwards my uncle had married Elizabeth, the daughter of the Duke of Buckingham. She was very strong-minded and considered to be one of the most accomplished ladies of her time. She entertained poets and the like.

It was not a happy marriage. I think my uncle was a very arrogant man and she was not of a temper to tolerate that. She complained that when their daughter Mary was born, he neglected her; and soon after that he became attached to a woman of his household.

If this lady had been of good family it might have been an ordinary enough situation, but she was a washerwoman in his wife's nursery.

The Duke and his Duchess separated and he refused to give her anything but the scantiest of allowances. There was quite a scandal about this. I had heard nothing of it when it happened, but perhaps I was not as alert for gossip then as I was at this time. There were attempts to bring about a reconciliation; the Duchess refused to divorce him and the Duke went on living with his washerwoman.

And this was the man who, I was sure, would be very censorious towards his poor little niece who had been too young to understand what she was doing.

I must forget my exploratory adventures with Henry Manox. My relationship with Francis Derham had been charming while it had existed, but it was in the past. If the Duke could sport with his washerwoman, how could he condemn me for what I had done?

～

I liked to walk in the gardens. It was very pleasant down by the river. I enjoyed watching the barges sail past and I would look in the direction of Greenwich and wonder if the Court were there, and what it would be like to be among those interesting and exciting people.

One day, as I stood there, a young man came out of the house and started towards the privy stairs where a small craft had drawn up. I thought this might be waiting for him. There were often callers at the house, especially when the Duke was there. He was not there at this time, but the young man could have been visiting my grandmother.

He looked familiar to me.

He hesitated and then smiled and came swiftly towards me.

"We have met before," he said.

"I thought it might be so," I replied.

"Tell me. You are . . . ?"

"Katherine Howard, granddaughter of the Duchess of Norfolk."

He gave a delighted laugh. "That is it. Well met, cousin. Do you not recognize me?"

I knew then. It was his voice . . . his smile. "Thomas," I said. "Thomas Culpepper."

He bowed.

"Do you remember . . . ?" We were both asking the same question.

"It was a long time ago," he said. "I was so sad when I left you."

"I was sad when you went."

"We were the greatest of friends, as well as cousins. How wonderful it is to see you again!"

I felt lighthearted, experiencing a deep pleasure.

"You are more beautiful even than you were then, when I thought you the prettiest girl I had ever seen."

I flushed with happiness. I had always hoped to

see my cousin, Thomas Culpepper, again.

"We have grown up since," I said.

"In which I rejoice." He took a step nearer. "Mistress Howard, may I give you a cousinly kiss, for this is a very special occasion?"

When he had given me the "cousinly kiss" on the forehead, he held me by the shoulders, and looked searchingly into my face.

"Oft times I have thought of you, little cousin," he said. "And now we have met again. You are under the protection of the Dowager Duchess, I believe."

"'Tis so. And you?"

"I," he said, with an air of mock importance, "am a gentleman of the Court."

"You are at Court!" I cried in excitement.

"Yes, indeed, I have a very important post in the service of His Majesty."

I clasped my hands together. "That is wonderful. How I long to go to Court!"

"It may be that you will. Your uncle, the Duke, doubtless will arrange it."

"I hope he will. Tell me. To what part of the Court are you attached?"

"The Royal Bedchamber."

"You are Gentleman of the Bedchamber!"

"I am concerned with the royal leg."

"What mean you?"

"The leg in question is subject to an unfortunate affliction which causes His Majesty great torture at times. My duties are to dress the King's ulcer. It is one of the worst I ever saw. It greatly provokes His Majesty's temper. Sometimes I fear I take my life in my hands when I kneel before him to remove the bandages."

I wrinkled my brows in disbelief.

"I tell you truth," he went on. "I have a certain knowledge of unguents and that serves me well with His Majesty. There is none who can dress his leg as I can."

"So you are a kind of doctor?"

"Say a nurse rather. I sleep in his room, or close to his door, so that he can send for me at any time. You are disappointed. You thought I was going to tell you I was his chief adviser."

"I did not."

"Mine is perhaps the safer post. The bouts of anger which are directed against me are brief, and, as I say, he does always remember that I am more deft with a bandage than any other. He loves me more than he hates me; and although I am sorry I cannot tell you I have a high post in the King's entourage, I believe my head is a little firmer on my shoulders than those of some in higher places."

"I am glad of that," I told him.

"I know you speak from the heart, cousin."

"We do little of interest in our household. I am always hoping to come to Court."

"You will one day, I am sure."

"It would be good if we could both be there together."

"I can think of nothing better."

"Tell me of the Court."

"It is as you would imagine, full of drama, full of comedy. All are seeking favour, so hoping to climb a little higher up the ladder to fortune."

"And you?"

"I am happy as I am . . . and particularly at this

moment, when I am near my dear little cousin whose company I have been denied so long."

"Have you seen the Queen?"

"I have."

"And what is she like? Is she really so unattractive?"

"By no means. She is a very gracious lady."

"They are always saying the King is not pleased with his marriage."

"In that they speak truth. He does not accept her as his wife. There are times when the lady is very uneasy. No doubt she remembers Anne Boleyn. Such a memory is enough to make any lady in her position somewhat uneasy."

"She must be very unhappy."

"She is fearful."

"To be so . . . unwanted!"

"Mayhap that is not such a hardship, for 'tis my belief that she wants him no more than he wants her."

"She does not like the King!"

"My dear little cousin, dare I whisper it? The King shows his age. His leg . . . . But no more. They could send me to the Tower for such talk."

"Send you to the Tower!"

He laughed. "Ah, when one lives near the King, one must take account of one's words."

"It is so exciting! How I wish I were there! Did you come here to see the Duchess?"

"She sent word that she wished to see me. She asked me a number of questions, stressing the connection between our families, my aunt being your mother, Jocasta. I told her that you and I met years ago. Then she asked me about my service to the King, and I mentioned that His Grace had a liking for me on account of my gentle fingers."

I laughed. "Does that mean that she will invite you to come here and we shall meet again?"

He paused. "I pray that that may be," he said. "But in the service of the King, one is moving all the time. There are those peregrinations around the country. The King must show himself to the people. We leave Greenwich tomorrow and when we shall return I cannot say. But when we do, depend upon it, I shall find some reason for calling on my little cousin."

I clasped my hands together in delight and he said: "And now, I must away. *Au revoir*, cousin." He placed his hands on my shoulders. He held me against him for a moment and kissed my forehead.

Then he stepped back, bowed and ran down to the waiting barge.

~

My grandmother sent for me. Her legs were giving her great pain and she would have me rub in a new unguent which had been recommended to her by the apothecary.

"I declare," she said, "they bother me more than they ever did."

I set to work and she talked. "Your cousin, Master Culpepper, called on me lately."

I paused. A fear had come to me. Had someone seen him give me that "cousinly kiss"?

"Go on, child," she said impatiently. "A goodly young man, Master Thomas. I heard he had a post at Court. It seems he has become a favourite of the King."

I did not say that I had met him and that he had told me what that post was.

"Yes. His Majesty favours the young man. I believe

he often sleeps in the King's chamber, and, with the King's favour, doubtless will advance himself."

"I am pleased at this."

"You are not a child now, Katherine Howard. Eighteen, is it? It is time a match was made for you. I have spoken to your uncle and he agrees with me that the time has come. You have some qualities, but little education."

She looked at me reproachfully, and I was tempted so remind her that I had none because it had never been given to me; but I restrained myself.

She went on: "Your uncle is considering whether a match might be arranged for you and your cousin, Thomas Culpepper."

A great joy swept over me. My hands trembled. I could not believe this. My cousin—whom I had now convinced myself I had loved from the moment I saw him—and I to be husband and wife! Now that I had seen him again, he seemed to me all that a man should be; and I believed he was as ready to love me as I loved him. It was a dream come true.

"The idea does not seem to displease you," said the Duchess.

"Your Grace, I am sure it will be a very suitable match."

"Master Culpepper has the King's favour, and that means a great deal."

"Yes, Your Grace."

"Well . . . if he will have you, and if the Duke—and I tell you, he is considering this—if the Duke comes to the conclusion that it is right for the family, then there will be a match for you and Culpepper."

I spent the rest of the day in a haze of contentment, recalling every word he had said to me at our last meeting and going back to that childhood encounter. I think I imagined that we had plighted our troth then as children.

What mattered it? The prospect of marriage with Thomas Culpepper made me very happy indeed.

~

I was hoping for a speedy conclusion—marriage and happiness ever after. However, the Court was travelling round the country and not only Thomas Culpepper but the Duke of Norfolk was with it.

Nothing more was said of the proposed marriage and I must try to restrain my impatience.

It was difficult to do this, for I wanted to tell everyone.

They noticed the change in me.

"Mistress Katherine Howard looks as though she has come into a fortune," commented Mary Lassells.

"Or is it love?" asked Dorothy. "Do tell us."

"Oh, it is not yet settled," I said guardedly.

"So . . . there are plans afoot."

"As yet there is nothing to say," I answered, regretting I had mentioned the matter.

"I saw you talking to a very handsome young man in the gardens. Indeed, I saw him kiss you."

"Oh, it was only a cousinly kiss."

"Your cousin?"

"Yes. Master Culpepper. He had been sent for by the Duchess. As he is my cousin, it is meet for him to give me a cousinly kiss."

"And who is this Master Culpepper?" asked Dorothy.

"He has a place at Court. The King favours him."

They exchanged glances; and I left them, chiding

myself for having mentioned him. But I was often careless and therefore frequently telling myself that I should not have said this or that.

It was a week or so later. The Duchess had not referred again to the match, and when I tried to bring it into the conversation, she brushed it aside, so that I knew that the negotiations had gone no further.

Then I had a shock. I was in the gardens near the privy stairs, gazing along the river to Greenwich, when a barge drew up. Immediately I thought of Thomas Culpepper, but to my horror I saw that the occupant was Francis Derham.

He sprang out and, seeing me, gave a cry of pleasure, and came hurrying towards me. I quickly moved away, lest the bargeman should see our meeting. But Francis followed me.

"Katherine," he called. "What ails you? Are you not pleased to see me?"

I turned and faced him. "Why have you come?" I demanded.

He looked amazed. "I have come to see you."

"You should not have done so."

"I do not understand."

"It is over, Francis."

"What say you?"

"That which was between us is no more."

"Katherine! We are troth-plighted."

"That was long ago."

"Not so long. And what has that to do with it? I am husband to you and you are wife to me. You cannot have forgotten how it was between us."

"It should not have been."

"Katherine! My love! It *was*."

I cried: "No, no. You must go away. It is over. We were too young. It was play."

"Play!" he said. "It was not play for me."

"It is over. You went away. That ended it."

He was looking at me with utter desolation, and I was deeply sorry for him. He had really loved me. He was not like Manox. Oh, I could not bear to think of Manox. But to see my poor Francis looking so lost and sad made me want to weep. I must not relent though. Francis must go away. We must not return to that intimacy which we had once shared. What I wanted more than anything was that he should find another lover. It was all over between us two as far as he was concerned.

But all he could do was look at me with those sad, bewildered, yearning eyes, which assured me that he had always been my true and faithful lover.

"Francis," I said. "I am sorry, but it is over. I love you no longer. I was only a child. I did not understand. I was fond of you, and it was all so exciting. Can you understand? Please Francis. Will you fall in love with someone else?"

"I shall never do that . . . having known you," he assured me.

How I should have loved to hear those words at one time. Now they filled me with alarm.

~

Francis Derham was really very daring. He was, of course, one of the Duke of Norfolk's pensioners and he must have presumed that the Duke knew nothing of the reason for his sudden departure. He was evidently right, for the Duke made no objection to his return.

It was only the Duchess who knew, and she evidently decided that no good could arise from reviving the scandal.

I was sure that she could not be very happy about Derham's return.

But there he was—back in the household, which made me very uneasy, for I could come face to face with him at any moment.

My fear was great when, shortly after Derham had returned, my grandmother sent for me and, in a state of great apprehension, I presented myself.

She was seated in her chair and, to my intense relief, beaming with pleasure.

She said: "Sit down. I have some good news for you. You are to have a place at Court."

"At Court!" I cried. My first thoughts were: I shall not have to wonder whether Francis Derham is going to spring out on me at any minute. To Court! It was my nature to be able to forget unpleasantness and be quickly transported to blithe euphoria.

"You may well be joyful. 'Tis good news indeed. A chance for you, my child. You must make the most of it."

"Yes, Your Grace. Oh, I will."

She looked at me, nodding approval. "Stand up," she said. "And come closer."

I did so while she peered at me, assessing me.

"You are very small," she said. "Some would say too small. But I am not so sure. You are slender withal and you have a certain grace. You look girlish . . . young for your years . . . and that has an appeal. You are fair enough. Light brown hair . . . curly and plenty of it. Good eyes . . . hazel . . . and those long dark lashes. Your nose is good . . . face round . . . childish . . . you are a worthy Howard."

I was giggling with pleasure. To go to Court! To be away from Derham and near Thomas Culpepper. I assured myself that I was deeply in love with Thomas Culpepper and soon there would be a betrothal—one which would have the approval of all.

"You are indeed fortunate," she went on. "You owe this, of course, to your uncle. He has noticed you of late. He says your manners leave much to be desired, and he chides me for allowing your education to be neglected. But I fancy he thinks that one of the reasons why your cousin . . ." Her voice faltered as it always did at any mention of Anne Boleyn. But she went on quickly, for this was a happy occasion which must not be spoiled by unhappy memories.

"The Duke thinks that too much education can make a woman over-saucy, so he does not regret overmuch the fact that you have none of that of which your cousin had too much. You are not without charm, and your looks favour you. So he decided to put your name forward and, as the King has not protested, there is a place for you. It is great good fortune. Unfortunately for the Queen, she does not regard it as such, to lose her own countrywomen and perforce take ours in exchange, but she is no fool and must know that when queens come to new countries they must lose those attendants they brought with them and take others from their new country. So this is what is happening. The Queen's ladies—those she brought with her—are being sent back and you are to be one of those who will replace them."

I clasped my hands together in ecstasy. To serve the Queen, that poor neglected lady, to be at Court where everything happened, to be near Thomas Culpepper, who slept in the King's chamber and was favoured by him! I could hardly contain my happiness.

"I see you are overcome with joy, my child. That is right. So should you be. This is a happy day for you and for the family. It will be for you to show your uncle that he was right to put his faith in you."

"I shall!" I cried.

"There. I am happy for you. You will do your best, I am sure."

She was smiling at me. "And do not let this make you over-vain, child, for that would detract from your charm. But you are indeed a pretty child."

I found the courage to ask: "And there will now be my betrothal?"

She looked a little puzzled.

"Your Grace mentioned to me that Thomas Culpepper . . ."

"Oh yes, yes. There was talk of a match between you two. Well, now this has come to pass, who shall say? It is not a matter to be decided rashly . . . in particular now. Your uncle will have other matters on his mind."

I was a little disappointed, but nothing could spoil the prospect of this wonderful future which was opening out before me.

I wanted to run round telling everyone: "I am going to Court!"

~

Francis Derham came upon me in the garden. I suspected he had been watching for me. He caught my arm and angrily I wrenched it away from him.

"I have told you," I cried. "Francis, please understand, it is all over. It is no more as it was."

"I have heard that you are betrothed to a certain Thomas Culpepper."

"When did you hear such a thing?"

"It was from one of the Duchess's women. She had overheard it, she said. Is it true?"

"If she says I am betrothed, then she knows more than I do. As far as I know I am not betrothed to anyone."

He looked relieved. "I could not bear that you should go to any other," he said.

"Francis, do please understand. I am very sorry, but I no longer feel love for you."

"You did love me. You said many times that you were my wife. You said that you would wait for my return."

"It was all child's play, Francis."

"It was not to me."

"Please leave me, Francis. I am going away . . . to Court. Please, please, let us forget what happened."

"How could I forget that you are my wife?"

"I am not. I am not. We were children playing at love."

"You cannot deny that we were lovers in truth."

"Please, Francis, please . . . I am going away."

"To Culpepper?"

"No . . . no, only to Court."

"You must not do this."

"It has all been arranged for me. I am commanded to go. I am going to be a lady-in-waiting to the Queen."

"That must not be!" he insisted. "You must tell them how it is between us. If you go away, I shall not stay in this house."

"As to that, Francis, you must do as you list."

"Katherine, at Court, you will be exposed to all kinds of profligacy which you do not understand. You are so sweet and innocent. No, Katherine, I will not have it."

"It is not for you to say, Francis, whether or not I go to Court."

"I am your husband."

"Say that no more, Francis. If you love me . . ."

"You know I love you. How many times have I told you? How many times have you said you love me?"

"That is in the past. It is all over now."

"It will never be over for me."

"I am going to Court, I tell you."

"To be betrothed to Culpepper?"

"I am not betrothed to anyone any more."

"But to go to Court. You . . . in that den of vice."

"Can it compare with the Long Room in this house?"

He was silent. It was as though he were thinking of that innocent girl who had already been thrust into something like that den of vice to which he referred, and I saw a great tenderness in his eyes.

"Francis," I said. "I did love you, but it is over. Please understand. We could still be good friends. If you love me, you will understand."

He said slowly: "I do love you, Katherine. I have

193

always loved you. I would never do anything to harm you."

I believed him, for I was convinced that he was speaking the truth.

A Meeting with the King

It appeared that the King's marriages—and this to Anne of Cleves was his fourth—must always be overshadowed by death.

When he had married his first queen, many years ago, that had only been possible because of the death of his elder brother, Arthur; and King Henry had inherited a wife as well as a throne through that death. Then, when the first wife was put aside that the King might marry my cousin, the great Cardinal Wolsey, although he escaped the axe, died, it was said, of a broken heart and despair. Many deaths had followed that marriage: the noble Thomas More, the saintly Bishop Fisher, many monks—most barbarously— and all traced to that second marriage. My tragic cousin had gone to the block; and Jane Seymour's brief reign had ended in her death. Now there was the new Queen, and Thomas Cromwell—one-time favourite—appeared to be in danger.

There was a charge of treason, and his enemies—chief among them my Uncle Norfolk—had been quick to seek the opportunity to destroy him. The King's anger against him had been fuelled by the fact that it had been Cromwell's activities which had saddled His Majesty with a wife who did not please him.

I learned something of Cromwell then and marvelled at the hazards people risked when ambition drove them on. I wondered how Cromwell, who had once been so powerful, was facing the fact that he was in growing and acute danger.

Many people were pleased to see him in this plight. I was amazed at the constant references to his humble birth. His father was sneered at for being a blacksmith and a shearer of cloth who kept a brew-house in Putney which was also a hostelry. And this Cromwell, a blacksmith's son, had had the temerity to climb to the position of Lord Great Chamberlain of England.

I said, in my naive way, that the blacksmith must have been very industrious to have done so many things. As for his son, he must have been very clever indeed to have climbed so high from such humble beginnings.

Patronizing glances were turned on me. What did frivolous Katherine Howard know of such matters? They were determined to hold Thomas Cromwell's origins against him, but it did not seem logical to me.

"Too much climbing up high from low places can bring his sort to the headsman," I was told. I wanted to say that a great number of our noble families went that way too—in fact more often than humbler men. But I did not. I was not clever at arguments, and most of my expressed opinions were generally reduced to ridicule.

I gathered that when Cromwell became a member of Gray's Inn he was singled out by Cardinal Wolsey as a man who could be useful. When I did go so far as to say that Wolsey thought highly of him, I was reminded that Wolsey was a butcher's son. "Like to like," they said. "And look what became of Wolsey in the end."

"There had been a time when the King was very fond of him, as he was with Thomas Cromwell," I pointed out.

It was obviously dangerous to be favoured by the King. My cousin Anne had surely been more favoured than any. I dreamed sometimes that I saw her, with her head on the block, and the axe descending. Unpleasant dreams, to be dismissed as soon as it was daylight.

And now it was Cromwell's turn. Poor Cromwell, who had risen so high, from working in his father's hostelry—as he might well have done—to supping with princes. And where had that led him? To the Tower.

I heard that my uncle and the Earl of Southampton were to visit the Tower to talk to him, to learn for what reason he had beguiled his master into making this unsatisfactory marriage. What was Cromwell's arrangement with her family? Was he serving the interests of others rather than those of his master?

My uncle, I knew, was his greatest enemy. I was not sure of Southampton; but it was clear that there would be no mercy from them, and Cromwell would know that, too.

I wondered, when my uncle visited him, whether he had been aware of the Duke's triumph, which I knew must have existed. He had been very annoyed when Cromwell had been made Chamberlain and the title of Earl of Essex had been bestowed on him. The Duchess had let that slip during one of the massage sessions.

She said: "The Duke has discovered faults in this man. It was his duty to expose them and, fearlessly, before the others at the Council table, he stood up and accused Cromwell of treason."

I later discovered what the charges were. Cromwell, it was said, had liberated people for bribes, and also taken payment for licences to export corn and other food; he had helped to circulate heretical books; and there was one other ridiculous charge against him: He had planned to marry the Princess Mary and take the throne.

The Protestants would have saved him if they could, but they were powerless to do so.

Poor Cromwell. He wrote appeals to the King from prison, begging for mercy and a chance to talk to him; but the King turned his back on the man who had once been so highly favoured: Cromwell remained in the Tower. And, on a hot July day, he was taken from there to Tower Hill where he laid his head upon the block.

~

I was caught up in the dazzling prospect before me. My uncle, the Duke, had given orders that the garments I should need for my new position were to be supplied. I loved clothes and it was wonderful to be fitted by the seamstresses and feel the softness of the beautiful materials which were being provided. I had always wanted to possess such clothes. I was required to parade before the Duchess in my new gowns while she nodded approvingly. I swear she had never been so fond of me as she was then. There was a faint hint of sadness in her expression though, for seeing me in the splendid clothes naturally reminded her of my cousin.

But this would pass quickly and soon she would be watching me, her eyes sparkling with anticipation of my future. When I left her I basked in the envy of the ladies.

There was a shadow overhanging my happiness

that came from my encounters with Francis Derham, which were more frequent than I liked. He was very sad and angry at the prospect of my going to Court.

"You think it is all balls and banquets . . . dancing and such pleasures," he said. "My dear Katherine, that is how it seems on the surface. Beneath there is intrigue . . . scheming . . . treachery. It is the most dangerous place in England."

"I am to serve the Queen," I replied. "There can be no harm in that. They say she is a very gracious lady."

"I do not wish you to go, Katherine. I forbid you to go."

I looked at him in horror.

"Hush!" I cried. "What would anyone think to hear you talk thus. People listen. They repeat what they hear. Have a care, Francis, you will destroy yourself. It is you who will be in danger if you talk like that."

"You must not go to Court, Katherine. Something tells me it would be bad. Let us go away together. We could go to Ireland. They would never find us there. Think! We should be together. Then you would feel towards me as you did before."

I was angry. He was trying to spoil everything.

I ran from him and tried not to see him again. I could not bear the sight of his sad face. What I was trying to do with all my might was to forget the past. I wanted to think only of the glorious future . . . and Thomas Culpepper.

~

The Court was at Greenwich and thither I was to go in the company of the Countess of Rutland and Lady Edgecombe, who would teach me what was expected of a lady-in-waiting to the Queen.

To a novice like myself they appeared to be very formidable ladies, and they certainly made me feel how lucky I was that this post should have been given to one as ignorant of Court procedure as I was.

"In the first place," said the Countess, "you are very young."

"I am eighteen, my lady," I told her.

"She looks much younger," said the Countess to Lady Edgecombe, who agreed.

I must remember that my mistress was the Queen. They told me how I must address her, speak only when spoken to, act quietly and always in a seemly fashion. I must never forget that I was in the presence of royalty, and if the King should appear at any time, I must make the deepest curtsy I had ever made in my life, and not stare at him. I must behave as though I were in the presence of a dazzling greatness and keep my eyes averted. I was not quite sure how I was going to convey my awed respect if I were to act as though I were not there; but I supposed I should know when and if the time came.

One of the younger ladies was more approachable. She said: "You will be all right. Just keep quiet and speak only when spoken to. That is best. We shall soon be in Greenwich. I like it better than this place. Did you know it is called Whitehall because of the white towers the King built here? It was York House before."

When I learned that it had once belonged to Cardinal Wolsey, I remembered what I had heard of him. It could not have been so very long ago when he had lived here in splendour, as he had at Hampton Court. I had heard it said that his love of grandeur was one of the reasons why he had begun to fall. He had gained a great deal but he stretched out his hands for more and it was said he kept a more splendid court than that of the King. Derham was right. The Court could be a dangerous place. But surely not for humble ladies-in-waiting like little Katherine Howard, who only spoke when spoken to?

Hampton Court had gone to the King, a present from the great Cardinal. So had Whitehall. But even the presentation of such magnificent gifts had availed him nothing. Those were foolish thoughts which would intrude.

"And this," I was told, "is the chamber in which the King married Queen Anne—not the present Queen, but Queen Anne Boleyn. It was here that they celebrated her coronation."

Here were memories again. There was so much to bring back what was best forgotten. Stop it, I admonished myself. Think of the good things. Velvet gowns, the jewels my grandmother had given me, dances, banquets, grand occasions and being under the same roof as Thomas Culpepper.

Then we went to Greenwich—beautiful Greenwich, which had been made magnificent by the King who loved it dearly. Was it not the place of his birth? Here his marriage to his first wife, Catherine of Aragon, had been solemnized; jousts were frequently held here. The King liked to celebrate Christmas here. The Princess Mary had been born here, so had the Lady Elizabeth. Then again, I was thinking of my cousin. How had she felt when the longed-for boy turned out to be a girl?

I could not understand myself. It was as though some devilish imp were at my elbow, whose sole purpose was to intrude into my carefree mood and destroy it.

I would be merry. I would rejoice in what was happening to me. This was Greenwich. The Court was here, and I was to be presented to the Queen. Life was going to be amusing and exciting.

From the moment the Countess of Rutland presented me to the Queen, I knew I could be happy serving her. There was a kindliness about her. She seemed to be aware of my nervousness, and wanted to make me understand that there was no need for it.

"Katherine Howard," she repeated my name in a guttural accent which was not very attractive, but her smile was warm.

"The Countess will tell you . . ."

I could not understand the rest of the sentence, but then the Countess said: "The Queen tells you that I shall inform you of your duties and she is sure that you will do them well."

I realized that the Queen's knowledge of English was somewhat limited and that, when she arrived, she had been unable to speak a word of it.

I made my curtsy and retired. I felt very happy that I was to serve such a gracious lady.

I could not understand why the King had been so displeased with her. She was no beauty, of course. I was thinking again of my cousin and pretty Jane Seymour. I had never seen Catherine of Aragon, and in any case had I had the opportunity to do so she would have been quite old, so I could not have judged her, but I could see that this Queen was different from her immediate two predecessors. She was not very tall, but she gave an impression of largeness. It must have been because of her big bones. Her forehead was unusually high; her eyes were large and dark and with long dark lashes that were quite beautiful. I thought that she would have been good-looking, in a rather heavy sort of way, but for her pitted skin. The poor lady had suffered from smallpox at some time and it was the ravages of that disease which had spoiled her appearance and horrified the King. I had heard of the miniature which Hans Holbein had painted of her and which had so pleased the King when he had seen it that he had gone ahead with plans to marry her.

She did nothing to improve herself, in my opinion. Her gown was unbecoming, and with its light sleeves and close-fitting, high collar, reminded me of a man's. The gown opened in the front to show a kind of chemise drawn up with a ribbon, at the neck of which she wore a large brooch. Her hat, turned up at the front, would have been difficult for the most beautiful woman to have worn to advantage. On her, it made her rather large features look quite masculine.

Queen Anne of Cleves had no idea how to make the most of what personal attractions she had. I started to think of what I would have chosen for her if I had had the chance to do so. I saw her in a beautiful scarlet gown, velvet, of course, rather severely cut, for there is nothing more detrimental than to try to appear feminine when one is not fashioned that way. The Queen had a good, kind face; but I could see now that her pockmarked skin, together with her lack of femininity, had made her unacceptable to the King.

In the days that followed, I settled into my role. I lived now far more luxuriously than I ever had before. My duties were light, and it was very rarely that I was in the presence of the Queen.

The Duchesses of Richmond and Suffolk and the Countesses of Rutland and Hertford, with Lady Margaret Douglas, were those close to her. I should have loved to be nearer the Queen and to know what she was really thinking. I realized that the King neglected her and made little effort to hide his disappointment in his marriage; I was sure she was not of a nature to show her feelings and, if she were embittered and humiliated, she hid this very successfully.

It was at Greenwich that I met Lady Rochford. She was a distant connection, through her marriage to my cousin, George Boleyn, who was, of course, brother to Anne; he had died at the same time as his sister, charged with incest with her. Lady Rochford had given evidence at the time against her husband.

I remembered my grandmother's saying of her that she was a vindictive woman and had been jealous of her husband's devotion to his sister. Anne and George were two of a kind—brilliant, witty, clever and handsome. Poor Jane Rochford was different. It was natural that George and Anne were fond of each other's company and the love between them was that of a gifted brother and a clever sister.

Jane Rochford was the neglected wife. Well, how could George be expected to spend his time in her company? So Jane had her revenge. All those wicked lies . . . it was just what poor George did not need at that time.

I remembered this now, but I did feel a little lonely, and Jane was friendly.

"My little cousin!" she cried. "So, you have come to Court. His Grace of Norfolk has arranged this, I'll warrant. I believe your uncle has great influence in high places."

"Yes," I agreed. "I believe it was my uncle who persuaded them to accept me."

"Nothing pleases him more than to see Howards filling high places at Court."

She was very talkative and so determined to be friendly that I found her company welcome. The ladies of the royal household were inclined to look down on me—a newcomer, very young, an unimportant member of the company.

I discovered that Lady Rochford was not only a great talker, but a reckless one and, as our acquaintance grew, she became more and more outspoken in a manner which might have caused trouble if it had been reported in certain quarters.

For instance, she was very frank about the relationship between the King and the Queen. She told me how the Queen had arrived in England and how disappointed the King had been on that first occasion when he saw her. He had been waiting for that moment for so long, ever since the death of Queen Jane, for the King was a man who must have a wife. There were some men like that. Many would be content to take a mistress, for it seemed unlikely that any marriage the King made would bring him a son. But he was a man with a conscience. Had I ever heard mention of the King's conscience? I would sooner or later. All his marriages had brought forth his conscience.

Conscience made him rid himself of his first wife. Was she in truth a virgin when he married her? Had her marriage with his brother been consummated? Didn't it say something in the Bible—Leviticus, was it not?—that a man might not marry his brother's wife? Then, of course, he was infatuated by our ill-fated cousin, Anne, and the old conscience was up in arms again. He'd find some work for it to do over the present Queen, she'd warrant.

That was the manner in which she talked. It amused me and, innocent as I was, I could not see the danger. Perhaps I did have a notion that I should not be listening, but I did learn a great deal of what was going on.

"Oh, he was shocked, I can tell you, at that first meeting," she went on. "He could not hide it. He cut short the visit and could not bring himself to give her the furs—beautiful sable, they were—which he had brought as a gift. Anthony Browne had to present them to her instead. And ever since, he has been trying to find a way to be rid of her. It was not only her face which he did not like. There was her Dutch accent. He found it grating. She had so little

English and he no Dutch. Doubtless he welcomed it as a reason for not spending much time with her. Then he tried to think of reasons why he could not marry her. It was like that time when he tried to be rid of Queen Catherine so that he could marry our cousin. I will tell you something." She came close to me, looked over her shoulder and then began to whisper. "Now that he is married to her and she is truly Queen, he does not spend his nights with her. He says, 'Farewell, sweetheart,' and leaves her. And when she was asked if she were hurt by his neglect, her answer was that she was quite happy and she received as much of his attention as she wished. That will tell you how matters are between the King and the Queen."

"Dost think the King will send her back to her own country?"

"You may trust him to find a way of being rid of her."

"But her brother is the Duke of Cleves. It is not as though she were a subject like . . ."

"Like our poor cousin? No. But you may be sure that the King is looking for a way to be rid of her, and he is not one to give up what he has set his heart on. I would not like to be in Her Majesty's shoes, but then, who would, I wonder?"

She laughed, and I could not help thinking of the kindly, gentle face of the Queen.

~

Then I met Thomas.

I was in the music room playing the virginals, for I loved music. I could sing quite well and I liked to accompany myself on the lute, which was a favourite instrument of mine. As I played, the door opened and, to my intense joy, there stood Thomas.

"Katherine!" he cried, and ran towards me. He put his arms round me and we clung together.

"I heard you had become the Queen's new lady-in-waiting, the prettiest lady-in-waiting at Court—that is what they are saying."

"You lie," I said, laughing, well pleased.

"'Tis God's truth, I swear, and I'll challenge any who denies it."

"This is what is called Court manners, I'll swear."

"I tell you, I only say what is clear to us all. Let me look at you. Ah, sweet Katherine, how glad I am that you are here at last."

"How fares it with you, Thomas?"

He lifted his shoulders. "Good . . . at times. At others . . . well, the royal temper is not as clement these days, for His Majesty is not a happy man."

"Is it because of the Queen or his leg?"

"Neither gives him cause to rejoice. Most of those around him receive some abuse, and there is the occasional blow."

"Oh, Thomas, that must be very distressing."

"It is part of our duty to accept what comes our way. I do not suffer as much as some. At times, curses are thrown at us and we are told we should all be in the Tower."

"Thomas!"

"Do not pity me. I am safe enough. He knows that none can dress his leg as I do. Is that not amazing, Katherine? The deftness of my hands and my ability to deal with an ulcer have elevated me to favour. But enough of me. Are they kind to you?"

"Oh yes. I have friends already."

"It is wonderful to know that I shall be able to see you."

"Shall we meet often?"

"It depends. I must be at hand when I am needed, and I am never sure when that will be. As for you, I suppose you have your duties. But depend upon it, I shall contrive to see you at every possible moment."

"I cannot cease to marvel at the good fortune which has brought me here."

"Oh, my Lord Norfolk would make sure that there is a place for his niece at Court."

He suddenly kissed me with passion, and then said, as though to excuse himself: "We are to be betrothed."

"I do not forget."

"We shall marry and then mayhap go away from the Court. How would you like to go to Hollingbourne?"

"There is nothing I should like more."

"We shall go there one day, Katherine. We will have done with the Court. I should be happy to be away from it—not to be at the beck and call of an irritable old man. What am I saying?" He looked around him. "No one heard," he said with a grin. "Only my sweet Katherine, and she would never betray me. We shall go away together, my love. Hollingbourne is beautiful. There we could find perfect happiness . . . ourselves . . . and the children we shall have. We shall be happy for the rest of our lives."

"Is it possible, Thomas?"

"We will make it so."

"When?"

"First we must have the approval of my Lord of Norfolk. But why should that be denied us? My family is noble enough. But perhaps not noble enough for my lord. Do you know if he has any other plans for you?"

"He has not. The Duchess told me I was to be betrothed to you."

"Then she must have His Grace's approval."

"So it will come to pass."

"It must," he said. "If it did not, I should die of a broken heart."

It was wonderful to hear him talk thus, and to know that there would be other such meetings. This one was cut short by the sudden appearance of Lady Rochford, for while Thomas and I had stood there close together, the door had quietly opened and she had come in.

She said: "So it was here you came."

"I was playing the virginals," I stammered.

"And Master Culpepper found you here?"

"I was passing and heard the music," Thomas explained.

"Mistress Howard plays very well, does she not?"

"She does indeed."

"I am not surprised that you were attracted by it. I thought you might be here, Katherine, but I heard no music." She smiled mischievously. "So I looked in."

Thomas bowed and said he must be gone. I felt irritated with Jane Rochford for intruding. I had been so deeply engrossed in talking to Thomas.

"What a handsome young man Master Culpepper is!" said Jane.

"Yes, I suppose most would reckon him so."

"Do you not?"

"Oh yes, of course I do."

"I thought so." She smiled. "Well, you make a pretty pair—the two of you standing there, close, by the virginals. Does Master Culpepper play?"

"I do not know."

"Oh, I thought you were discussing music."

I was silent.

"You seemed so absorbed," she added.

I often spoke without thinking, and something prompted me to do so then.

I said: "We are to be betrothed."

She was really surprised. "What? You and Culpepper?"

"My grandmother told me before I left Lambeth that it was to be."

"I did not know."

"There is no reason why you should."

She laughed. "Well, I know now. That accounts . . . I mean, you seemed to be talking . . . intimately." She raised her eyebrows slightly, as though to imply that she meant more than she had said.

"We are cousins," I explained. "I knew him a long time ago."

"That is good. It is always well for people to know each other before they are betrothed."

I felt irritated that she should speak as an expert on the subject when she herself, as was well known, had suffered a most unsatisfactory marriage.

Then she leaned forward, still smiling, and kissed my cheek.

"I wish you all the happiness you deserve, dear Katherine," she said.

"Thank you."

She slipped her arm through mine and together we left the music room.

~

Those were happy days. There was so much to interest me at Court. The main topic continued to be the relationship between the King and the Queen.

"If it were not for his leg, the King would have taken action by now," said Jane Rochford.

There was an occasion when I saw the King. I was looking out of the window at the time so I could stare to my heart's content. He was a majestic figure in his splendid padded garments, scintillating with jewels. He was with my uncle. I had never seen the Duke looking humble before. The King was talking; his face was red and I gathered that he was not very pleased about something. My uncle bowed slightly as he spoke. I was laughing inwardly, pleased to see him, for once, so deferential.

The King seemed very old to me. I knew he had been born in 1491, so he must be nearly fifty. There was a purplish tinge to his face and, although I was too far away to see him clearly, when he suddenly turned in my direction, I noticed that his mouth was thin and tight and his eyes seemed to disappear into his fat face. He was clearly angry; he lifted the stick on which he had been leaning and waved it at the Duke. I thought he was going to strike my uncle. He did not, however, but lowered the stick and they went on walking—the King leaning on the stick, my uncle hovering reverently a pace behind him.

I realized that I was staring directly down at them and I shivered, contemplating what would have happened if either of them had looked up and seen me at the window.

It was all very interesting, and it was a great relief to me that I could not come face to face with Francis Derham here at Court. I wished I could forget the past, but I could not entirely. Poor Francis, when he had said that his love would endure forever, he had meant it. His face haunted me.

A few days after my meeting with Thomas in the music room, the Duchess of Richmond and the Countess of Rutland sent for me. I was still rather nervous and I wondered if I had been discovered by others as well as Lady Rochford in "intimate conversation" with Thomas. I suppose I was still remembering that occasion when the Duchess had caught me "romping" with Derham.

I was relieved to discover that the summons had nothing to do with that incident.

"Mistress Howard," said the Countess, "you have been with us for some little time, and I believe you have not yet attended a banquet of any importance."

I smiled and blushed, as I had a habit of doing.

"We have been thinking you might attend this one which the Bishop of Winchester is giving at his house in honour of the King."

"The King . . ." I stammered, seeing in my mind's eye that huge, magnificent figure whom I had observed walking in the gardens with my uncle.

"Do not look startled. You will not be presented to him."

My relief was noticeable, and they smiled.

"I should like to see the gown you plan to wear," said the Duchess.

"Mistress Howard has some really fine clothes," commented the Countess.

"I know," replied the Duchess, "but I should like to see it all the same."

The Countess nodded.

"Will Her Majesty the Queen be there?" I asked.

"The King will be, so it is unlikely that the Queen will."

"I am sure Mistress Howard will conduct herself in seemly fashion," said the Countess kindly.

I was excited. A banquet! And the King would be present!

~

"So you are going to a banquet," said Lady Rochford. "What shall you wear? You must show me. I will tell you whether it is meet for such an occasion."

"The Duchess of Richmond is looking after that."

"And it is to the Bishop of Winchester that you

go. A very important gentleman. At least, he believes himself to be so."

"I'll dare swear that, as he is the Bishop of Winchester, he must be."

"I have heard that he is the son of a clothworker in Bury St. Edmunds."

"Whether it was in Bury St. Edmunds or London would matter little, I'll trow," I said coolly. I was beginning to challenge her statements in this way, for it was her custom to attempt to lower all those in high places, especially people who were of lowly birth.

"He is another such as Wolsey," went on Jane. "A butcher's son of Ipswich. And Thomas Cromwell, a cloth weaver's son, from I know not where. And look where they ended."

"As I have said before, many of noble birth have gone the same way."

"Well, the Bishop is a clever man. I'll grant you that. He made his way to Cambridge, and had an education to match any, they say. He sidled his way into a great family. None other than your own, Mistress Howard. Did you know that the high and mighty Bishop, when he was plain Stephen Gardiner, was once a tutor to the son of the great Duke of Norfolk?"

"No, I did not."

"I swear that was so. And there he was, under the patronage of the noble Duke, all set to take the leap to fame and fortune. All he had to do was ingratiate himself with the Duke—and that he clearly did. I will grant you, he has been of service to the Duke ever since. Is it not true that these two great men go hand in glove together, and doubtless will do so until it suits either of them to do otherwise."

There were times when I was sorry for Jane. She was clearly an unhappy woman. Life had not been kind to her, but that was perhaps due to herself. I believe she had loved her husband passionately, but he was not of her kind. Erudite, witty, a courtier to his fingertips, another such as his sister. And they had both ignored poor Jane. Perhaps if they had been more thoughtful of her, kinder to her, she would have been different, not so embittered that, when the time came for revenge, she took it. And now, she must live with that. Was she, I often wondered, haunted by memories?

"Do you think I shall make some mistake, Jane?" I asked. "I believe Court etiquette is very strict."

She looked at me through narrowed eyes and smiled grimly.

"That," she said, "I will not deny is a possibility. You learned little of courtly ways in the Duchess's household."

I was not too put out. I would pass through the ordeal somehow, I was sure, and in any case, Jane was only trying to alarm me because she was piqued, not having herself been invited to the banquet.

~

The Countess of Rutland sent for me.

"You are prepared for the banquet, I hope," she said.

I told her I was. "The Duchess thinks my gown suitable," I added.

"That is well. The King likes to hear ladies sing at the table when the meal is over. The Bishop has arranged for a lady of his choice to entertain the King thus. Alas, she has some malaise of the throat and may not be able to perform."

She paused and her next words startled me. "I believe, Mistress Howard, that you have a low and pleasant voice. One or two ladies will sing, of course, but if it should be necessary to include another . . . you could be called on."

"I . . . to sing at the King's table . . . !"

"Oh, he will not notice you. He is just fond of music, and likes to hear it at all times. If the need should arise, I want you to be prepared. You play the lute, do you not?"

"Yes, Countess."

"Well, be ready. You could sing and strum as you do so. Do you know 'Greensleeves'? It is a favourite with the King."

"Oh yes . . . but I am not very good. I am sure someone else . . ."

"Do not be nervous. I will hear you sing and if you are practised enough . . . I should think you could do very well. Let us go to the music room and I shall judge whether you should sing . . . should the need arise."

We went and I sang, nervously at first, and then I was carried away by the music. I had always loved the haunting melody of "Greensleeves." It was said that the King himself had written the words and composed the music. It seemed strange that such a majestic and terrifying looking man should write so gently of love.

"You will do very well, if you are not nervous," said the Countess. "So, if it should be necessary, I will tell my Lord Bishop that you will sing."

It had spoiled the pleasure a little. I told myself that it was hardly likely that I should be asked. And yet, uneasy as I was, I should be a little disappointed if I were not.

≈

How excited I was as we took the barge to the Bishop's residence. All the ladies and gentlemen of the Court were laughing and merry and no one took any notice of me.

I was dressed in a gown of scarlet velvet which my grandmother had provided when I came to Court, and I knew it became me. It had seemed very grand until I mingled with the dazzlingly clad ladies of the

Court. This was my first grand banquet, and the King himself was to be there. Perhaps I should be able to observe him at closer quarters than I had hitherto. But perhaps not. I should certainly not be seated near him at the table.

Should I be called upon to sing? Now that I was at this brilliant assembly, all my delight in the prospect disappeared. I wanted to hide away, watch them all and not be seen. Even more did I feel this when I saw among the guests arriving at the Bishop's house was my Uncle Norfolk. I hoped his eyes would not alight on me.

To my surprise, I was given a place at the high table.

"Because," whispered the Countess, who happened to be close to me, "it may be that you will be called upon to sing. Be ready. Have you your lute with you?"

I said I had, and began to tremble with apprehension. I felt very insignificant.

The King sat in the centre of the high table, looking out over the room; on his right was the Bishop, on his left my uncle. I recognized others; the King's brother-in-law, the Earl of Suffolk, the Earl of Southampton, the Earl of Hertford and Sir Thomas

Seymour. I was right at the end of the table with my back to the room.

It gave me an opportunity to look at the King. I had to do this surreptitiously, as I had been warned not to stare; and I knew that if I were found guilty of any unseemly conduct, this would be the last time I went to a banquet.

There sat the King, grand and glittering in his padded surcoat, with its puffed sleeves, which made him look even bigger than he really was. Jewels as big as eggs glittered in his garments, and his fingers shone with them as they moved.

The table was laden with food. I had never seen so much. I thought fleetingly of the days in my father's house when there was often not even enough for all of us. There were several kinds of fish and pies of all shapes; the pastry of many of these had been formed into the shape of crowns or Tudor roses. Scullions were dashing to and fro, carrying dishes of sucking-pig, hot and steaming.

The King took the food in his hands and ate with relish, while the Bishop watched him eagerly, well pleased. Whenever the King spoke, everyone was silent, listening attentively. My uncle looked subdued and humble, as he had in the gardens.

The meal had been going on for some time and several of the guests were nodding over their wine. Then one of the ladies started to sing in a high treble voice which could scarcely be heard above the conversation. Her song over, another began to sing.

They will not want to hear me, I comforted myself. They really pay little attention to the singing. I wonder why they want anyone to do it.

The singing had ceased, and I was suddenly aware of my uncle's eyes on me. I felt uneasy. Had I committed some fault? What? I had just been sitting quietly, listening. What could I have done?

The Duke nodded to someone. I could not see to whom. I told myself I was mistaken. He had not really been looking at me.

Then I felt a tap on my shoulder. A young man was standing immediately behind me. He picked up the lute, which was at my feet, and put it into my hands.

"My Lord Duke wishes you to sing, Mistress," said the young man.

"My Lord Duke!" I looked along the table. There

was no doubt now. His eyes were on me, cold, critical. My fingers trembled. They would not do as I wished. Frantically, I forced them to pluck at the lute and the feel of the instrument immediately gave me courage. I made myself think of the music room, and pretended I was alone. I would play and sing as though to myself. I knew I could both play and sing well. I had so few accomplishments that I must be aware of this one which was mine. And no one was listening. They were all too interested in their own conversation.

I began to sing. I was playing a tune which I loved, and I was playing for myself.

When I stopped I was aware of a silence around the table. I looked in the direction of my uncle, and I saw that the King was gazing straight at me. There was a glazed look in his eyes.

He spoke then. "'Twas well sung," he said. "Who is the lady?"

My uncle replied: "She is Katherine Howard, Your Majesty."

"Ha!" said the King with a laugh. "One of your brood, Norfolk, with such a name."

"My niece, Sire."

"Is she of the Court?"

"Lady-in-waiting to the Queen, Your Majesty."

At the mention of the Queen's name, the King's expression darkened. Then he glanced at me and looked pleased again.

"Niece, eh?" he said.

"My brother Edmund's daughter," the Duke told him.

"Very pretty," said the King, smiling directly at me.

"Your Majesty is gracious," replied my uncle.

"'Tis but the truth, Norfolk. Methinks I should speak to her, compliment her on her singing."

My uncle came round the table to where I was sitting.

"The King wishes to speak to you," he said quietly. "Come."

I followed him and, as I stood before the King, I felt my uncle's hand on my shoulder, reminding me that I must make the most humble obeisance that I had ever made in my life.

I went down to the floor and was afraid I was going to lose my balance in doing so. I almost did, and was aware of my uncle's annoyance.

But the King was smiling.

"Come, come," he said. "Rise, my dear young lady."

A hand shining with jewels took mine. I was drawn close to him and I was looking straight into that fleshy face; the little eyes were glinting.

"You are very young, Mistress Howard. Tell me, how many years have you graced this earth?"

"I am eighteen years old, Your Majesty."

"Eighteen?" he said rather wistfully. "'Tis a goodly age, eh, Norfolk? You and I left it behind some time since."

"Your Majesty is right."

"I liked your song," he said to me. "It is one of my favourites."

Everyone applauded and there was laughter, in which the King joined.

"You sang it with feeling. Did she not?" He looked round the table.

"She sang it as it deserved to be sung, Your Majesty," said someone.

"'Twas so indeed. You will sing for us again, Mistress Howard, and you shall sing that song. It would please me much to hear you."

I was not quite sure what was expected of me, and I was blushing. My uncle was frowning, and I guessed he was urging me to say something.

I stammered: "Thank you, Your Majesty."

My uncle's obvious exasperation told me that I had failed to come up to his expectations.

"My niece has but recently come to Court," he said. "She is nervous and overwhelmed by Your Majesty's kindness. Your Majesty must forgive her lack . . ."

"Lack, Norfolk? I see no lack." The King was glaring at my uncle and I could not suppress my pleasure at seeing him disconcerted. "I like well her manners," went on the King, patting my hand and looking affable again.

He bent closer to me. "Heed him not." Then he said loudly: "I would have Mistress Howard sit beside me. I would speak with her."

The chair next to the King was immediately vacated and I began to feel a little less nervous. He was the King, and it was clear that they were all in great awe of him, even my formidable uncle, but he was very pleasant to me.

"Now," he said. "You and I will talk. We will pay no

attention to Norfolk's carping. You and I understand each other, do we not, Mistress Howard?"

I giggled, lost for words, and again he did not object. In fact, he laughed with me.

"And you have recently come to my Court. I guessed that, for I have not seen you before, and if I had, I should have remembered you. Perhaps you would have remembered me?"

I knew that was a joke, because everyone would remember him and count it an experience to have seen him. So we laughed together over that.

There appeared to be no need to worry about making the courtly remark. The King did not seem to mind if I just acted naturally.

"Your singing pleased me greatly," he went on. "You have a pretty voice, but methinks, Mistress Howard, that everything about you is enchanting."

I did manage to murmur: "Thank you, Your Majesty."

"Oh," he said jocularly, "that is one blessing for which you do not have to thank your King. But let me tell you this, it pleases me. It pleases me indeed. I like to see freshly innocent young ladies about my Court, and you are that, Mistress Howard."

I was very pleased to discover that I was not expected to say much. I merely had to listen to him, and laugh when he laughed and put in the occasional "Yes, Your Majesty," to be varied with "Your Majesty is gracious."

He talked a little about my family and how the Howards and the Tudors had been friends.

"For the most part," he added. He remembered my father, who had done well at Flodden. He asked questions about me, which did not strike me as unusual.

I found myself talking naturally to him, and if I forgot to say "Your Majesty" or "Your Grace" all the time, that did not seem to matter. I told him that I had been brought up in my grandmother's establishment and how poor we had been when I was very young. He listened and nodded sympathetically.

He kept me beside him for the rest of the evening and together we watched some dancers whom the Bishop had engaged for his entertainment.

As we took the barge back to Greenwich, I realized that people's attitudes towards me had changed. They no longer regarded me as the insignificant newcomer, ignorant of the ways of the Court.

I had been favoured by the King in an unmistakable manner.

~

The next day my uncle came to see me. That in itself was significant. Before I had always been summoned to see him.

"Your singing was a success," he said almost grudgingly.

"The King liked it, did he not?" I replied.

"I fancy he liked more than your singing."

I laughed. I had changed. I would not have dared laugh like that before in the Duke's presence.

"You must not be foolish. You must act warily. You will be advised."

I wondered what about.

"You are very ignorant of Court ways," went on the Duke.

"The King liked that."

"Hmm." He was thoughtful. "You must not be too . . . free with the King." He looked at me with some exasperation. "You must not act in an unseemly fashion."

I did not understand what he meant. I wondered how anyone would presume to act in an unseemly fashion towards that great and glittering creature.

"You are such a child," he said quite irritably. "You are young, even for your years."

I was silent, not knowing how to apologize for that.

"I shall speak to your grandmother. You may need new dresses . . . some jewellery." He lifted his shoulders and frowned, as though he were puzzled. I think he found it difficult to understand not just why the King could have liked my playing so much, but more, that he had talked to me during the evening. "But it may come to naught," he went on, as though to himself. "Just a whim of the moment. Bored with Gardiner's efforts to entertain him. Perhaps wait a while . . . and see."

I thought he was going to explain, but he just said: "We shall have to wait and see how deep the interest went. The song was his own. That could have been it."

Then he left me.

❧

The ladies were talking about the King's interest in me.

The Countess of Rutland said: "You were honoured indeed, Mistress Howard."

"She played very well and sang with deep feeling," commented Lady Richmond. "I think that was what interested him. He gets sentimental over 'Greensleeves.' It was a brilliant idea to choose that piece."

"Mayhap," added the Countess thoughtfully, "it was more than the song."

They exchanged glances and smiled.

"It is not everyone who pleases the King," said Lady Richmond. "His leg gives him great pain . . . among other things."

"Which," put in the Countess, "may possibly be more painful to him."

Then they seemed to come to an understanding, which I guessed meant they realized they were talking too freely before someone who was not included in their circle.

Lady Rochford was quick to seek me out.

"There is much talk about Mistress Howard," she said, her eyes sparkling with mischief. "The King was most impressed by her singing."

"Oh yes, he liked it. It was because it was 'Green-sleeves.'"

"Was that so? Then we shall have all the ladies singing it. May the good Lord spare us! And what of my Lord Norfolk? He was, I'll warrant, proud of his little niece on this occasion. That is somewhat rare with my lord, is it not?"

I laughed. I could always laugh with Jane Rochford.

I said: "I think he was more surprised than anyone. You know, he has not a very high opinion of me. Indeed, he always makes me feel more stupid than I am."

"Oh come, Mistress Howard, you are not stupid. Methinks you have become a very important lady."

"My uncle does not think so. But it was amusing, Jane. When he presented me to the King, he was very different from what I have ever seen him before."

"That is the power of royalty, my dear Katherine. It is good to bask in it, but one must never forget it can soon be withdrawn. 'Well done, thou good and faithful servant' can quickly be followed by 'off with his—or her—head.'"

"Oh, Jane, you are very funny."

"There is truth behind the mirth, dear child. I should like to know what the mighty Duke thought of the King's interest in his little niece."

"I think he was afraid I was going to disgrace the family. He was surprised."

"You may do that yet."

"What? Disgrace or surprise?"

"Both." She laughed and went on: "Well, I think we may assume that at this time His Grace the Duke is not displeased with his niece."

"I am not sure."

"But the King was certainly not!"

"He did not seem displeased with me, of a surety."

"'Tis a beginning, and where there is a beginning there must be an end."

~

Some of the Queen's ladies were invited to the Bishop's house once more—I among them—and, to our surprise, we had not been there long when the King arrived; and among the courtiers who accompanied him were my uncle and the King's brother-in-law, the Duke of Suffolk.

I noticed a look pass between my uncle and the Bishop, and it seemed to me that there was something conspiratorial about it.

My uncle came to me and looked me over with that critical manner to which I was accustomed. He took my arm and led me away from the others to the King, bowed, and said: "Your Majesty, may I present Mistress Katherine Howard."

The King smiled broadly. "Of a surety you may," he said, turning that smile on me.

"Your Majesty was kind enough to commend her for her singing. Your Majesty may remember the occasion. My niece was overwhelmed."

"Now, let me think," said the King, his eyes twinkling. "Sing, did you say? Ah, I recall the lady."

"Your Majesty was most gracious."

"The grace was not mine," said the King. "Rather that of the young lady. Sit beside me, Mistress Howard. I would speak with you for a while."

He waved his hand to dismiss my uncle, who bowed and moved away.

Then the King talked to me, asking me questions which he had asked before. Did I like living at the Court? It must be different from what I had done before—and so on.

On this occasion I was less shy. In fact, the King was so friendly that I forgot that he was the King. I am afraid I laughed rather immoderately until I remembered who he was and curbed it.

He realized this and, taking my hand, patted it gently. I was fascinated by those fat, glittering fingers, and could not take my eyes from them.

"You must not be afraid of me," he said gently. "You are a good girl, Mistress Howard. I know that well. I like young ladies to be modest and virtuous. Such gifts are rare, and especially so in surroundings such as these. You are newly come and know nothing of this, so, prithee, Mistress Howard, do not adopt too many of the habits of my Court."

His mouth fascinated me. It was so small and seemed particularly so because his face was so big. Such a thin straight line of a mouth. Such little eyes that seemed to peer forth from all that flesh. When I had seen him at first, I had thought it was a cruel face.

It was quite different when he talked to me. There seemed something young about it now—almost like a baby's. And then, talking about the morals of his Court, it was almost prim and definitely disapproving.

He noticed how I looked at him, for he said: "You study me, Mistress Howard. What do you think, eh? What do you think of your King?"

I was unsure how to reply and I stammered: "I think Your Majesty is very kind to me."

He looked pleased and a great sense of relief swept over me because I must have found the right answer to this difficult question.

"To those who serve me well, I can be very kind." He was smiling now and there was something very soft and sentimental about his face. I was amazed by the speed with which it could change. Now there was a glitter in his eyes and it was different again. It was a look which sent a shiver of alarm through me. I had seen it before, and suddenly I was thinking of Manox and Derham and my dear Thomas. The King was pressing my hand.

"I could be very kind to you, Mistress Howard," he said.

"Your . . . Your Majesty is gracious."

"And will be more . . . and will be more, I swear to you."

He looked sentimental again, with that glazed expression in his eyes, and suddenly he said: "Tell me of your music. You play the lute, I know."

I told him that I also played the virginals.

"You shall play for me," he said. "I like much the virginals. We share this love of music, you and I."

It grew increasingly easy to talk to him. I completely forgot he was the King. I pulled myself up sharply, putting my finger to my lips to prevent the informal words coming out, and he said to me: "What ails you, Mistress Katherine?"

I sought to explain. "Your Majesty is so gracious to me. I forgot you are . . . Your Majesty."

That seemed to amuse him. His laughter boomed forth and everyone was looking our way.

For a moment I thought he might be angry, but his smile was more soft and sentimental than ever.

"I like that, Katherine," he said. "I like it well."

~

The Duchess asked me to visit her. This was not the command to which I was accustomed, more a request.

I sailed upriver in a barge which had been sent to take me from Greenwich to Lambeth.

She greeted me warmly.

"Ah, granddaughter," she said, "you have become a success at Court."

"I am not sure. But the King has spoken to me."

"Spoken to you indeed! I heard he had you seated beside him and that you talked together. What could you have had to say to the King?"

"It was easy. I just talked. I forgot he was the King and I told him that."

She looked at me in horror.

"It was all right," I assured her. "I am not to be sent to the Tower."

"Do not say such things . . . even in jest!" she cried, and I knew she was thinking of my cousin.

"Oh, it mattered not."

"And it was at the Bishop's residence that this happened?"

I nodded.

"Stephen Gardiner does not forget his allegiance to

your uncle. That is as it should be, for where would Gardiner be without His Grace? He came up from nothing . . . his father a clothworker, was it? Something such. And if your uncle had not brought him to the attention of Wolsey . . . poor Wolsey. These people . . . they come and go. Wolsey . . . Cromwell . . . who next? We have to walk through life with the greatest care . . . those of us who live near the Crown. It is well to remember that. So, it was at Gardiner's place . . . and your uncle was there . . . and you did not know that you should meet the King."

"No . . . no one knew. The King came without telling them that he would."

She gave me a slightly supercilious smile.

"And the King paid attention to you . . . had you sit beside him? He talked to you and you forgot he was the King and he liked that. Is that all?"

"What else should there be?"

"I was asking you. Ah, I think I hear sounds of arrival. It will be the Duke himself."

The Duke saluted his stepmother and acknowledged me with a nod.

"Katherine is here, as you see," said the Duchess.

He turned to me then and I recognized the speculation in his eyes as he looked at me: There was a certain interest there which had never come my way before.

"You stand well with the King," he said. "It is good that you have pleased him."

"I have done as you asked," put in my grandmother. "She shall not be short of a gown or the occasional trinket. The seamstresses are here now. They are waiting to fit her as it is necessary."

The Duke was actually smiling at me. "I doubt not that you are eager to try these new gowns, and I'll warrant you are as fond of finery as most girls are, eh?"

"Yes, Your Grace."

He glanced at my grandmother, who nodded.

"Then go, child," she said. "Try the blue velvet. They used one of your old gowns for size. It should fit. There are some beautiful materials and the colours should become you well. Let me see how you look in the blue velvet."

I was always glad to get away when my uncle was present. Moreover, the prospect of clothes always excited me.

How they had changed towards me! The King's attention had done this. I felt a warm glow of gratitude towards him. I was beginning to lose my awe of him. He had been so friendly, and he had shown clearly that he did not think me in the least stupid—or, if he did, he liked it. I was as a young girl should be, he implied.

I gasped with pleasure at the materials when I saw them. I may not have had much book learning, but I did know something about clothes. I held up the material against me and the two seamstresses cried out in delight.

"Oh, how that scarlet becomes you, Mistress Howard! I think we should make it with the flowing sleeves."

The flowing sleeves were a fashion which had been introduced to the Court by Anne Boleyn, because she had a deformity on the finger and the full sleeves helped to hide it. They were graceful and becoming and were still in fashion.

I examined the materials and we talked of styles. I tried on the blue dress. The bodice had a square-cut neck and the skirt hung open in the front to disclose a beautifully embroidered kirtle decorated with a tracing of silver thread. The women hovered round me, straightening the skirt and patting the material here and there.

"Ah, but you are beautiful in that gown, Mistress Howard," one of them said.

They stood together, looking at me in admiration— I suspected as much of their own work as of me.

I was delighted. So often I had seen the Court ladies in splendid gowns and wished they were mine. And now, it seemed, they were.

"The Duchess wishes me to show her this gown," I said.

They nodded to each other. They had no doubt of her approval.

I went back to my grandmother's apartments. As I opened the door to the little anteroom which led to her chamber, the sound of her voice and that of the Duke made me pause. They must have left the door of the chamber open, so I could hear distinctly and I realized that they were talking about me.

The Duchess was saying: "It is not easy to believe that this could be happening . . . to her."

"He is in a strange mood at this time. The shock of the Queen's arrival . . . the disappointment."

"Our girl is exceedingly pretty . . . in a simple way, of course."

"But witless."

"That could be an advantage. Remember . . ."

"I remember well, madam, and need no reminder. That was a disaster. He turned against the family for a time."

"But has been won back," said my grandmother. "If indeed it did come to pass . . . oh, she is not like that other. *She* was bold and thought herself clever."

"More clever than she was in truth," retorted the Duke grimly.

"Oh . . . this could be of great good."

"Gardiner will do his best."

"So should he, when it is considered what good you have brought to him."

"But we shall have to be watchful . . . of her. She is so untutored . . . young even of her years. But as yet it is merely an interest. His moods are less predictable than ever."

"We can only wait . . ."

"Yes, and be watchful."

There was a slight pause and I wondered whether they had become aware that I was in the anteroom. But, as they had been talking about me and their words were revealing, I was reluctant to go into the room and stop this interesting discussion.

I waited for a few more seconds and, as they had fallen into silence, I went into the room.

"Ah, here is the child," said my grandmother. "Let me look at the gown. Marry, and it becomes you well. Think you not so, my lord?"

He nodded; and he was smiling to himself.

I thought a great deal about that conversation I had overheard. They were not the only ones who were excited by the King's interest in me. I was myself. It was so unexpected, after having been ignored, to be treated with a certain degree of respect.

What made it so pleasant was that I could be natural and that was what the King liked about me. He, who was surrounded by the cleverest and most beautiful women at Court, had shown a preference for the society of little Katherine Howard—witless, as her uncle called her, without education and unable to converse amusingly. All she had to recommend her was a simple prettiness; she was small but slender with it; she had an air of helplessness, a look of innocence, which seemed to make the King want to be gentle with her.

That was what they were saying about me. I did not care. I was going to enjoy being in favour.

Soon after this, I met Thomas Culpepper in the gardens.

"There is much gossip about you and the King," he said and he looked uneasy.

I laughed. "It is wondrous how people talk," I said. "I sang and the King liked my song because it was his own. He spoke to me, then I went to the residence of the Bishop of Winchester and the King happened to be there, so he talked to me again. That is all. Is it so very important when the King talks to one of his subjects?"

"It would depend on the manner of the talk," said Thomas.

"Oh, it was just . . . talk. He asked if I liked being at Court and I told him what it was like when I was a little girl in my father's house, that he might judge the difference between that and the Court. Then we talked about music. He loves music. He was very kind."

"Did it not strike you as strange that he should talk thus to you?"

"Of what else should we talk?"

Thomas looked at me in faint exasperation.

"You know you are very pretty, do you not?"

"I have heard it said," I replied with some satisfaction.

"Has it not occurred to you that that was why the King spoke to you?"

"He is an old man," I said.

Thomas's exasperation increased.

I went on: "My uncle, the Duke, and my grandmother are very pleased. My uncle has never been so gracious to me as he is now."

"I can well believe it," said Thomas grimly. "Oh, I like it not."

Then he put his arms round me and held me tightly.

"Katherine," he said. "Never forget that you are betrothed to me."

"We have not been . . . formally, but I do not forget it was to be. I often think of going away to Hollingbourne. That is what I long for."

"It *shall* come to pass."

"Oh yes. Perhaps soon."

"They will not accept me now."

"My grandmother talked of it once."

"Perhaps it might have been possible . . . once. But now . . . not yet."

"I am eighteen years old. I am no longer young."

"It must be so, Katherine. It must be."

"And it shall, Thomas. Be of good cheer. Why are you so downcast?"

"I am afraid, Katherine."

"You must not be. I love you and you love me— and do not forget they once spoke of our betrothal."

"That was before you came to Court."

"It has not changed me."

He kissed me sadly.

"No," he said, "you have not changed. It is the world around you that has changed. Katherine, do not cease to love me. I should not wish to live if you did."

"Thomas," I assured him. "I shall always love you. No matter what, I am yours."

A Royal Wooing

There were rumours about the Queen. The King wanted to be rid of her and was more determined on this than he had been even before.

"Poor lady!" said Jane Rochford. "She is very uneasy. Who would not be in her position? She remembers what happened to those who went before her."

As usual, Jane made it her task to find out all that was going on. She sparkled with excitement, for nothing delighted her more than intrigue and I believe that when it concerned the relationship between the sexes it was of special delight to her.

"They say there is only one way by which he can rid himself of her, and that is to send her to the block, as he did on another occasion with another queen. But she is too important for that. True, the Duke of

Cleves is not a great emperor, but His Majesty cannot afford to offend even a minor power when it could mean sending that power into the camp of one of his enemies. Depend upon it, there will be a divorce."

"How can he divorce the Queen? She is a good and virtuous lady."

Jane looked wise.

She said: "Kings have their ways. It is not a matter of turning against her. He disliked her from the moment he saw her. He even said he liked her ill and that she was different from what she had been made out to be by men who had deceived him, and it was woe that she ever came to England. Those were his very words."

"I think she is a very pleasant lady."

"It is not for you to judge, Katherine Howard. It is for the King who had to marry her. Let me tell you this. I have heard that his friends are trying to find a way out for him."

"But how can they? The King is married to her."

"Oh, marriage can be proved to be no marriage. Did we not see that, with the King's first wife? His Majesty would forgive a queen a great deal if she gave him a son. It is his great desire to have a son . . . in his own image . . . one whose education and upbringing he himself can watch over. He wants another King Henry to follow when he has gone."

"To have a son just like himself . . . that would be the ambition of most men, I believe."

"Ah, but with the King it goes more deep. He has a throne, and the House of Tudor must stand forever." She lowered her voice and came closer to me. "It is not very firm on the ground, is it? There are many who think that the Tudors' claim to the throne is not very strong. Who was Owen Tudor? True, he was said to have married Queen Catherine, the widow of King Henry V, but was there actually even a ceremony? Who can be sure?"

"Jane!" I cried in dismay.

She laughed, and I noticed that her colour had deepened. "Don't you dare repeat a word of what I have said."

"You cannot believe I would betray you. But, Jane, be careful. People have lost their heads for voicing such opinions."

"I go too far, but I trust you, Katherine. You see, I

trust you with my life. And are they not interesting . . . these times we live in? But I go too far. I know I must have a care, eh? You would never betray me. If you did, I would come back after death and haunt you. You would have no peace from me, Katherine Howard."

"I swear I will say nothing."

"I know. You are my very good friend, as I am yours. And, in any case, how would you stand? You listened. You joined in."

"Have no fear. I shall not whisper a word."

"And I will remember not to be so indiscreet," said Jane, and went on to be more so.

"The King needs a son. As I said, it is more important to him than anything. It is odd, but the meanest scullion can get a woman with child, yet kings cannot."

"There are the Lady Mary, Lady Elizabeth and Prince Edward."

"Poor little boy. A puff of wind would blow him over. Do you know that in his nursery they live in perpetual fear lest some ill befall him and they be blamed? Holy Mother, it would go ill with them if they allowed the boy to get as much as a rheum. You know His Majesty's wrath when things go wrong! The

King blames his wives for his lack of a strong and healthy male heir. He himself is as virile as he has always been. And time is running short for him." She clapped her hands over her mouth and laughed.

I could not help laughing with her.

"Jane," I said, "you are the most reckless woman I know."

"You can go somewhat far in that direction yourself," she retorted.

"Not as far as you."

"We will not quarrel about that. What was I saying? He does not think the fault lies with him. He believes that, if he could find a woman who would bear him sons, all would be well."

"The Queen might do that."

"She would have no chance when he cannot bring himself to do that which would produce them. What he wants is someone whom he can love, and he believes that one will give him the boy he so much desires. All those years with his first queen frustrated him. Stillborn, weakling . . . one after another, and only the Lady Mary after all those years; and she is always ailing. Then, of course, our cousin gave him only the Lady Elizabeth, when he had so fervently believed she would give him a son, and she would have done so had she not miscarried."

"I heard it was because she found the King with Jane Seymour."

"That may be, but she lost the child. Then there was Queen Jane who had the boy, but no one believes he will survive long. So the King dreams that somewhere is that woman who will give him not only the pleasures he craves, but the son he so desperately wants. He is sure the inability to get a son does not lie with him . . . because of the Duke of Richmond."

"But the Duke of Richmond is dead. He died years ago."

"Not so many. Four years, to be true . . . just after the King's second queen. He was a healthy young man, and how the King doted on him! He was the living proof that the King could get a healthy son, and the perpetual miscarriages of Queen Catherine were not due to him."

"The Duke of Richmond married one of my uncle's daughters . . . my cousin."

"Oh, there were always strong ties between the

Tudors and the Howards. My Lord Duke, your uncle, sees to that. He seeks to unite the families on every occasion. I remember the young Duke of Richmond well—such a handsome young man, with a look of his father—strutting about the Court. It was a pity he was born on the wrong side of the blanket."

"But even so, he did not live. What of his mother?"

"She was Elizabeth Blount—lady-in-waiting to the Queen Catherine. It was long ago, before you were born."

"Did the King wish to marry her?"

"No. He had not thought of divorce at that time. The queen was not so very old then and he had not begun to despair of having a child by her. So young Richmond was born and proved to be a healthy boy. The King was overjoyed, and at the same time frustrated. If only the child had been Prince Henry instead of Henry Fitzroy."

"What happened to Elizabeth Blount?"

"She received honours and was in due course married to Sir Gilbert Talboys. Manors were bestowed on her for life. As for the boy, he was only six years old when he was made Knight of the Garter and Duke of

Richmond. He was married when he was about fourteen to His Grace the Duke's daughter, your cousin Mary. The King loved him dearly, not only, they say, as a son, but because the boy was a living proof of his own virility."

"But he died . . ."

"Yes, very soon after Anne Boleyn. Young Richmond was only seventeen."

"Did that not show the King that he could not, after all, get healthy sons who lived the normal span?"

"No, they said Richmond had been poisoned."

"Was it really so?"

"Who can say? Rumour had it that the late Queen and her brother . . . your cousin and my husband . . . had poisoned him before they had died. And the result was poor Richmond's eventual death."

"Did they really believe that?"

"People believe what they want to believe—the King more than any." Again she gave that half laugh and looked over her shoulder. "If he *were* poisoned, then it seems that the King can get healthy children. If he died of some natural cause, the question arises, can he? So it is best to say that the Duke was poisoned.

Do you not know that, Katherine Howard? So now the King is looking for a new wife. He needs to give the nation a boy who will grow up in the shadow of himself. He is also not averse to a young and pretty woman who will keep him warm and comforted at night. Therefore, I say to you that however pleasing Queen Anne is to Katherine Howard, you should be very wary, for the King is seeking the road to divorce; and Her Majesty, bearing in mind what had gone before, must be growing very uneasy."

~

Tension was growing throughout the Court. The King and Queen were never seen together now and we heard that the Queen was to go to Richmond, where she would take up temporary residence. As one of her ladies, I should, of course, go with her.

It was a few days before we left and we were still at Greenwich when my uncle came and said he would like to talk with me. He would prefer our conversation took place in the gardens, that we might be more private.

Such a pronouncement aroused inevitable apprehension in me and I immediately feared that I had been guilty of some misdemeanour.

We walked under the trees in silence for a moment while I waited for the storm to break.

Instead he said: "It seems that you have been conducting yourself well while you have been at Court, Katherine." His voice was friendly. "Your grandmother is most pleased with your progress."

I was aware of that, because of the dresses she had provided, and I was very pleased, for life had become much more pleasant now that I could appear as well dressed as the others.

I was still waiting for what he was to say when the King appeared, surprisingly unaccompanied. I immediately curtsied, and when I raised my eyes I saw that the King was regarding me with the benign smile which I had come to expect from him.

"Well met, Katherine," he said, and he looked from me to my uncle, still smiling.

"It was a happy choice when my niece and I decided to walk in the gardens," said my uncle.

"It was indeed," agreed the King. "I doubt not you have much to engage you, Norfolk?"

"Your Majesty speaks truth. May I have your permission to retire?"

"'Tis granted," said the King benevolently.

I was preparing to follow my uncle when a plump bejewelled hand was laid on my arm.

"You would stay awhile and talk to your King, Mistress Howard?" he said.

I was overcome with embarrassment, which I believe pleased him, for, as he had said, he liked me to be natural.

There was a seat nearby on which about four people could have sat in comfort.

The King said: "We shall sit there and talk awhile."

He took my hand and with the other held the stick on which he leaned as we walked.

He sat down and indicated that I should sit beside him. His large person and padded garments took up a good deal of the seat, but there was room for me close to him.

I had rather expected I must kneel at his feet.

He noticed my surprise and that pleased him too. He laid his hand on my thigh and kept it there, patting me now and then.

"You must not be afraid of me, Katherine," he said.

"Oh no, Your Majesty."

"You must think it strange that I, your King, should so honour you."

"Yes, Your Majesty."

"Katherine, shall I tell you something?"

I was completely disarmed by this playful mood.

"Oh, yes please, Your Majesty."

"I feel honoured to be with you," he said with a meekness which, even in my inexperienced eyes, seemed too ostentatiously assumed.

I stared at him in astonishment, but I knew again that he was delighted by my response.

"You are such a little girl, are you not?"

"I beg Your Majesty's pardon, but I was born small."

He laughed out loud and shook with merriment. I felt uplifted, as though I had said something very clever. I was wondering why they were all so much afraid of him, when he could be so kind, so affable.

"Well, so you were." He squeezed my thigh again.

"And I will tell you something else, shall I, sweet Katherine?"

"If it please Your Majesty."

"I like it well. You are little, Katherine Howard. Women should not be like great mares." His face darkened. "I never liked that sort. Katherine, I will tell you this. You are the exact size that pleases me."

I laughed. He was watching me closely, his lips slightly parted so that they no longer looked cruel; his eyes gleamed, and there was an even deeper colour than usual in his plump cheeks.

"You continue happy with Court life?" he asked.

"Oh yes, Your Majesty."

"And you sing and dance and pass the days merrily? Oh, Katherine, you are a happy young lady. I see it in your face. You bring happiness to those about you. Do you know that?"

"I . . . I did not know."

"And you think that your King is the happiest because he is the master of them all . . . this brilliant Court, these men and women—they are here to serve him. You think there must be naught he lacks. Is that so?"

What could I say but "Yes, Your Majesty," for he was looking at me, expecting an answer.

"Then you are wrong," he said in a voice of thunder. His face was distorted in anger which alarmed me. My simple "Yes, Your Majesty" appeared to be the wrong answer. Thomas had said that in the service of the King one must take great care. A careless word could result in one's being sent to the Tower.

He saw my startled face and reached for my hand. He lifted it and, to my astonishment, raised it to his lips, kissing it.

"My dear, dear child," he said. "My dear Katherine, your King is not a happy man. There are times when I wonder why it is that Heaven persecutes me so. Have I done aught wrong? Is there some fault in me of which I know nothing, but which has displeased my Maker? Do you think so, Katherine?"

I was abashed. I looked up at the sky, as though hoping to find the answer there. How easy it would be to make the wrong answer to such a question.

But apparently no answer was needed, for his expression changed again to one of abject self-pity.

"It is a cross I have to bear," he said. "Through

the years I have borne it. All I asked was a wife who would be good to me . . . and the nation. I was a good and faithful husband."

I looked sharply at him. I could not stop thinking of Elizabeth Blount—lady-in-waiting to Queen Catherine—who had been the mother of his son, the Duke of Richmond. I thought of my cousin's miscarriage, which might have been the means of giving him—and the nation—the desired son, and which had been brought on because my cousin had come upon him, fondling Jane Seymour.

Yet he looked so sad, and quite unaware that he could be speaking anything but the truth, that I found myself almost believing him.

"Why . . . why?" he went on.

How I dreaded these questions. Why did I have to be so inadequate? Why had I not been like my cousin? Oh no, I must not think of her.

But apparently again he did not need an answer. Though I did wish he would not keep putting his words in the form of a question.

He was saying: "There is nothing I ask more than to be a good and faithful husband to a wife who will love me in return. Yet I am plagued. It would seem there is a curse on me."

There was silence while I tried to think of what I ought to say. He was still holding my hand.

He said: "I believe you to be a good, sweet girl. You know nothing of the evils of the world, sweet child. You are untouched by the wickedness of the world. I find great pleasure in the company of one such as you."

Again silence. What could I say? Was I good? I had never wanted to *harm* anyone. But to most people goodness meant virtue. An image of Manox rose before me. I thought of the slighting manner in which he had spoken of me to Dorothy Barwike.

But I was going to forget all that. Perhaps soon they would agree to my marriage with Thomas. I should go to Hollingbourne and in the years to come tell my children about the time I was at Court and how the King had liked my music, how I had met him in the garden and he had talked to me.

I could hear myself saying: "There was something very kind about him."

"Yes," went on the King, drawing me back to reality, and almost as though he were talking to himself.

"Ill luck has dogged me. There are times when I ask myself, what have I done? There was my first marriage . . . only a form of marriage, that was. I was not married all those years when I thought I was. Then I married a witch. A spell was put upon me then. And after that there was Jane . . . good Jane . . . but she died and left me the boy Edward. There are times when I think I shall outlast him. And then . . . and then . . ." His face was dark again.

"But, Katherine, the Lord has shown me the way out." He leaned towards me and put his face close to mine. "What think you of that?"

I realized that this question had to be answered, and desperately I sought for the right words.

"I . . . I rejoice for Your Majesty."

"And not only for him, Katherine. You should rejoice for another."

I did not know to whom he was referring, so I remained silent.

"You are a good, modest girl. It pleases me that there are still such as you in my realm. You have a good heart, Katherine. I would not be deceived in you, would I?"

"Oh no, Your Majesty."

"Of course not. It is clear in your sweet face. You will be a good and honest wife, will you not? You will love your husband as he will love you?"

I was on the point of telling him that I was all but betrothed to Thomas Culpepper and that we planned to settle at Hollingbourne, but something restrained me. Moreover, he went on immediately: "After my tribulation, it may be God's will that I come to happiness."

"Oh yes, Your Majesty. I pray so."

"We will pray together, Katherine," he said. "You and I, eh?"

I smiled happily.

"You please me greatly, Katherine," he said. "Have they told you how pretty you are?"

I blushed and he squeezed my thigh again. I thought, it will be bruised, I doubt not, and I giggled inwardly, asking myself if it were an honour to be bruised by the King.

His face was creased again in tender sentimentality.

"My dear little flower," he said. "I like you, Katherine."

"Oh, Your Majesty is very kind to me," I murmured.

"And will be kinder. There is much we shall talk of when the time is ripe. Ere long it will be so for, as I have told you, you please me. You please me greatly. What say you to that?"

I did not know what to say, and he went on: "Eh? Eh? What say you?"

"Your . . . Your Majesty pleases me." I stopped short.

That was a terrible mistake. I was glad that my uncle could not hear. But it seemed I could do no wrong in the eyes of the King. He slapped his thigh this time. He was laughing.

"I like that, Katherine," he said. "The King has found favour with little Mistress Howard. What better news? What better?"

I laughed with him—which was easy enough—while I marvelled that my uncle could offend him so easily and that an untutored girl such as I was could so easily say what he wanted to hear.

～

There was an apprehensive air of expectancy in the Queen's household at Richmond. On the rare occasions when I saw the Queen, I was aware of tension, as though outwardly she were serene but she was aware of our watchfulness. The only attendant left to her from her own country was known as Mother Lowe; and she was constantly at the Queen's side.

I gathered that the Queen had always been gracious to her English attendants, but I supposed it was only to Mother Lowe that she would reveal her true feelings.

There was something else. Attitudes towards me had changed considerably. Those who had previously ignored me seemed eager to show friendship. They watched me closely. It was, of course, because the King had spoken to me.

I did not see Thomas. I wondered why, because usually he had sought some way of meeting me.

Lady Margaret Douglas, who was chief of the Queen's ladies, had, among others, noticed me. She talked to me now and then and we had become quite friendly. She was very handsome and I judged her to be about six years older than I. I had always been interested in her because at one time she had wanted to marry Lord Thomas Howard, one of my cousins.

Lady Margaret was, of course, a very important lady, being the daughter of the King's sister Margaret by her second husband, the Earl of Angus. She had had a very adventurous life and must have passed through many dangers. I think she felt drawn towards me because she had loved a member of my family.

She was closer to the Queen than any of the ladies—except Mother Lowe—and one day I mentioned to her that I had seen the Queen in the gardens; she had looked sad and Mother Lowe seemed anxious.

"Well," said Lady Margaret. "Who would not be . . . in her position?"

"Do you think she misses her home?"

"It would seem so. But I think she fears most what is going to happen to her."

"Because she does not please the King, you mean?"

Lady Margaret looked at me quizzically, and she said, with a lift of her lips: "The King looks elsewhere."

"What will become of the Queen, think you?"

"Ah, that is what we are all wondering. Oh, Katherine, it is not all pleasure and honour to be royal."

"No," I said.

"How old are you, Katherine?"

I told her.

"You seem younger," she said. "I know how you lived in your early days, and then you were with the Dowager Duchess. It is only recently that you have come into royal circles, is it not?"

I nodded.

"Think of me, the daughter of a queen. It sets one apart. People are inclined to think it is a glorious position to hold, but it does not always work out that way, Katherine. Terrible things can happen to some of us."

I knew that she had spent a time in the Tower and I wondered whether I should refer to it.

She went on: "One is moved this way and that. It all depends on how one is being used. I often think how much happier some of us might have been if we had not had royal connections. One should consider a great deal, Katherine, before one moves close to the throne."

"But if one is born there, one can do nothing about it."

"No, they are caught in it from the moment they are born. The fortunate ones are those who have a choice. You have seen ambitious men . . . and women . . . move too near the throne and what can happen to them. There was your own cousin."

The vision of Anne came to me then. I saw her beautiful head bent over the block, awaiting the fall of the axe. But it was not an axe, of course; it was a sword sent specially from France for the purpose. How like her to die in elegant style.

"She might have married Northumberland," Lady Margaret was saying. "He adored her, and she loved him. But fate had a different destiny for her." She looked at me steadily. "I would be very wary before I sought favours of the King. For me there has been no choice. When the Ladies Mary and Elizabeth were declared illegitimate—that was when Jane Seymour became Queen—I was in line to the throne. There were no male heirs for the King, and I was the daughter of his eldest sister, you see. My mother was a very forceful lady; my father was a very ambitious man. They quarrelled and there was much ill will between them. My mother fled from Scotland, bringing me with her, and I was brought up in the palace of Greenwich."

"Greenwich is beautiful," I said. "I love Greenwich."

"I, too," she said. "The Lady Mary was there. She is close to my age. In truth I am a few months older. We spent our early years together and friendship grew between us. But in time I was taken away. Oh, the wars and the troubles and the effect they have on our lives! I have told you once, Katherine Howard, and I will tell you again. It is not good to be too close to royalty."

"I have often wondered about the Lady Mary," I said. "How strange life must be for her. She was once adored as the King's daughter and then she became of no importance at all."

"Yes, yes. Again and again I tell you. It is not good to be too close to royalty." She was looking at me very intently. "It is dazzling, but it is dangerous, to get too close. Many have found that. Remember the Cardinal? Who will forget him? He was my godfather. He went too far . . . you will learn that I speak truth."

I believed that to be true for some; but there were others. I was thinking of my own family, which had survived its disgrace at Bosworth Field. But on the other hand I was aware now that my uncle, the Duke, was always on the alert lest he should make a false move.

"Do not deceive yourself," went on Lady Margaret. She was studying me intently. "Do you know, you remind me of your uncle, Thomas . . . my Thomas. Not that your looks resemble his . . . except perhaps your expression at times. Well, you are a Howard, as he was."

I saw tears in her eyes and she put an arm round me.

"Oh, I am foolish," she added. "It was just that memories came back. They put us in the Tower . . . just because we became betrothed . . . secretly."

"I am sorry," I told her. "How you must have suffered."

She withdrew herself, perhaps remembering that she was the King's niece and I the humblest member of the Queen's ladies-in-waiting. But her lover had been my kinsman, and that brought us close.

"I loved him," she said. "But I was royal, you see. I could be Queen of England, and so a match would be made for me. I was not allowed to choose. Your cousin, Queen Anne, had been my friend—even though the Lady Mary and I had been as sisters, and you can guess there had been enmity between Mary and Anne Boleyn. It was natural enough. Mary was devoted to her mother, and to see her replaced and so cruelly set aside was too much to be lightly borne. I am saying too much. Thomas Howard and I were sent to the Tower, just because we loved each other and had betrothed ourselves . . . and he was not the match they wanted for me."

"How sad for you. I can never pass the Tower without shuddering."

"As well you might. You should bear that in mind."

"You feel badly because you were there once. Was it a long duration?"

She shook her head. "I fell ill of a fever and they thought I might die, so they took me away and I was sent, still a prisoner, to Syon House. I remember at length being released. It was an October day, just over two years after they had beheaded the Queen. Two days before my release, Thomas died."

"What a sad story!"

"I tell you because . . . oh, Katherine, do you know why I tell you?"

"You are telling me because you think I ought to know how easily one can make a mistake at Court."

I thought: I, too, am betrothed, as she was . . . or almost. Does she know? But I shall marry Thomas and we shall go to Hollingbourne. Did not my grandmother say that this would be?

She was watching me closely. Then she said suddenly: "And now I am restored to favour—lady-in-waiting to the Queen . . . and the King's niece . . . accepted at Court."

"But you still remember my Uncle Thomas."

She nodded. "But 'tis over, is it not?"

"The Queen appears to be a very gentle lady."

"I believe her to be."

"Lady Margaret, she is very much afraid now, is she not?"

"She has not found favour with the King. I suppose it is not easy to choose a wife . . . or a husband . . . on the account one receives from other people. They praised her too much, and, alas, she is not the King's idea of a beauty."

"I thought she had a very kind face."

"The King looks for more than kindness. She is not graceful, and he looks for grace, it seems. She is too learned. Some men do not like learned women."

"That seems strange. Would they not wish to talk of interesting matters with their wives?"

"You do not know men, Katherine Howard."

Did I not? There was Derham. I had regarded myself as married to him once. Thomas Culpepper, to whom I was almost betrothed. I knew there were such men as Manox, too.

"If you did," she went on, "you would understand that they like to be the masters. Superior in matters of the mind. Clever women disturb them. There are those who say that Queen Anne Boleyn was too clever for her own safety."

"None would find me too clever, I'll warrant."

She laughed with me, which I realized meant she agreed.

"And the Queen," I said. "She is too clever?"

"Chiefly she lacks the kind of beauty which is to the King's taste."

"Lady Margaret, what will happen to her?"

"I believe there will be a divorce."

"Can that be?"

"Assuredly it can. The King does not have to get a

dispensation from the Pope now, does he? He is now Head of the Church, and can command archbishops and bishops to obey him when he needs them to."

"But there would have to be reasons."

"I will tell you this, Katherine, but it is not generally known as yet. There has been a convocation, and the matter has been referred to the two archbishops with four bishops and eight other members of the clergy; and there are reasons why a divorce is possible. The first and most important is that the Queen was precontracted to the Prince of Lorraine; the second is that the King was married against his will and has never completed the marriage; and the third is that the nation wishes the King to have more children, and in view of his feelings for the Queen, he could never have them through her."

"But he did actually marry her."

Lady Margaret lifted her shoulders.

"Depend upon it, the King will have an annulment if he wishes it enough. And there is no doubt in my mind, and those of many at Court, that the King will have his way."

I thought a good deal about that talk with Lady Margaret. I had vaguely heard about the death of my uncle in the Tower and that he had been foolish enough to act unwisely with a lady.

My uncle, the Duke, was contemptuous of such conduct, although he continued to act scandalously in his own marital concerns, and was still involved in his liaison with the washerwoman, Elizabeth Holland.

But that was the way of men. I thought fleetingly of the King's assertion that I was a good and modest girl and how he approved of such conduct at his Court; and I could not help remembering Elizabeth Blount and the Duke of Richmond and the King's conduct with Jane Seymour, which had been seen by my cousin.

And I was very sorry for the poor Queen.

~

It appeared to be as Lady Margaret had said.

Some of the ladies-in-waiting on the Queen and some of the gentlemen of the King's bedchamber were called as witnesses to the fact that the royal couple did not spend their nights together. I wondered whether Thomas Culpepper was called and what he thought about the matter.

It was clearly proved that the marriage was no ordinary one. The Queen was not present during the proceedings, as her English was not good enough for her to understand what was going on. But she had learned a little of the language and, when she was asked if she had informed Mistress Lowe or any of her ladies of the King's neglect, she had replied that she had not done so as she received quite as much of His Majesty's attention as she wished for.

Then came the announcement that the marriage was null and void and that both parties were free to marry again. A bill was produced to prove this. The Archbishop of Canterbury announced the end of the marriage, and the Lords passed the bill which afterwards went to the Commons, where approval was readily given.

The King had had his way.

Several of us were in the Queen's apartment when news came that the King was sending a deputation to the Queen that she might agree to the terms which were set out.

I could not but be aware of the brooding sense of foreboding which hung over those apartments at Richmond.

The Queen, outwardly calm, sought to hide the fear which beset her. She remained in her apartments and would see none but Mother Lowe.

Lady Rochford said: "Poor lady! One can guess her feelings. Three have gone before her. One discarded as a wife after many years, another to the block and the third no sooner married than she died in childbirth. You can understand her fears. It seems as though a curse has been laid on the King's wives."

"All will be well," I said. "The King can be very kind."

"When he gets his way," said Jane, with a look over her shoulder.

The deputation had arrived. I was surprised, because my Uncle Norfolk was not with it. Instead there were the Duke of Suffolk, the Earl of Southampton and Sir Thomas Wriothesley—all men to inspire fear.

I was with Lady Margaret when she was told that the men were waiting. I followed her, keeping a discreet distance, so I heard what was said.

Suffolk was the spokesman.

"My lady," he announced. "We come here on the King's business, and would be taken without delay to the Queen."

"I will go to Her Majesty at once and tell her of your coming," said Lady Margaret with the dignity and authority becoming to the sister of the King. "She may wish to receive you here."

Suffolk replied: "It matters not where, my Lady Margaret. But it is imperative that we are received by the Queen without delay."

Lady Margaret bowed her head and left them. I followed her to the Queen's apartment and stood at the door waiting. I should disappear before they came out, but I felt an urgent desire to know what was happening.

I heard Mother Lowe cry out sharply in those guttural tones which I could not understand. There was a brief silence and then Lady Margaret seemed to be giving orders.

Lady Rutland came to the door and saw me standing there, but she was too shocked to ask me what I was doing. She said, in a voice of shock: "The Queen has fainted."

I said: "The King's messengers are waiting to see her on the King's business."

"I know. It is for that reason. Go to them. Tell them Her Majesty will see them as soon as it is possible for her to do so."

I went back to the hall and told Lord Suffolk and the others what Lady Rutland had told me.

Suffolk looked impatient, but he thanked me courteously, and I was amazed that he could be so respectful towards me—more so than he had been towards Lady Margaret.

I came back to the Queen's apartments to tell them I had spoken with the Duke of Suffolk, who would be waiting with his friends until the Queen was ready.

Nobody noticed me when I entered, for all attention was fixed on the Queen, who was lying back in a chair, and one of the ladies was fanning her.

She had recovered from her faint, but she looked pale and was clearly disturbed.

The Queen stood up suddenly. She said: "I will go now. There is no sense to wait."

Mother Lowe took her arm and they talked rapidly in their own tongue.

"*Ja, ja,*" said the Queen, and then she turned to Lady Margaret. "Come," she said.

And they went down to the hall to face the King's messengers.

～

As I had expected, Lady Rochford would know what was taking place.

"They have come to take the Queen away," she said. "It was as one expects in these matters. She fainted, poor lady. That was how it was with your cousin. Depend on it, she will be in the Tower this night."

"But why? Why? What has she done to deserve such treatment?"

"She has not been beautiful enough to suit the King's taste."

"Oh, no . . . no."

"But yes. How did the others go? Remember? Well,

you are thinking. It was not the Tower for Queen Catherine. She had the Emperor to support her, do not forget. Of course, the Queen has her brother, the Duke, but he is not the Emperor Charles, now is he? But mayhap the King will have to take a little care. And then that other queen. We know now how it went with her. And this is the fourth. Yes, it will be the Tower for her."

"Do not say that. Lady Margaret thinks there will be a divorce. Why should they come here to talk to her in that way if there was not to be a divorce?"

"Mayhap the King thinks a divorce is not binding enough. Mayhap he has something other in mind. There might be some to say his new marriage was no marriage at all . . . the one with this new queen. I mean the one he will take next. These doubts can cause great trouble in the realm. Whereas when he married Jane Seymour, none could say that she was not really the Queen because of Anne Boleyn, because Anne was a dead woman."

"Jane, you should take care of what you say."

She took my arm and put her face close to mine, smiling at me in that sly way of hers.

"I only speak this way to little Katherine," she said. "She is my friend. She would never speak against me. She knows full well that if she did, they would say she had joined in the talk and was as guilty as I."

"Oh, Jane," I said, "let us not speak of such matters."

~

The Queen faced those men in the hall. They talked to her and I heard afterwards that, when she heard what they had to tell her, she could only think she was living in a dream. It was not as she had feared. And a great joy came over her, such as she had not known since coming to England.

I soon learned why. It was Lady Margaret who told me.

The messengers had brought word of the King's intentions, and it was their task to obtain the Queen's acceptance of his terms.

"She was to cease to be his wife," said Lady Margaret, "and if she would agree to this, he would adopt her as his sister. She must give up the title of

Queen. But she would have precedence over every lady in the land, except the King's two daughters and, if he married again, of course, his Queen."

"And she accepts that most willingly, I'll vow," I said.

"You speak truth there. Moreover she will have estates to the value of £3,000 a year."

I gasped in astonishment.

"I was with Her Majesty," went on Lady Margaret. "At first, she thought she had not heard aright. But I assured her that she had. I thought she was going to faint again, she turned so pale . . . and then the colour was flooding back into her cheeks. I think this day the happiest lady in England is the Queen . . . who is Queen no longer—and well content not to be. She is to write to her brother and tell him how wholeheartedly she accepts the King's conditions."

"Does she not want to return to her own country?"

"Indeed not," said Lady Margaret. "To have been rejected . . . unwanted. Imagine it! And the alternative? To stay here . . . as the King's sister."

"But she is not that."

"Indeed not!" said Lady Margaret. "The King calls

her sister and she has £3,000 a year and is one of the most important ladies in the land. Oh come, Katherine, can you not see why she wants to stay there?"

"Poor lady. I am so happy that it has been settled in this way."

"I hope she did not betray her great desire to be rid of the King. I'll swear it was as great as his to be rid of her."

"Then it is a most happy solution for them both," I said.

"And there you speak wisely, Katherine Howard."

I think it was the first time in my life that anyone had thought words of mine wise.

~

My grandmother requested me to call on her, so I took a barge to Lambeth.

I found the Duchess in an exultant mood. She seemed more spritely and much younger.

"Katherine, my dear child!" she cried. "You look in excellent health and good spirits."

"There is no reason why I should not be," I replied.

She laughed. "Of a surety there is not. Indeed, you are going to be much honoured. My little grand-daughter, Katherine Howard, of all people! Who would have thought it? Your uncle says he finds it hard to believe, and that you will need much guidance. You must do exactly as he tells you."

"Have we not always done so? And why has he become so interested in *me?*"

"Katherine, my child, can it be that you do not know?"

"It is because the King has noticed me. I know that."

She laughed. "Noticed indeed! Well, you were always a pretty child." She screwed up her eyes and studied me intently. "Many girls are pretty, but you have something more. Plump as a pouter pigeon and yet still the little girl. A pretty creature, who needs to be cherished and cared for, being somewhat unworldly. Yes, I can see it."

I smiled complacently. It was good to meet with this approval—something rare in the past.

"The King will be here soon."

"Here?"

"Here indeed. You must be prepared for him. Let me look at you. Hmm. Shall I bring the ruby necklace for you to wear? No, I think not. You are better as you are. Simple. I believe that is the quality which attracts. Now, you must be prepared when the King speaks to you."

"How shall I know what answers I should make? I never know and he asks so many questions. Some of them do not need to be answered, but that is not always so . . . and I am never sure."

"You have pleased him as yet. It is true that he is in a mood to be pleased with you. He has fallen in love with you, Katherine. It must be because you are so different from the others."

"In love with me!"

She nodded. "It is hard to believe that you . . . a simple girl . . . could win the affection of the King. But it appears to be so. It is for this reason that he is so eager to be rid of Queen Anne."

"Oh no, you are wrong! I have amused him with my simple ways. He is kind."

"You must not be so foolish, Katherine. We know the King likes an innocent and unworldly girl—such a contrast to those who have gone before. It is a novelty. But you must not take that too far. If you seem too stupid, he might turn from you."

"You cannot mean that I . . ."

"Could be the next Queen of England."

I began to tremble at the thought. *I* married to the King—that old man with his bad leg, which had to be dressed by Thomas—and I was betrothed to Thomas.

I said: "Your Grace, I could not. I am already betrothed."

She stared at me in amazed horror.

"Betrothed! What mean you?"

"You said I was to be. Do you not remember? To my cousin Thomas Culpepper."

"Thomas Culpepper? Are you crazy, girl?"

"I am not," I said defiantly. "We are going to marry, leave Court and live at Hollingbourne."

A sudden fury came over her. She brought up her hand and slapped my face.

"Do not let me hear you say such a wicked thing again," she gasped.

"But . . ."

"Silence! Your uncle would be furious. He would make you sorry you ever saw Thomas Culpepper, and him sorry he ever saw you."

"We love each other."

"Be silent, I said. You must be mad. Never a word of this must pass your lips again. Do you want to ruin us all?"

"Ruin you? How?"

"Ruin the whole family. You were always addle-pated. The King has a fancy for you. Your uncle says he has never seen him so determined since . . ." She faltered. "We do not want such as that to happen again. He was set against the family then . . . but it was only for a time and we did return to favour. Not a word of this so-called betrothal to Culpepper, or it will be the worse for you . . . and for him. Not a word, not a word. Is that understood?"

"Do you mean . . . ?"

"What I say. There must be no more talk of Culpepper. You must forget there was ever any mention of you and him. And . . ." Her voice dropped to a whisper. "There was that other. Derham . . . Francis

Derham. He is away. In Ireland, I believe. He must stay there and, Katherine Howard, you must forget you ever saw him."

"I cannot forget as I will. I could never forget Francis Derham."

"He came back . . ."

"I told him it was over between us."

"It is not only over, it never happened. It must never be mentioned. You did not know Francis Derham. You did not make any arrangement with Thomas Culpepper. Holy Mother of God, Culpepper is still in the King's service."

"But I cannot believe I did not know Francis Derham because I dare not speak of him. And I love Thomas Culpepper."

"Be silent. You love none but the King. This is what he will demand. You are his subject, remember. He has singled you out for great honours. You must be worthy of them." She drew me to her, half-pleading, half-threatening. "Katherine, you have come too far. You cannot go back now. The King has chosen you. What greater honour could there be than that? You must accept what life offers you.

Think of all those who, were they in your position, would be rejoicing in their good fortune."

I said slowly: "The Queen rejoiced to be free of him."

"He did not love her. If he had, she would have been the happiest woman in the country. Now . . . that is for someone else."

"I wish," I began. "Oh, how I wish . . ."

"You will have nothing to fear. Think of it. Queen of England. The King's much-loved Queen, who only has to be as she is, and is sure to please him. You need have no fear. I shall be at hand to help you, and there is your uncle. He will tell you exactly what you have to do. So . . . as I say, there is nothing to fear . . . unless, of course, you play the fool and throw away good fortune by prattling of love for this and that one. Listen to me, Katherine. That did not happen. You must put all thought of it from your mind and do as you are told by your uncle and me . . . and so please the King. You cannot be blamed for what happened in the past."

I kept thinking of Derham in the Maids' Chamber, where we had rolled on the floor and made merry, until my grandmother had come in and found us.

There was so much of the past which I wanted to forget, and now I was overwhelmed by the confirmation of that which had haunted me for some time, and while evidence had pointed to the fact that there must be some truth in it, I could not entirely believe it.

The manner in which the King had noticed me should have made me realize the truth. I was not, as he believed, an inexperienced girl. I had seen the expression in his eyes, as I had in those of others. It was merely because he was the King that I had not accepted what it really meant. I had thought of myself as insignificant Katherine Howard, accepted at Court because I was the niece of the Duke of Norfolk.

The glittering prospect was now revealed to me. The King—the much-married King—had chosen me.

I remembered all the excitement there had been when his desire had fallen on my cousin, and how it had brought our family into closer connection with royalty—which seemed to be the ambition of everyone at Court.

I was flattered, and on the other hand alarmed. I kept thinking of the poor Queen, who had fainted with fear when the King's commissioners came to talk to her and then had nearly fainted again, this time with joy, because she discovered he wanted her to be his sister instead of his wife.

But he liked me. He liked my simple ways. He had never shown any anger towards me, not even that tetchiness which my uncle could sometimes arouse in him. He had smiled at my simplicity and liked me the better for it. He might frighten others, but he had always been very kind to me. And he was the King.

My grandmother was smiling at me now. "Your cheek is a little red," she said.

"That is because you slapped it."

"Ah, you are not the Queen yet, child, and I did it for your good. Never . . . never speak to the King of Thomas Culpepper . . . nor . . . that other."

"I will not," I said. "It is past and done with."

"You cannot be blamed for what was done so long ago," she said, frowning deeply, and I had the idea that she was trying to convince herself.

"Is this thing really true?" I said. "How can you be sure?"

"The King has spoken to your uncle."

"But do you think he really means it?"

"Of course he means it, child. It is a serious matter. Let me tell you this. Your uncle is very pleased with you."

"It will be the first time he ever has been."

"He is proud of you. You must always remember to do what he tells you. Now, we must compose ourselves. The King will be here at any moment. I hear sounds from below. It means the barge will be at the privy stairs."

There was brief pause while my grandmother studied me, patting my hair and looking anxiously at my cheek.

"You are flushed," she said. "That is quite becoming. It hides the mark on your cheek. Now . . . remember. Be yourself. Ask for nothing. Be natural. Be surprised."

"How can I, when you have already told me?"

"Heed that not. Show yourself overwhelmed by the honour."

"I *am* overwhelmed," I said.

The Duchess nodded, smiling.

My uncle came into the room. He looked at me

with more affection than he had ever shown me before—or anyone for that matter I thought rather frivolously, which was strange at such a moment, except perhaps the laundress, Bess Holland. I supposed he was already seeing the crown on the head of another Howard.

"Well," he said, "you have heard of the honour which is about to come to you."

"Yes, Your Grace."

"That is well. Indeed, you have pleased us all. I know you have little knowledge of worldly matters. That is in your favour. His Majesty will not want to be plagued with women's arguments. All you have to do is to be as you are. It is this which has won his regard. Now he is impatient. I will conduct you to his presence."

I followed him into one of the smaller rooms where the King was waiting. He was standing by the window, his hands clasped behind his back. He looked larger than ever in his padded surcoat; and there was a large ruby at his throat.

"My niece, Mistress Katherine Howard, Your Majesty," said my uncle, pushing me ahead of him.

The King was smiling, his little eyes brilliant. He regarded me with fondness. I would have knelt, but he laid his hand on my shoulders and drew me towards him.

"You may leave us, Norfolk," he said to my uncle, who immediately bowed and obeyed.

"You are not shy of the King, Katherine," he said. "I think you care not as some would for the honours I am about to give you. I think perhaps you have more regard for my person than for those. Tell me, is that so?"

"Oh yes, Your Majesty."

"You please me very much, Katherine. In fact, so much that I want you to be my queen."

I believed he was waiting for me to go down on my knees in an ecstasy of joy and thank him. That would be difficult for me to do, and I remembered the injunctions to be myself, so I murmured: "Your Majesty cannot . . ."

"Katherine, there is little the King cannot do if he sets his heart on it. And this I tell you. The matter I am here to speak of is my will, and I will allow none to gainsay me. Katherine, you have pleased me greatly, and I am going to make you my queen."

"But Your Majesty . . ." In spite of my grandmother's warning, I was on the point of telling him of my betrothal to Thomas, but he had silenced me.

"No buts," he said. "I will have none . . . not even from you, sweet Katherine. You are overwhelmed, I know. You did not think this could be so. Now tell me, did you?"

"No, Your Majesty. I . . ."

He laughed and said tenderly: "You are over-modest . . . as a maiden should be. You cannot believe this good fortune which has come to you. I like that. But let me tell you this: It shall be so."

There was something in his demeanour which told me he would be very angry if I confessed my feelings and my proposed betrothal to Thomas, and that the anger might be directed not only against me but Thomas too.

"My dearest little Katherine," he was saying, "think only on this. I shall raise you up to be my queen."

I did not know what to say. My feelings were so mixed. I . . . to be the queen! Honoured throughout the Court! It was such a dazzling prospect that it was as though it blinded me. All those who had been faintly contemptuous of me would now bow the knee and call me Majesty. It made me want to laugh. That was hysteria, I imagined. And Thomas? Oh, Thomas, I thought, we should have been so happy at Hollingbourne. I could see clearly that there was no choice for me. This glittering and powerful King had decided my fate. And so had my uncle. They had done it between them. I could see that I should never marry Thomas.

The King was smiling at me very kindly. There must be great kindness in him, for he had never shown anything else to me. I was aware of that immense power in him. For some extraordinary reason, after dignified Catherine, dazzling Anne, pretty Jane and unwanted Anne of Cleves, he had chosen me to be his fifth queen.

I was not the sort of person who could make things happen the way I wanted them to—although those like my uncle could. I must just let events carry me along.

For a moment I felt trapped. It was not my will, but theirs. I had no recourse but to obey. They had decided my fate, and I was trapped—a golden cage it might be, surrounded by treasure, but I had no means of escaping from it.

Mine was a serene nature. I was not clever enough to devise plans for escape, and I was not sure, when I realized what all this would mean, whether I wanted to.

I was at least wise enough to know that if I did escape from this fate, I should bring the wrath of my family down upon me and would never be allowed to marry Thomas Culpepper.

"You do not speak," said the King. "I will tell you why. You do not know what to say. Is that so?"

"Yes, Your Majesty," I mumbled.

He took my hand and drew me near to him. He looked closely at me and put out a hand to touch my cheek.

"You are beautiful," he said. "I never saw one that pleased me more than you do. And that pleases *you*, does it not?"

I nodded.

He drew me even closer. I could feel the warmth of his flesh against mine. He kissed me gently on the forehead.

"Always remain as you are at this moment and you will please me," he said.

"I . . . I will try, Your Majesty."

He gave that rather loud laugh of his.

"You will always please me, I know," he said. "At last I have found you. I have looked so long. You are like a rose. My favourite flower, Katherine. The flower of England . . . most beautiful of all flowers. But roses have thorns." His face darkened, and there was a certain petulant droop to his lips. For a moment he looked angry, then he was smiling again. "And you are my rose without a thorn. That is how I see you, Katherine. Do you wonder that I want to keep you at my side forever?"

I was sitting on his knee now, his arm round me, holding me tightly against him. The ruby on his coat touched my skin, it was so close to me. I wondered about his leg and thought of what Thomas had told me of it. I was about to ask him if it were better but, innocent as I might be about matters of importance, some natural instinct told me that this was not a time to remind him of his infirmities.

"I am blessed in you, sweet Katherine," he said. "I

believe that, through you, the curse which Heaven has put upon me is about to be lifted."

I wondered how even Heaven would have dared put a curse on such a powerful person, but again I said nothing.

"I am a simple man," he went on, and I almost showed my amazement at such a statement. "I ask but little. Just to live in peace with a wife who will care for me as I care for her. Katherine, my sweet child, that joy has, till now, been denied me. What have I done that God should punish me, eh?"

Another of those unanswerable questions—and one I had heard before. Fortunately, he supplied the answer, and as I cast down my eyes he continued: "I will tell you. Through no fault of mine, I went through a form of marriage with my brother's widow. That was no true marriage, and for years I lived in a state of sin with a woman who was not my wife in the eyes of Heaven."

"Oh no, Your Majesty," I murmured.

His arm tightened about me and then his face hardened.

"And then . . . I married a witch . . ."

Visions of my beautiful cousin came to me. He had broken with Rome for her sake, and now he said she was a witch.

"Then Jane . . . she was a gentle creature, but she died and, though she gave me a son, he is not strong. And now . . . this woman from Flanders. You see what I tell you is truth. But you have come to me and you are going to give me all that I ask. The curse is lifted and so, Katherine, I shall make you my queen."

His expression had undergone many changes as he was speaking. He had looked both forlorn and angry. At times he reminded me of a little boy, and then seconds later his face was so twisted in anger that he was like a cruel tyrant.

I felt suddenly sorry for him, and I realized at once what a pretentious attitude that was. On impulse, I put my arms round his neck and kissed his cheek.

The effect of my action was immediate. His eyes filled with tears; his expression was soft and sentimental.

"Sweet Katherine," he murmured and held me close against him.

And in that moment I was reconciled to whatever lay before me.

The Queen

The whole country was now aware that Anne of Cleves was no longer the Queen and that the King and she had come to an amicable agreement. The King had made her his sister and Parliament had obsequiously begged him graciously to consider marrying again for the sake of the nation.

The marriage was secretly arranged. There was to be no grand ceremony and coronation, as there had been for my predecessors. Whether the King considered these would follow too closely after those of his fourth marriage, or whether they would prove too costly, I was not sure.

I felt as though I were being hurried along in a fantastic dream. I could not say that I was unhappy. I had always loved excitement and I certainly had my share of it at that time.

There was a quiet ceremony with only a few people present, including my uncle, the Duke, who was clearly pleased that we had progressed so far, and I had the rare sight of recognizing the approval in his face for *me*. I had to admit I enjoyed that.

My grandmother was present, her eyes full of pride as they rested on me, and perhaps I did detect the faintest apprehension.

I realized afresh the immense power of this man who had chosen to be my husband. Yet I was not afraid of him. How could I be? Nothing but the warmest affection had he ever bestowed on me. His hand constantly reached out to touch mine; there was a caress in his very smile. I knew, of course, what lay before me. I was indeed no innocent child.

The King had given me several jewels on our wedding day when he told me that the happiest man in the country was the King.

I know now that I am one of those women who must have physical love. It was something I had greatly missed when Francis Derham went away. Now I could indulge legitimately, and I need have no qualms of conscience. Thomas and I had always been afraid to give way to our desires, lest we might jeopardize our future. Derham and I had deceived ourselves into insisting that we were in truth married. But this was different. This was duty. This was my husband, and there was no need for guilt. Did it add to the excitement? Perhaps that was due to the fact that this was the King. I believe that power is a strong element in the attraction of the male to the female. The man is all-conquering; the woman submissive. Henry was the most powerful man in the country. I had been of no consequence until he had singled me out for his approval.

I had an uneasy moment or two when he seemed to show surprise at my ready responses. He had been expecting an entirely innocent girl. That was something I could not feign, and I was never good at pretending. My grandmother had insisted that I must be natural, and I found it difficult to act otherwise than my impulses directed. If he had expected a reluctant child, who must be carefully initiated into the mysteries of the senses, he was mistaken. This was one sphere in which I was not ignorant, as I seemed to be in all others. But I think Henry attributed my reaction to a delight in the great honour which was being bestowed on me, and it seemed to add to his pleasure.

He said I was the perfect wife—the rose without a thorn.

~

We were at Hampton Court—one of the King's favourite palaces, presented to him by Cardinal Wolsey in an attempt to regain his favour. It held many memories for me—later less pleasant ones—but at that time I shared the King's pleasure in it.

Cardinal Wolsey had made it one of the most desirable residences in the country. I had heard that there were 1,500 rooms, and so lavish had been the Cardinal's hospitality that at times all these rooms were in use; and the fireplaces in the kitchen were each large enough to roast the whole of an ox. I had not seen proof of this, but I believed it to be true.

It was a pity that the palace for me was haunted by Wolsey—only now and then, of course. I used to think of him there at the height of his glory, no doubt imagining it would always be thus for him. But he loved power too much for his own safety; he loved pomp and splendour and surrounded himself with it, so that people used to sing: " 'Why come ye not to Court?' 'To which Court? To the King's Court or to Hampton Court?' " That was his downfall. A subject should not seek to rival his King. It was small wonder that the King asked if it were meet and proper for a subject to outdo the King in his manner of living. There was nothing Wolsey could do then but offer Hampton Court to the King, yet even that did not save him. So I was a little saddened thinking of him during those days.

The King was very happy at that time. He continually kissed and caressed me; he gave me valuable jewels. He sensed that I did not care for them a great deal and, as he liked everything I did, that seemed to please him. He was proving to be the most uxorious of husbands. I think he really did love me dearly.

I said to him one day: "There is to be a grand banquet in the great hall here. You are proposing to present me to them as your queen."

"That is so, sweetheart," he said. "You are going to have the honour which you deserve."

"There is something I would ask Your Majesty," I said, a little hesitantly.

"Ask me, and I doubt not that it shall be yours."

"It concerns your daughter, the little Elizabeth. She is but young. She has done no wrong. I would ask that she may be present at the banquet and seated in a place of honour . . . near me where I can see her."

He hesitated for a few moments. Then he said: "Why do you wish this?"

"Because she is young. She is your daughter, yet she is shut away. I think she may be sad and wish to see her father now and then. And as she is *your* daughter—I would know her too."

I saw that look of sentiment in his face. It was so often there for me.

"As you ask, sweetheart," he said, "it shall be. The child has done no wrong. She could not be held responsible for her mother's ill deeds."

So Elizabeth was to come to the banquet.

In due course I was brought to the great hall where all the greatest in the land were assembled, and they came to kneel before me and pay homage to me as their queen, while the King looked on benignly; and

I could not help but be proud to have won so effortlessly that favour for which they were all striving.

Afterwards we went to the royal chapel and I sat beside the King throughout the service.

In the banqueting hall, Elizabeth was seated opposite me. She was a striking-looking child; her reddish hair must have been very like the King's, when he was her age, of course. She would be about seven years of age, but she looked more. There was a wariness, an alertness, about her. Poor child, she had been but three years old when her mother had gone to the block. How much did she know of that? I wondered.

I smiled at her to show her that I would be her friend, and she responded cautiously. I was very pleased though that I had arranged for her to be brought to Court.

It was a successful occasion.

When we retired, the King looked at me with that indulgent expression to which I had become accustomed.

"Well," he said. "Did your presentation please Your Majesty?"

"It was wonderful. You are so good to me."

I enjoyed bringing that soft, sentimental look to his face.

"You shall see, sweetheart, what I shall do for you."

"You do too much."

He laughed aloud. "The feeling of most around me is that not enough is done for them." He added: "Were you disappointed not to have a coronation?"

I shook my head. "What do I care for a coronation when I have the King?"

He was so happy that, although I did think of Thomas now and then, I could be happy too.

"And I have something to show you," he went on. "I was not going to let our marriage pass unnoticed."

"Unnoticed? Oh come, my lord, that was not possibly what you wished. It is not every day the King marries." I stopped myself in time. That seemed a rather tactless remark and might have provoked some merriment if any had been there to hear it—and dared show the flicker of a smile. Every day might be an exaggeration, but five in a lifetime was a goodly tally.

In his uxorious mood, he had not noticed. He drew a coin out of his pocket.

"What do you think of this?" he asked.

"It looks like a gold coin."

"It is a gold coin. Look. Here are the royal arms of England."

"With the initials H.R. I have a notion that might mean Your Majesty."

"My Katherine is a saucy wench," he said. "Turn it over."

I did so. Then I saw what it meant. It was done to honour me.

"K.R.," I read. "*'Henricus VIII Rutilans rosa sine spina.'*" He had named me his rose without a thorn. I felt a faint shiver of uneasiness.

I hoped he would not ask too much of me.

I did not lose much time in visiting the nurseries, which at that time were situated at Hampton Court. I missed my own brothers and sisters and had always wished to be in the heart of a family. Now I had three stepchildren—one of them older than myself; but I did not think the Lady Mary would wish to see me. She was a sad creature; she had never recovered from the suffering her mother's ill treatment and death had caused her. I had heard it said that when Catherine of Aragon's heart was broken, Mary's was too. I had seen her only once or twice, and she had seemed to be a very tragic figure.

It was the children I wanted to see—Henry's daughter Elizabeth and his frail little boy, heir to the throne.

Lady Bryan, who had brought up Mary and was in the process of doing the same for Elizabeth, now held the office of Lady Mistress in the Prince's household. She was greatly loved by the children, I had heard, as was Lady Penn, who was now their chief nurse.

These ladies greeted me with the utmost respect, although they must have thought I was very young, quite inexperienced and quite unfit to hold the important office which the King had thrust upon me.

I had told them that I had come to see the Prince and that I believed the Lady Elizabeth was often in his company.

"'Tis so, Your Majesty," said Lady Bryan. "It is a source of great pleasure to me that they are so happy together. The Lady Elizabeth is a very clever child, and the Prince dotes on her."

"It would seem you have a very happy household."

"I trust so, Your Majesty. Children should live in happy surroundings."

"We are in agreement on that. Would you please conduct me to the Prince's apartment?"

The Prince was sitting at a table, with Elizabeth beside him. She sprang to her feet at my approach and curtsied. The Prince scrambled down.

I did not wish for any formality, and I said: "Let us all sit down, shall we? I saw you, Lady Elizabeth, at the King's banquet, and, my Lord Prince, I am very happy to make your acquaintance."

Elizabeth said: "You must bow, Edward. This is the Queen."

Edward studied me intently and said: "She does not look like a queen."

"You must not say that," Elizabeth chided.

I laughed. "Please do not think you must show me ceremony. I am not merely the Queen, am I? We are closer than that."

Edward looked at Elizabeth and waited for her to reply.

"Your Majesty is gracious," she said with dignity.

I could see that she clung to ceremony, but when I asked her about her lessons she changed. She was really devoted to her books, and I realized that she was teaching Edward to be the same.

I felt I must not pursue the subject of learning too far, for I feared it was possible that, at seven years of age, Elizabeth would discover my lack of it.

I asked them about their outdoor activities. Elizabeth apparently rode well, as she did everything else; but Edward did not care so much for it.

"They are constantly telling him he must do this and that because one day he will be King," she said. Then she glanced over her shoulder. "We should not speak of that time," she added, "because my father would have to die before Edward became so." Then she looked annoyed at herself for having made such a statement. "Edward likes me to be with him," she went on. "Then I can look after him."

"You must be a great help to him," I said.

"Yes," she agreed coolly. "He relies on me, do you not, Edward?"

He nodded, smiling, and slipped his hand into hers. She was very self-assured for one so young, I thought. And she was more like her father than the boy was. How perverse life was! If she had been a boy, how different everything might have been. How she would have delighted her father then; she looked so like him at times. I could see nothing of her mother in her. But perhaps there was a certain pride and that indomitable spirit.

And what was she thinking now? That I was her mother's cousin. What did that make me? Her second cousin perhaps? I wondered if she was thinking, as I was, of that beautiful head on the block and the sword descending. Would she be thinking that I was one of the women who had taken her mother's place?

I had heard that she had become friendly with Anne of Cleves. I could not believe that she had felt the same towards Jane Seymour. I wished I could stop thinking of my cousin's coming upon Jane Seymour seated on the King's knee while he smiled at her as he did so often at me. It was really such a short time ago, and since then Jane had become Queen and so had Anne of Cleves; and now it was my turn.

Feelings of doom descended on me. Oh no, he loved me. Indeed, all I had to do was smile and say what he wanted to hear. And I was fond of him. Who would not be fond of a husband who indulged one so? It was so easy to satisfy his demands. At last I had accepted that there must be no contact with Thomas Culpepper, and he had gone from my life forever. It was the only way—not only for me, but for him.

I was quite happy in my new life. I had never had perfection and perhaps I did not hope for it. Now I looked forward to having a share in that family which I had inherited. It amused me to realize I had stepchildren—that frail little boy and the intriguing Elizabeth.

I did not expect friendship from Mary. She would naturally turn from her father's wives. But in time, who knew?

Yes, on the whole, I was pleased with life.

Warning Signals

Then came a rumbling of disaster. I had been married not quite a month when it happened.

It was mid-morning when the King came bursting into the apartment. His face was flushed; his eyes had almost disappeared into his fleshy face so that they looked like glittering beacons seen through slits; his mouth was a thin straight line.

"What think you of this? By God's blood, that priest shall suffer for this."

I went to him, put my arms round him and attempted to soothe him.

"What mean you, my lord husband? You seem very angry today."

He turned to me, his face softening at once. "I would never believe this of you. He shall suffer for this. Good Lord, spare me from priests!"

"What has he done to disturb you so? I cannot bear to see you thus. Is there aught I can do?"

He put his arms round me and looked into my face. "This dastardly priest has dared to utter words . . . words . . ." He spluttered. "Words against you."

I felt myself begin to tremble.

"Against me!" I cried. "What could he say against me? I know him not. What has he said?"

"What has he said? By God, he has spoken against your virtue . . . that is what this scoundrel has done. He shall hang for it."

Uneasiness was gripping me now. "What . . . what . . . has he said?" I murmured.

"What has he said indeed . . . this priest of Windsor?"

Windsor. I felt a little better. I knew no one at Windsor.

"What has he said? Please tell me. I must know. I beg you to tell me."

"It is just tittle-tattle. 'The Queen is guilty of conduct unbecoming to her rank. There have been whispers about her.'"

"Windsor?" I said. "But I was not at Windsor. How . . . ?"

"Sweetheart, you must not let this disturb you. I will not have it. The priest has been placed in Wriothesley's care. He swore he did nothing but repeat what had been told him. The other . . . the one who, he declares, said this slanderous thing to him, is under arrest in Windsor keep. We will let them wait there while we decide what shall be done with these scoundrels."

I was feeling a little easier. I knew no priest of Windsor. That was the fact I was clinging to.

"You do not believe them?" I asked.

"By God's Grace, I know you for what you are. No one is going to say a word against my queen in my hearing . . . nor that of any other . . . or it will be the worse for them. Nay, sweetheart, there are those who cannot abide the good fortunes of others. These priests, they would tutor us all. We must do this . . . they say . . . we must do that . . . if we would please them, and if we do not always follow them, they will stand up and slander us. Priests . . . monks . . . there are times when I have had my fill of them. They would have us all go the way they want. I do not like these self-righteous men. Depend upon it, they see how you have been honoured, and they are filled with envy of you. I have raised you up, and, by God, it has pleased me to do so. And priests . . . and such . . . should keep their mouths shut. They should look to themselves."

"This has caused you much sorrow, I fear," I said in a low and trembling voice.

His eyes took on a misty look.

"Nay," he cried. "You must not fret. It is slander, ill-founded lies." He was fierce again. "And I will not have slander spoken against my queen."

I had been easily frightened. I waited for what would happen next. I started to think again of what had taken place at Lambeth. Why had these rumours come to the priest of Windsor? Who had spoken them in the first place? Derham? Not Derham. He was a man of breeding, an honourable man. He had really believed he was going to marry me; after all, he was one of the Howards. Nor would Thomas have betrayed me. He would die rather. Then I thought of Henry Manox. Could it have been Manox? He lacked the scruples of the others.

But Manox was not mentioned. And who would have gone to Windsor to whisper to the priest?

So my mind worked and during that week nothing further happened.

The King noticed my uneasiness and was eager to put an end to it.

"This foolish matter has disturbed you, sweetheart," he said. "That must not be. I will teach these men a lesson. We shall let it be known that none speaks against the Queen."

I thought about this a great deal and wondered what would happen to these men. Perhaps they would be put to the torture. That was something the King was not eager should be tried on them. He would not want them to produce lurid "confessions," as people sometimes did to escape further torment. Yes, I was frightened. I supposed that, had I been the innocent girl Henry believed me to be, I should have felt differently. I tried to make myself act as such a girl would.

The King said that the sooner the men were brought to trial the better.

Trial! I could not bear that. I must do something.

There was no one whose advice I could ask. I had to obey my own instincts.

It was true that I had always hated to hear of torture and executions. My whole nature shrank from it. Priests, not being of the nobility, were submitted to the horrific death of hanging, drawing and quartering. I could not bear to think of this.

It suddenly occurred to me that, if they were freed, they would no longer seek to harm me; and when they considered what terrible fate might have befallen them, they would be very careful of what they said in future.

I went to the King and, going on my knees to him—a gesture for which he chided me but with which, I sensed, he was rather pleased—I begged him to save the lives of the priest and his companion, to warn them to be careful of their words in future and go on their way.

He lifted me up so that my face was on a level with his.

"My sweet Katherine," he said. "Your heart is indeed tender. These men had maligned you, and you would forgive them. You ask me to grant you this, and because you ask a boon of me . . . it is granted. It shall be as you wish. What a happy day it was when God gave you to me."

I was indeed happy. I cast aside my anxieties as though they were a heavy and burdensome cloak; and I would not let myself brood any longer on those uneasy days. The men were freed with a warning of the dire consequences which would befall them if they ever uttered another word against the Queen's Grace, and they must always remember it was due to her mercy that they were free men.

I had been right, I told myself.

Then the King and I set off for a voyage round the country. I was to be presented by the King to his people as the Queen who had, at last, brought him contentment.

~

The King seemed to have forgotten that unpleasant incident, and I had forced myself to do so too. He did not refer to it again. Now the matter was over.

The country might not have been able to afford

to give me a coronation, but I had all the clothes I needed, which, after so much deprivation in the past, was very much appreciated. I was becoming accustomed to my condition and enjoying it more and more every day.

The King was certainly a good husband to me. He constantly marvelled at my youth and energy. I never saw his leg without its dressing. When he came to me at night, it was always freshly bandaged. He was taking more exercise. People remarked on his healthy looks. I think his relationship with Anne of Cleves had had its effect on him, and there was no doubt that he was happy now.

He was almost always in a good temper and when his eyes alighted on me that soft and tender look would come into his face. I was becoming really fond of him and I often thought of the wonderful life he had given me.

Lady Margaret Douglas had ceased to be Anne's chief lady-in-waiting, and had become mine. I was pleased at that. I think most of the ladies had found it difficult at first to take a subservient position to me. I could understand that. It took time to accept the fact that little Katherine Howard was now the Queen. I did not mind that. I was not one who wanted a great deal of ceremony.

In my entourage were also the Duchess of Richmond and Suffolk with the Countess of Rutland and, of course, my old confidante Lady Rochford. She was the same as she had always been, reminding me that she was my very good friend. Mrs. Tyrwitt and Mrs. Leye were among the gentlewomen and Mrs. Tylney was one of the chamberers who, I remembered, had once been employed in the Duchess's household. There were so many of them that I forget the number.

It was about this time that I heard what was happening to the Countess of Salisbury. She must have been seventy-three years old and she was a prisoner in the Tower. The very word "tower" sent a shiver through me, but that an old lady, used to the comforts she must have enjoyed until now, should suffer so, horrified me.

"Poor, poor lady," I said. "How terrible for her!"

The Countess of Rutland glanced at me quickly. "She is the King's enemy, Your Majesty."

"What has she done?" I wanted to know.

I noticed that the Countess looked a little non-plussed.

"She . . . er . . . she has conspired against the King. She was in league with her son. Your Majesty will remember Cardinal Pole. He is the King's enemy . . . although the King once gave him his affection."

"But what were they quarrelling about, and do they need to keep that poor old lady in the Tower? She must be nearly frozen at night. It is very cold there, and does she get enough to eat?"

I saw that look on her face which she tried to disguise. She thought I was a little idiot who did not know when it was safer to leave things alone.

I could see I was not going to get very much information from those around me except from Jane Rochford, and, as I could not stop thinking of the poor lady's discomfort, I went to Jane for information.

"That would be Margaret Pole, Countess of Salisbury," said Jane. "It must be over a year since she was sent to the Tower."

"So she has been there all through the winter! Oh poor, poor lady!"

"Indeed yes, but then she is the daughter of the Duke of Clarence, and you know who he was."

I waited expectantly.

She raised her eyebrows, as though to express her amazement at my ignorance, and to remind me that, although I was the King's wife now, the same intimacy remained between us as always had. I would not have had it otherwise. I did not want her to shield me from the truth, as the others tried to.

"The Duke of Clarence, Majesty"—she used the title with a certain levity—"was the brother of Edward IV and Richard III, so you see his daughter might be a little watchful of the throne. What do you think of that?"

"Go on," I said.

"The real trouble is, of course, her son, the Cardinal Pole. There was a time when the King was quite fond of him. He paid for his education and looked after him generally. The Cardinal is a very clever man. It was the matter of the divorce from Queen Catherine of Aragon that came between them. Like Wolsey before him, Cardinal Pole did not see the matter as the King wished him to. So the rift began, and when the Pope made Reginald Pole a cardinal, there was real trouble. It would have been the Cardinal's head that went . . . if he had been here. Tempers ran hot. The King was determined to wed Anne Boleyn."

"And the Countess?"

"They say she was conspiring with her son, who was on the Continent."

"Was she?"

"That is not for me to say. But the Poles are very close to the throne . . . too close for comfort."

"I feel so much for her that I cannot forget her. Not so long ago, she was in her comfortable home, and suddenly there she is . . . in that place, with only jailers to attend her. She will suffer greatly from the cold . . . and does she get enough to eat, think you?"

"I doubt it. It is the lot of prisoners."

"Jane, I know what I shall do. I shall have them make something for her . . . by the seamstresses. A nightgown furred against the cold . . . some shoes she will need. Stockings. They will help to keep her warm."

"The King's enemy . . ." began Jane.

"Need the King know?"

"What, deceive His Majesty so soon after the marriage!"

"Oh Jane, do not be silly! It is not really deceiving. It is just not telling."

"Well, all you have to do is smile sweetly, tell him how wonderful he is and that you adore him, and he will be at your feet."

I smiled complacently.

"Send for the seamstresses," I said. "We will begin at once. That poor lady shall no longer freeze in that dreadful Tower."

Jane obeyed, and in a very short time I was able to send the Countess two nightdresses—one furred— together with hose and boots.

Jane entered into the scheme and was a great help. She was most excited and I wondered whether it was because she really cared about the comforts of the Countess, or because she felt it to be a rather dangerous undertaking, assisting a prisoner who was in the Tower by order of the King.

I was not afraid. If he heard of it, he would only smile, I was sure. Perhaps he would ask me jovially why I was sending comforts to his enemy, to which I would answer that I was so happy in the love of the King I could not bear to think that an old lady was in such discomfort.

Nevertheless, although it was probable that many knew what I had done—for the Queen's actions, however small, were certain not to go unnoticed—nothing was said.

There were other matters to claim the King's attention. A certain John Neville had started a rebellion in the north of England. I was with the King when the news of this was brought to him. I had never seen him in such an angry mood, since news of the slander the priest of Windsor was uttering against me had come.

He banged his fist on the table in an excess of fury. I cried out in alarm, but on this occasion he had no thought even for me.

"This," he cried, "is that fellow Pole's doing!"

He was on his feet, shouting. He strode to the door. He gave orders. There was an immediate Council.

I did not see Henry all that day, and when I did, he was preoccupied. I managed to soothe him a little. I listened to him. I sympathized with him while he shouted that he would subdue those Yorkshire oafs. It was of no great moment, but he was a sad man.

He was in a mood of self-pity.

"Katherine, I have given my life to this country. Is it not an amazing thing that there should be those of my subjects who can be so ungrateful?"

"It is," I soothed. "When you have given your life to them."

He took my hand and held it.

"You understand, do you not? You see how I suffer through these ungrateful people?"

"Oh I do, I do."

He kissed me.

"It was the happiest moment of my life when I looked across that table and heard you singing my song," he said.

❧

Sir John Neville was soon suppressed.

"They had not a chance," Jane told me. "They were defeated before they started. They will soon be wishing they had never been born."

The King said: "I have an unhappy people to govern. I could reduce them to such poverty that they would not be able to rebel." His face hardened and took on that cruel look which always made me uneasy.

I must see the parade of the prisoners with him. As they passed, I watched that cruel smile on his face. They were taken to the Tower from whence they would be taken to Tyburn, where they would be hanged and taken down before they were dead, to suffer that which I could not bear to contemplate.

It came to my mind to ask the King to spare them, but even I knew that would be folly. I must remember that I dare not go too far. So I saved myself in time from begging for their lives.

The King was happier that night. He was quite sentimental about his care for his people and how misguided they were to attempt this rising. It was all a matter of the Church again. He was the Head of the Church now, but there would always be those who would question it . . . until they saw the folly of it, as these men now did.

"It is this fellow Pole who is behind it," he railed. "I was fond of him. I cared for him. I paid for his education." There were tears in his eyes. "It was my conscience. His mother is the daughter of the Duke of Clarence, brother to Edward IV; and my mother, Elizabeth of York, was the daughter of that Edward, that King. You see how closely we are linked. It was the marriage between my mother and my father that united the Houses of York and Lancaster. Alas, men are ambitious. Reginald Pole could not forget that he was descended from Edward IV and Richard III. I even suspect him of having had his eyes on the throne. A king's lot is not always a happy one, Katherine. I know you have thought it is. You have seen the pageantry, the pomp and the feasting. But it is not always so. Then I need my Katherine to soothe me . . . not a woman who will argue of this and that, but one who will be there to comfort me, to take my mind away from the wearisome matter of governing. Do you understand that, wife?"

I nestled against him. "I understand that I always want to give you what you want."

He was happy then. The rebels of Yorkshire were all in the Tower. Tomorrow there would be the spectacle of their execution.

Neville would be taken back to York. He should perish where he had started the trouble, that the people might see the fate of those who turned traitor to the King.

~

There was a sequel to the Yorkshire rising. The Countess of Salisbury was sentenced to death.

I was horrified. I had thought of her comfortable in her furred nightdress, and considered how delighted she must have been to receive it. And now she was to die.

I was not so foolish as to think I could plead for her. I knew the King would give me a great deal if I asked it, but I had glimpsed his rage at the very mention of Reginald Pole, and I knew I must not stretch his indulgence too far.

As was my habit, I tried to forget what I did not want to hear, but it was difficult to banish thoughts of the Countess from my mind. I felt an urge to know what she felt about the manner in which she was being treated. I talked to Jane Rochford.

"It is reported that she has declared she has committed no crime," she told me.

"Is it true that she was not involved in the Neville rebellion?"

"It is what she says. But many will tell you that the revolt was supported by Reginald Pole, and she is his mother, so it is very likely that she helped her son. Ever since the King broke with Rome, there have been those who are for the King and others who cling to the Pope, and Cardinal Reginald Pole most naturally supports the Pope."

"Then she is guilty," I said.

"She declares she is not. But she would, would she not?"

"But if she is innocent, she must not be executed."

"She is certainly guilty of being in the royal line."

"Oh, Jane, you make the most daring statements!"

"I only say them to you. It is because I speak to you as I would to myself. You must forget what I have said as soon as I say it. It is because I am so close to you." She added, with a grin: "Your Majesty."

"Jane, I wonder how right you are."

"We can only wait and see."

"Be careful, Jane."

"Your Majesty must be so, too. Remember, what a Majesty says can mean more than the words of a simple lady-in-waiting. Forget not who sent clothes to her. That could be a rash act . . . more than making a remark as to whether she is guilty or not."

But Jane did look a little subdued. I think she was wondering whether she had gone too far.

The following day the Countess walked out from the Tower to Smithfield Green, which was close by.

The Lord Mayor, with several other prominent Londoners, came to witness the end of the Countess. The block was a low one and no scaffold had been erected. The Countess prayed for the King, the Queen and the young Prince Edward. She also spoke movingly of the Princess Mary, whose governess she had been, and whom she had openly supported when the King was trying to divorce her mother in order to marry Anne Boleyn. The poor Countess had not had a happy life since that time, and this was largely due to her opposition to the King's wishes. And now . . . she had come to her death. Having said her prayers, she held her head high and, standing by the hastily erected scaffold, she announced to the watchers that she was condemned to die as was the fate of traitors.

"But," she said in louder tones, "I am no traitor, and if you will have my head, you must win it."

I could not believe this when Jane reported to me. She was romancing, as she could do at times.

"It was a moment of horror," Jane went on. "The headsman caught her and dragged her to the block. He could do no other. Was he not acing on the King's orders? He forced her down. She was weak. Do not forget, she had spent a year in the Tower. He struck. The first blow missed her neck. So he hacked again . . . and again and again . . . until he had her head from her shoulders."

I covered my face with my hands. "It was not so! It was not so," I cried. "I do not want to hear."

"I was not present," said Jane. "But that is the tale as I heard it."

And if that account of the Countess's death was not exactly accurate, there was no doubt that something similarly horrific had occurred. People crossed themselves when they spoke of it. The King would not have it mentioned in his presence. The woman might have been royal. Her son might be a traitor. But, for the comfort of all concerned, she was best forgotten.

~

The Duke of Norfolk was begging an audience with me. I liked that. The mighty one humbly begging to see me! Graciously I agreed to see him.

He was looking embarrassed and uneasy as he bowed, which I supposed was because he must show the necessary respect due to the Queen, who was, after all, only the silly little niece whom he had hitherto despised.

His first words were: "Your Majesty, I trust this is a time when you will remember that I am your uncle, who wishes you nothing but good fortune."

"Your Grace is kind," I said, rather flippantly.

"I would serve you well."

"Your Grace has something to say to me?"

"That is so. We have just been made aware of the discord in the North."

"I was of the opinion that the King had settled that matter."

"Praise God, he has put down the revolt and punished those who have been responsible. But the King is uneasy."

I looked surprised. "He has not told me."

The faintly contemptuous lift of his lips was hardly perceptible, but it was there.

"The King, I know, is very concerned for your comfort. He would not wish you to be worried with such matters."

"The King does confide his troubles to me, I should tell you."

"Indeed he does. He often speaks to me of his growing love for our family, and he is grateful to the Howards for having given you to him."

I did not like this reference to the magnanimity of the Howards. Previously they had always considered me unworthy of them. But *I* was the one who had captured the heart of the King. They seemed to forget that I had, without effort, done that which they had all spent their lives striving to do.

The Duke went on: "I was referring to this trouble in Yorkshire which, as Your Majesty says, the King has settled. The King fears there may be other insurrections, and that is something he greatly wishes to avoid."

"Indeed he does. It is a most disturbing matter, with so many men going to their deaths."

"Traitors," said the Duke. "The King will not have traitors in his realm. There was the Countess of Salisbury." He coughed slightly. "It came to my ears that Your Majesty had supplied the lady with garments—furred garments."

"The nightdress was furred. She needed it against the cold. And there were hose and boots."

"The Countess was the King's prisoner."

"She was a lady unused to the hardships of prison."

"As she had been in the Tower for a year or more, it is to be presumed she was accustomed to them by that time."

"My lord, such hardships are something to which one never grows accustomed."

"It is the fate of prisoners. And this, Your Majesty, was the King's prisoner. I must stress that point. Now, if you had consulted me . . ."

"Your Grace was not one I would consult regarding an errand of mercy."

He flinched a little. I fancied he was growing angry. Oh, I had undoubtedly changed since I had become the Queen, beloved of the King.

He went on: "I should have warned you that it is a little unwise to . . . er . . . show friendship towards the King's enemies."

"The King has not mentioned this."

"The King is indulgent . . . to some. Your Majesty has not, I dare swear, discussed the matter with him."

"I had not thought it of any great importance."

He forgot then that he was talking to the Queen, for he said sharply: "Then 'twas a pity you did not give the matter more thought."

"I believe the Countess derived much pleasure from the gifts."

"I doubt not that she did . . . in more ways than one. There is much trouble in the country. I would speak to you of that."

"Pray do," I said. We were indeed changing. It was the first time he had ever thought it necessary to talk to me of the country's affairs.

"When the King removed the Church from Rome, there were many in the country who were deeply disturbed, and it is their intention to take it back. This the King will never allow."

"I am aware of that."

"It causes strife. There will be others like Neville. There is a division in the country. Times are dangerous. You are a great comfort to the King, and I rejoice in that, but do not try him too far. You must strive to remain as you are now. That brings good to the King . . . and our family. Your task is to soothe him. Never attempt to try his patience."

"Do you suggest that this is what I have done?"

"Your Majesty," he said, remembering who I was once more. "I am your uncle. I have always had your well-being and that of our family in mind. For the good of the family and the country, you must keep the King's favour. I hope you will allow me to speak my mind."

"I was under the impression, my Lord Duke, that you always did."

"If, when Your Majesty decides to take some action . . . something which might be misconstrued by some as being a little rash . . . if you came to me, I could advise you as to its wisdom. Believe me, there are some matters so intricate . . . so open to misconstruction by one's enemies, that they need the utmost care in handling." He meant, of course, that they were beyond the understanding of simple people like myself. "For instance, the clothes you sent to the Tower." He shook his head slowly. "If you had asked me, I should have advised against that."

"It is a matter long forgotten, my lord. The lady is now dead . . . hacked to pieces, I hear."

He held up his hand just like the uncle of old. I knew what it cost him to treat me with respect, and I was beginning to feel impatient with him. Did he intend to play the wise uncle of a stupid girl all my life?

"The King believed her to be a traitor," he went on. "She was aiding her son, who was aiding Neville. She died for that reason. That is enough. I would ask you . . . I would pray you . . . to consider before you take such an action again. A word from you will bring me immediately to your side."

"I suppose I might send for anyone if I needed them," I retorted with a laugh which, to my annoyance, seemed to border on a giggle.

"This is a serious matter. You could very easily

do that which would prove unseemly. You are not in your grandmother's home now. You are in a dangerous place, niece. I am here . . . ready to help you. I will advise you on all occasions."

"I have no doubt that you would do that, but let me tell you, uncle, that I have done very well so far without your help, and I propose to go on doing so."

He was really angry then. It was only because he was so accustomed to protocol that he could restrain himself from striking me, I was sure.

He stepped back a few paces and muttered: "I have done my best. I ask Your Majesty's leave to retire."

I gave it readily, fury raging within me.

It was some time after before I asked myself what I had done.

~

When I received the letter from Joan Bulmer, I read it with great concern; it was only after a closer perusal that I began to feel a qualm of uneasiness. It brought back memories I would rather suppress.

I had believed I had loved Francis Derham until I had met Thomas, then I had realized I had been overwhelmed until I came to know true love. I had indeed loved Thomas, and if events had turned out as we had hoped they would, I should have been very happy with him. But the King had seen me, and I had had no alternative but to go to him.

I was happy now. The King's devotion was wonderful. I enjoyed seeing his face soften when he looked at me. It was easy to keep him happy. Lovemaking was so much a part of my life. I think it had been meant to be since the day when Manox had begun to initiate me. I can only believe that there are some people like that.

And now Joan Bulmer. She had married and acquired the name Bulmer since our acquaintance. I really did not want those people whom I had known in the past to be near me now. I had been a little uneasy when I had heard that Katherine Tylney was in the household. It was not important, I told myself. It was just that I would rather they were not there.

I looked back over parts of her letter. It was quite a long one.

If I could wish you all the honour and good fortune you could desire, you would never lack health, wealth, long life, nor yet prosperity.

There was nothing wrong with that. It appeared that her marriage was not a happy one, and she went on to ask for a place in my household, for she desperately needed to get away from her present circumstances.

I know no remedy without your goodness. You could find the means to get me to London. If you could write to my husband and command him to bring me to you, he would not dare disobey. I beseech you to find a place for me. The nearer I were to you, the gladder I would be of it. I would write more unto you, but I would not be so bold for considering the great honour you are toward, it did not become me to put myself in presence, but the remembrance of the perfect honesty that I have always known in you hath encouraged me to do this.

I know the Queen of Britain will not forget her secretary, and favour you will show.

Your humble servant with heart unfeigned,

Joan Bulmer

No, I did not like it. The reference to my honesty, my humble servant. I tried to thrust my misgivings aside.

I did not reply to the letter for a few days, and then I found myself watching for another letter from Joan Bulmer.

This was foolish. Joan and I had been on fairly friendly terms. She was now in dire straits, poor girl. Had I not always been ready to listen to the trials of others and help if I could? Not that I had had much chance of doing so in those days, but they had always known I was sympathetic and would help if I were able.

No, this was just the letter of a woman in distress. She was unhappy. She wanted to be away from her husband, and at Court. I could understand that.

I was not quite sure of my feelings. Perhaps I was too uneasy to look clearly at how I felt. I kept wondering what the King's attitude would be if he knew that the Duchess had come into that room and had seen me rolling on the floor with Francis Derham. I pictured those little eyes sinking into his fleshy face with fury. I was wise enough to realize that by no stretch of the imagination could he picture himself in a similar position. His obesity . . . his bad leg . . . and I knew that thought would irritate him beyond control.

There was another matter which disturbed me, but only faintly.

I knew he longed for me to announce my pregnancy. There seemed no reason why I should not. But it was the familiar story. So far, there was no sign.

He was so enamoured of my youth and loving nature that he had not yet complained. But would he in time? My poor cousin had gone to the scaffold, many said, because she had only produced one child and that of the wrong sex; and when she might have given birth to a son, she had miscarried and he had lost his patience by that time.

I shut out all thoughts of such a thing happening to me. He adored me. But then he had adored Anne. He was an extraordinary mixture of ruthlessness and sentimentality. He always had a reason for his actions which made them right in his opinion. One could be in high office one day and in disgrace and disfavour the next.

Being lighthearted by nature, I did not dwell on these matters. The King loved me dearly. I was the wife for whom he had been searching all his life. I was safe.

Then I wrote to Joan Bulmer, offering her a place in my household.

~

When Joan arrived, I sent for her. She had changed a little. Her attitude towards me was different. But then, so was that of everyone—the outstanding example being that of my uncle, the Duke. I had seen little of him since my outburst, about which I was pleased. He must understand that he could not control my life.

Joan knelt and expressed her undying gratitude. I made her rise and told her that I hoped she would be happy at Court.

"I knew Your Majesty would help me," she said. "You were always so kind . . . to everyone."

There was a slight smile about her face as she said those words. I knew she was looking back, remembering.

"And now you are the Queen herself . . . and as

kind as you ever were. Your Majesty, I shall always remember. I shall never forget."

Why did it occur to me that it was not only my kindness she was remembering, but incidents from the past?

"I look forward to serving Your Majesty . . . in whatever capacity you wish . . . as I always tried to do."

There it was again . . . that covert smile. It would have worried me then if I had allowed it to.

I said: "I believe you were not very happy in your new life."

"I was not, Your Majesty. Oh, it will be a great pleasure to serve you . . . just as I did in the old days at Lambeth."

"Thank you," I said.

"Mistress Tylney has promised to show me what will be expected of me."

"You will find this different from the Duchess's household."

"Oh yes, Your Majesty."

When she had gone, I sat thinking of her. She brought back memories which I would rather forget.

She settled in and was soon a close friend of

Katherine Tylney and, in that lighthearted way, which was typical of me, I ceased to think about her.

~

Lady Rochford was the first to bring the news. I should soon have heard it, she said, for indeed the whole of London was talking about it.

"The Lady Anne of Cleves has been brought to bed of a fair boy," she announced.

"The Lady Anne!" I cried. "A boy! No, it cannot be. It is false. I do not believe it."

"'Tis bruited through the streets and they are saying it at Court."

"How could there be? She is no longer the King's wife."

"People do have children in the most difficult circumstances," said Jane with a laugh.

"Can it really be true?" I murmured.

"That we shall soon know."

"If it is the King's . . ."

"Ah," cried Jane, speculation in her eyes. How she loved the excitement of prying into people's lives. She was the sort of woman who would weave her own fantasy about people's actions to make a more dramatic story. I thought fleetingly of her evidence of the relationship between Anne Boleyn and her brother which had been given in such a manner as to make it seem like truth, and had resulted in sending her husband George to his death, accused of incest. And when it was considered, it seemed that all that had happened was that once, when Anne was in bed, Jane had come into the bedchamber and seen her husband sitting beside the bed while his hand rested on the coverlet. I wondered if she ever felt remorse for what she had done. If she did, it had certainly not cured her of the habit.

"One of the King's greatest desires is to have a healthy son," she was saying. "He will be most eager to see this child whom the Lady Anne has produced."

"Did no one know there was to be a child? It is strange that he is suddenly here."

"The King is deeply enamoured of you. He would never leave you, even if the Lady Anne does have a child." Her eyes were speculative again.

The courtiers were asking themselves which choice the King would make. It would be interesting to see which was more important to him: his healthy boy or his beautiful bride.

I think I never took the matter seriously. If I did, there was the fleeting thought that, if he divorced me, I could marry Thomas Culpepper after all.

I knew Thomas would want that. I had seen him only briefly since my marriage, although he was a Gentleman of the King's Bedchamber. He had avoided me; he was very much afraid that our friendship might be remembered. But I had caught a glimpse of something in his eyes which told me that his feelings had not changed. No mention was made of our suggested betrothal.

I knew people often thought of what had happened to Henry's wives, and it was not surprising that they might soon be wondering what my fate would be. Thomas must have realized how careful we had to be. More so than I did. And he still loved me.

And now it seemed that my future might be in jeopardy.

Then I had a visit from Anne of Cleves herself. She came without ceremony from Richmond, which was not very far from Hampton Court.

I received her at once, and she immediately told me that she had been extremely distressed by a certain rumour and wanted to tell me that there was no truth in it.

Her knowledge of our language had made great strides since her arrival. She was a clever woman and the first task she had set herself was to learn English. She was moderately fluent now and only occasionally did the pronunciation of a word betray her origins.

She said: "I have been confined to my bed for about ten days. Mother Lowe was mostly in attendance. She knows my needs better than anyone, for she has been with me, you know, since I was a child. Then these rumours started. It is quite ridiculous."

"I was of that opinion at the time," I told her.

"I was sure you would be. It is amazing how these rumours start. One says, I think this, or I think that, and then someone else says it is . . . and it goes on from there."

I agreed. I was thinking of Jane Rochford who, I knew, always had to embroider a tale.

"It was good of you to come and see me," I told her.

"I wished you to hear this from my own lips. I do not need to ask if Your Majesty is in good health. I see you are."

"And you also, my lady."

"I am when there are no foolish rumours to upset me."

"You have been indisposed, you say."

"It is over. What do you call it? A little matter of the chest, which kept me to my bed—so starting this gossip, mayhap."

"A rheum perhaps?" I suggested.

"But I am recovered completely." She smiled at me. I believe she thought I was concerned because I had taken her place, for she went on: "I am happier than I ever have been in my life before."

"I am so pleased to hear that."

"I have my little court at Richmond. The King has graciously given me other houses too. And I am rich. Life has become very good to me."

"I am happy for you."

She looked at me searchingly. Did I fancy I saw a shade of pity in her eyes? It might have been, for she had suffered great humiliation at the hands of the King when she had been Queen. And now I had stepped into her shoes.

I was so pleased that there was no child. I very much hoped that I should be the one to bring that joy to the King. I found I liked Anne of Cleves very much. There was something free and honest about her.

She asked me how the Court had seemed to me when I had first become her lady-in-waiting.

"I saw so little of you then," she said.

"I was kept in the background. They thought I was such a novice . . . and it was true. I had to learn everything. It was all so different from my grandmother's house in Lambeth. There was not the same order there."

She told me a little about her childhood too. How different it was from mine! Her father was John II, Duke of Cleves, who, when he had married, had become Count of Ravensburgh through his wife's inheritance. Anne had a sister, Sybilla. She wanted to know if I had any brothers and sisters.

"Several," I told her. "But I was taken away when I was so young that I hardly knew them. Because we were poor, I was sent to my grandmother, the Dowager Duchess of Norfolk."

Sybilla had married almost ten years before Anne came to England. It was a brilliant marriage to John Frederick, the great Duke of Saxony.

"It is good to remember the old days," said Anne. "When I think of my childhood, I remember the two white swans. This was because of an old legend of the Rhine. The Rhine was our river, you know. We always sang of it, and the story was that one of our ancestors came to us from nowhere and then left us in the same mysterious manner. She just arrived and then later, after bearing children, disappeared. She was supposed to be some messenger from the gods come to bless our family. She came down the river in a boat drawn by two white swans, and the swans have been our emblem ever since. Why do I tell you this?"

"Because I can see that we are going to be friends. How glad I am of that rumour, because it brought you to see me."

"I shall return, if permitted to do so."

"You have not only my permission, but my command."

Then she talked about the King's daughters and little son. She had made their acquaintance and was looking forward to improving it.

"The Lady Mary is very sad," she said. "I should like to see more of her and cheer her if possible."

"I have not yet spoken to her."

"She is not easy to talk to. She has—how do you say? She retires into herself."

I nodded, guessing that to be true. Poor Mary, she had suffered much.

We were silent for a moment, then she said: "The Lady Elizabeth is an interesting girl. She seems to be very clever. Wise beyond her years. And the boy, too, is clever."

So we passed an hour in talk and we parted on the best of terms, promising ourselves another meeting very soon.

I thought about her a good deal after she had left. What struck me most forcibly was that she by no means regretted the loss of her crown. In fact, she appeared to be remarkably relieved to have discarded it.

It had been a most pleasant morning, partly because

I was so glad to hear that the rumour about the baby was unfounded.

It had made me think though that it was time I was pregnant, and then I began to wonder whether this rumour about Anne of Cleves had started because it seemed that the King might have married another barren wife.

~

I had a visit from my grandmother. I could see that she was distraught.

She said: "Manox is back."

I felt a shiver of alarm. I did not want to think of Manox. I was trying to pretend he had never existed.

"Back?" I said. "Where?"

"At Lambeth."

"You have taken him into your household?"

"It seemed that I had no choice."

"But . . . why?"

"Let me explain. He arrived and asked to see me. I was disturbed and acting on my first impulse refused. He went away, and I thought that was the end of him.

I did not tell you then, because I thought it would disturb you. He came back next day and asked that a message might be delivered to me saying that, in view of the position he had once held in my household, he felt sure that I would grant him the honour of receiving him."

"And you did?"

She lifted her shoulders. "What he craves is a place at Court—with the musicians."

"Oh, no!"

She was frowning. "He heard that Joan Bulmer is back, and he said he was sure you would be as kind to him. You would remember how pleased you had been with his work when he was teaching you the virginals."

I stared at her blankly, and she went on quickly: "So I said I would arrange it. It seemed all I could do. You will not have to see him if you prefer not to. He can simply join the musicians. I can arrange that. He means no harm, I am sure. He is just a little . . . insistent. He always was."

"No," I murmured. "I need not see him."

"It is nothing to concern yourself with."

"No," I said. "That is so."

We were alike in some ways, the Duchess and I. We both shut our eyes to unpleasant possibilities.

She said: "If your uncle had been on friendly terms, I might have asked him. He would doubtless have ways of removing . . ."

"It is of no account," I said quickly. "Manox is only a humble musician."

"There is a certain insolence about the man which displeases me," went on the Duchess. "But then he always had that. The respect is so lightly applied that one can see through it. He has a great opinion of himself, our strutting little musician. He should be taught a little humility, and the Duke would have been the one to teach him. But I am not on the best of terms with my stepson; and I gather Your Majesty has offended him too."

"He really is overbearing and arrogant. I'm afraid I was not in the mood to pander to his wishes."

"Indeed not, and you Her Majesty! Who does he think he is? I will tell you. He is the premier peer of England. To tell the truth, I'd say he thinks he is as important as the King himself . . . or should be."

"You should see them together! Then you would know who the master is."

"Still, he has power, that one. It is well to be with him rather than against him."

"He must make amends to me."

"Well, little granddaughter, it is you who are the Queen. Tell me about last night's banquet. What did you wear? They say the King is so enamoured of you that he cannot take his eyes from you."

And so we talked, and I fancied that she, as well as I, was all the time trying to believe that Manox's return to London was of no importance.

~

When I was alone with the King a few days later, he took me on to his knee and said: "We are shortly to set out on our travels."

I was excited. I enjoyed travelling through the towns and villages while people came out to cheer us, and Henry was so proud when they commented on my beauty. I could not help being enchanted by it all.

He stroked my hair and went on: "We will not have

these risings every now and then on some small issue which some people think is their concern." His face darkened. "This man Neville ... he has paid the price of his folly and treachery, but you see, sweetheart, we have to make them see that we will have no more of it. That is why we shall go. We have to bring home to them what are the rewards of their conduct."

My heart sank. This was not going to be one of those journeys during which everyone was merry. It would be a sombre reminder of what happened to traitors.

"We shall drive through those counties which were involved in the trouble," he was saying. "We shall make them understand that on no account shall they defy us." His face was scarlet now, his mouth that straight line which I dreaded to see.

"It is one of the more unpleasant duties of the King," he went on. "He must keep his realm safe."

His mood changed and he was soft and sentimental again.

"It pleases me that I have my sweet little Queen to comfort me," he said. "I plan, during this tour, to meet the King of the Scots. He can be a tiresome fellow, and I must make him see that he will come to no good if he would play his devilish games with me."

His mood had changed again, but almost immediately he was once more the loving husband.

"Your brow is troubled," he went on. "Why, sweetheart, these are not matters for you. Alas, my lot is not always a merry one. A crown is not an easy thing to carry. That is why you, little one, are such a joy to me."

∼

I saw less of Henry during the short time before our journey began. He was busy with his ministers and plans for the journey. It was not a happy time for me. He began a fierce attack on those he suspected of working against him. The John Neville affair had affected him more deeply than I had at first imagined.

All the cases of those imprisoned in the Tower were examined, and, if the King's suspicions were strong, ended in execution. Even those who had not been found guilty of treason, if the suspicion was strong enough, were dispatched.

I was very uneasy. I could not stop thinking of

those people lying in that gloomy place, waiting to be summoned to the block or the hangman's noose. I had once or twice attempted to beg for their release, but Henry had made it very clear that he had not come to me to be reminded of his enemies.

I was horrified to hear of the case of Thomas Fiennes, Lord Dacre, who was at that time a prisoner in the Tower, although there was no reason why he should be there.

Jane Rochford told me there was quite an outcry over the matter, and that, if there had not been so much trouble over John Neville's rising, when many had been under suspicion, something might have been done about the case.

I always liked to understand these things, and particularly this matter of a man who was facing death for something he had not done.

"Then why is he in the Tower?" I demanded.

"I have heard," said Jane, "that one night he left his castle of Hurstmonceux with a party of friends. He is a youngish man . . . some twenty years old . . . and such can be high-spirited. He was only eighteen when he came into the title. You know what young men are.

Well, he and his friends found themselves on a gentleman's estate nearby and decided to indulge in a little poaching for fun. The party then split up and one of the groups was confronted by a gamekeeper. There was a fight, during which the gamekeeper was killed."

"How terrible! That was murder."

"When it was discovered who the young men were, it seemed doubly shocking. They were not even hungry men, desperate for food. It was all amusement for them. Lord Dacre was especially singled out, although he was not with the group who had killed the gamekeeper. There was a great outcry over the matter, as you can imagine, and Lord Dacre was sent to the Tower. They were there when the King decided that he did not want to leave his enemies in London while he was travelling north. The Dacre family were not in favour with the King, who suspected them of disloyalty, and when Lord Dacre's name was put before him, the King ordered that he should be one of those who were executed."

"But all he had done was go out with this wild party! And he was not even with the group who killed the gamekeeper!"

"The King was in no mood for trials. The Dacres had offended him. And so . . . His Majesty decided to be rid of this one. Dacre was not the only one, I swear. There were others."

I was very distressed. I said: "I do not wish to hear of them."

Jane nodded. She knew me well. It had ever been my way to put aside that which disturbed me.

~

It was just before we left on our journey that the Duchess came to me.

"I have to tell you," she said, "that Francis Derham is back in England."

I must have shown how shocked I was.

She went on: "He has been to see me. What a handsome young man he is! He is more handsome than ever. A real man. He was such a delightful boy."

"He is back in your household?" I asked fearfully.

"No. He has had adventures. What he was doing in Ireland, I can only guess. He was determined to make a fortune and come back and marry you."

I was trembling and desperately trying to forget that part of my life, and now it seemed that it was coming back to haunt me. Henry Manox was now one of my musicians. I had seen him from afar, and I had felt a twinge of disquiet, although his manner had appeared to be most respectful.

Derham was a different matter. I remembered his passionate insistence that he would come back and marry me. He had said we were husband and wife. He called me wife; I called him husband, and we were as such.

I experienced a moment of horror. They were all coming back: Manox, Joan Bulmer, Katherine Tylney and now . . . Derham.

My grandmother could guess at my fear.

She said: "Derham is a gentleman. He would never harm you. He would protect you if the need arose. You must have no fear of Derham."

I clutched at that belief. It was true. He had genuinely loved me. I knew in my heart that he would never harm me. I had nothing to fear from him. A great relief swept over me at the thought.

"Why did he come to see you?" I asked.

"Because he knew me for a friend. He is a good young man, he has done well in Ireland. Oh, what a reckless fellow! There is something of the pirate in him. Indeed, I fancy he might well have been engaged in something just outside the law."

"Piracy?" I said.

"I know nothing." She laughed. She had always had a weakness for handsome young men, especially those who flattered her.

"He talked of you," she went on.

"What said he?"

"That you were beautiful and that he knew of none to compare with you. He said you had had some regard for him. The King is not a young man. He thought that, if the King died, it would be his turn, and it could be just as you and he had once planned."

I had grown up a little and I realized, if she did not, the importance of what she was saying. I looked at her in horror.

"You have not said that in the hearing of anyone, I hope."

"Do you think I should be so foolish as that? I am telling you . . . and you only."

"It could cost him his head," I cried, thinking fleetingly of Lord Dacre, who had lost his for a murder he had not committed.

"You can be assured I shall say nothing of the sort to any. One must never mention that a king could go the way the rest of us do."

She laughed. She was reckless, I thought. God preserve her. I had been reckless, too, but how was I to have known that I should one day be Queen of England?

Secret Lovers

It was July when we set out. It was not a very happy journey. The King was in an ill mood, because the knowledge that some of his subjects could revolt against him depressed him. He wanted jubilation and expressions of affection wherever he went. In his youth he had been handsome, strong, in sports excelling all others, now it was obvious to everyone that he was no longer so. He often needed a stick to support him, or an arm to lean on. His leg was often painful, and I believed it was most unsightly beneath the bandages. He had lost his once healthy colour and his skin was tinged purple, his face bloated. It was small wonder that he needed a young wife to delude him into thinking he himself was young too. That was my task, and I believed I performed it well.

I might have been unlearned, far from agile with the pen, in complete ignorance of the classics, but I did understand the physical needs of men, and I was able to partake in these exercises with an acceptable skill. He told me that, while God had seen fit to plague him with some miserable and ungrateful subjects, He had at least blessed him with a good and loving wife.

There was heavy rain in Lincolnshire, which resulted in heavy flooding. Travel was impossible for two or more weeks. This delayed our journey and all through the month of July we made very little progress.

It was late August when we arrived in Pontefract. Henry was eager to meet the King of Scotland, which was the main reason for the journey. I had been rather depressed by the reception we had received on the way. There had been lavish entertainments for us, and rich gifts for the King, but I guessed this was due rather to fear than affection.

Henry was not displeased with it though. Had he not come to achieve their submission? They fêted him because they feared him, and subjects should firstly be in awe of their King.

Because of the delays, he had gone off ahead to

York with a few important men in the company, and I stayed behind in Pontefract.

It was here that I received a visitor.

I stared in amazement when Jane Rochford brought him in to me.

"Francis!" I cried.

He bowed low. It was Derham.

I was overcome with mixed emotions. This was due to the sight of him, as handsome as ever, a little more distinguished. He had grown older. He had had stirring adventures, I was sure. He was indeed a man.

I noticed Jane lurking by the door, her eyes alight with excitement, and I said: "You may leave us, Lady Rochford."

With a disappointed and reproachful look, she obeyed.

Derham said: "Your Majesty is well, I perceive . . . and more beautiful than ever."

"What are you doing here?" I demanded.

"Craving the indulgence of Your Majesty, and begging her to tell me in what way I can serve her best."

"You should not have come here."

"Where else can I serve Your Majesty? I have heard that Mistress Bulmer is in your service with Mistress Tylney, and Henry Manox has joined the musicians. You are surrounded by old friends, so I thought I could serve as her secretary. She will have need of those whom she can trust to serve her well."

He was appealing; he was very handsome, and I could believe that the love he had once borne me still existed. I could hear my grandmother's words. He would always serve me, he would always love me. I believed she was right. He would always act for my good. Sometimes I felt lost in this Court. It seemed that people were watching for me to make mistakes—I fancied some of them looked at me critically, though they dared not put their feelings into words. Yes, it would be good to trust those around me, and I could trust Francis Derham.

Playing for time, I said: "You have had adventures since we last met."

"Many," he replied.

"Did you make your fortune?"

"To some extent."

"Breaking the law?"

He shrugged his shoulders. "It is not always easy to keep within it."

"On the high seas?"

"'Tis as good a place as any."

"I think you are a very reckless man, Francis Derham."

"I would be as reckless as was necessary in the service of Your Majesty."

"Thank you."

"And," he went on, "I'll warrant there is one thing Your Majesty lacks."

"And what is that?"

"A good secretary."

"I know I was never happy with the pen, but I have improved."

"You still need that one who understands what you really mean to say."

I smiled. He wanted so much to be at Court. He was still devoted to me. He always had been and he was a faithful man. He had gone away to save me as much as himself.

I was reckless. Why did I not think before I made these rash decisions? There was a great charm in

Derham. My grandmother had been aware of it, too. Had she not said he would give his life for me if need be? I had nothing to fear from Derham.

So . . . I gave way and Derham came to Court as my secretary.

~

We arrived in Lincoln, where we were to stay a few nights. The King and his advisers were still not with us.

It was late in the evening when Jane Rochford rapped on my door. I bade her enter, and she was not alone. I started up, in a state of great excitement, for with her was Thomas Culpepper.

"Your Majesty," said Jane. "The hour is late, but Master Culpepper was insistent."

"Yes, yes. What is it?"

Thomas bowed. "May I speak alone with Your Majesty?"

Jane glanced at me, bowed and went out.

"Thomas!" I cried, when she had gone. "Why have you come at this hour?"

"It was the only time for seeing you in secret. It

is important. None knows that I am here save Lady Rochford, and I believe she is your close attendant."

"That is so. Thomas . . ."

He took a step towards me and suddenly put his arms round me, holding me tightly.

"No . . . no, no!" I cried, yet clung to him.

We remained thus for a few seconds, and I knew that to be with him was what I wanted more than anything.

Then I remembered what had happened to me since I was last with him and I knew that this was the most foolish thing we could do. I imagined what would happen if we were discovered. The King would never forgive me, and Thomas . . . I shivered. It must stop at once.

I drew sharply away from him.

"Why are you here?" I cried. "Why have you come?"

"I came because it was necessary to speak to you at once. I could think of no other way. If I were seen speaking to you about the Court, it would be remarked on immediately. I dare not . . . for your sake, Katherine."

"What is it of such moment that you must come like this?"

"You do not realize that you are in danger. Katherine, you are the King's wife."

"He would kill you if he were to find you here."

"I know. But I had to see you in secret, and I could think of no other way—I know Lady Rochford is your close friend. I had to trust her. Only she knows I am here. I came by way of a secret stair. Katherine, there are whispers about you. There was that priest at Windsor. He talked of your past life."

"That was no whispering. It was said aloud, and it came to nothing."

"It is not forgotten. There is talk here in the Court. They are whispering of the life you led before you came to Court. They are saying you are unchaste, Katherine. Do you not realize the danger of this? And now you have let Francis Derham into your Court! He is the last one who should be here. Why did you do that?"

"He came and asked. He wanted it so much. Our friendship is over. He knew that. I have told him so."

"But he is here! People will talk of it. You have

others of the Duchess's household with you. Do you think they will remain quiet? And when I heard that Derham was here . . ."

"Derham would never say a word against me."

"That may be so. He is an honourable man, I believe. But he is here!"

"I cannot send him away."

"Nay. Perhaps it would cause more talk if you did. I have come here because I had to speak to you. I know you well, my dearest Katherine, and I know you have not always been aware of the scheming people about you. But now you are the Queen . . . do you not see?"

"Do you think people will listen to the whispers? The King did not believe the priest of Windsor."

"It is not only the whispers. Katherine, you are so innocent. There is this conflict throughout the realm. It will remain while the Church is divided. There will always be those ardent Catholics who deplore the break with Rome and those who want to join the Protestant League. There are some who regard you as the puppet of the Catholics, and Queen Anne stands for the Protestants. They want her back and would do anything to remove you. Not only that. There are

Cranmer, Audley and the Seymours against the faction led by your uncle, the Duke of Norfolk. You have become a figurehead in the Court and are no longer in command of your own destiny. You are used by scheming and powerful men. You must understand these things."

"I do not understand. Nothing has been said to me of religion."

He smiled at me tenderly. "Of a surety, none would say aught to you of these matters. You are as innocent as a child. That is why you do not realize the danger in which you stand. It is an amazement to me that your uncle has not warned you."

"It is some time since I have seen my uncle. We are not on good terms."

"But you should be. This is very strange. If your uncle is not working for you, might it be that he stands with your enemies?"

"Thomas, it is because you love me that you see this danger. The King shows me nothing but kindness. I am certain that he would never allow any of them to say a word against me."

"All I know is that the King is very pleased with

you now, but his moods can change quickly. We have seen it with another. There was one time when none could doubt his love for her, and then it changed to hatred."

"You are frightening me, Thomas."

"It is the last thing I would do. All I ask is that you take care. That is why I have risked so much to come to you at this hour."

"I think you are unduly worried. It is because you love me . . . and I am glad you came."

"I have seen so little of you since you came to Court. I have deliberately done this, for I could not trust myself, caring for you as I did."

"Oh, Thomas . . . I wish you had not kept away."

"I tell you, I could not trust myself. I knew how it would be if we were together."

"Yet you came here . . . to my private apartment . . ."

"It was necessary. I had to warn you. I had to be with you somewhere where we could be alone. Take heed of what I say, Katherine, I beg of you."

"I would always take heed of you, my love."

Then his arms were about me. I was no stranger to passion, and I knew he was desperately fighting a losing battle in his attempts at restraint—and so was I.

This was Thomas, my true love, the man whom I should have married and with whom I should have lived in perfect harmony forever after. I was more mature now and my senses were more demanding than ever. Neither Thomas nor I could hold back the flood of passion and desire which swept over us. I cared for nothing but their fulfillment. We knew the danger in which we were placing ourselves, but we persisted.

I drew him through to my bedchamber.

"Katherine," he said. "I care not what happens after."

And I answered: "Nor I."

～

It was several hours later when he left. Jane Rochford was still up. She was smiling when she came into my bedchamber. She glanced meaningfully at the bed.

"So," she said, "my lord has gone."

"We had much to discuss," I replied.

"What a handsome gentleman!" she murmured. "I doubt there is one to match him in the Court. There is no doubt of his feeling for you."

"Was it noticeable?"

She nodded, her eyes bright with mischief.

"It was a mercy," she said, "that none of the others were here. After I had brought him to you, I made a point of seeing them and telling them that you had retired. I said I would summon them if they were needed."

"Thank you, Jane."

She smiled at me conspiratorially. "Your Majesty, if the gentleman should have cause to visit you again, may I suggest that it might be more convenient to receive him in my room? It is easily reached from yours by that pair of steps and is closer to yours than any. If the need arose . . . it would be a simple matter to slip back to your own room."

I looked at her in amazement and said sharply: "He came with a special message of great urgency, Lady Rochford. It is not likely that he will come again."

She bowed her head. "A thousand pardons for my forwardness, Your Majesty. I wished you to know that, if ever you need my services, they are at your command."

"I know your good intentions, but it is unlikely that the gentleman will have cause to visit me again."

Jane bowed her head and looked humble, but her excitement outweighed her humility.

The King had rejoined us. He was in good spirits. In spite of this, he seemed very old to me. It must have been because I was comparing him with Thomas. I had not stopped thinking of Thomas since that night in Lincoln when he had come to me. How I loved Thomas! How I longed for him!

Strangely enough, I did not feel as guilty as I supposed I should. I had had no choice. I had been forced into this marriage. If I could have chosen between a comparatively humble life as Thomas's wife at Hollingbourne and my royal state, I would not have hesitated for a moment. It would have been Hollingbourne for me.

But there had been no choice, and I had done the

best I could. I had made the King happy. If it were ever known what had happened, I knew what my fate would be. Had I not seen it come to pass before? I did not really believe that my cousin had been guilty. It had never been proved. But the verdict the King wanted had been given, her fate decided; and I *was* guilty.

But who need ever know? Thomas would not tell. Nor would I.

If I had made the King happy, could I be blamed? I had certainly pleased him. I was pleasing him now. I tried even more than I had before because of what had happened. It was not in my nature to concern myself with trouble which had not yet come. I could be even more loving with Henry because I could delude myself into thinking he was Thomas; and Henry was more delighted than ever with his queen.

We arrived in York, where Henry was to meet the King of the Scots, and, to his fury, a deputation arrived from Scotland with the news that the King would be unable to keep the appointment.

Henry's rage was great. The journey had been arranged, in the first place, with the express purpose of this meeting, and now his Scottish nephew was acting in a very arrogant manner. It was most humiliating. He had a false notion of his own importance if he thought his petty little kingdom could so flout its mighty neighbour.

People were afraid to approach him. I was the only one for whom he had a gentle word; he needed a great deal of soothing, and I performed that duty admirably.

Perhaps it was inevitable that, having taken the first step, Thomas and I found the temptation to take more irresistible.

There were occasions when the King was away on state business and Thomas contrived that he stay behind, and it was only to be expected that we take advantage of this.

I realized, of course, that Jane Rochford knew what had happened in Lincoln, and there was no sense in trying to hide it—particularly as I needed her help.

Jane was very sympathetic.

"Indeed," she said. "Thomas Culpepper loves you, and there is no doubt that you love him. He is young and handsome and you were betrothed to him once."

"No Jane, I was not really. There was only talk of it."

"Well, there would have been a betrothal. I can see no harm . . . as long as no one knows." Her eyes sparkled. "Now we shall have to go carefully. We do not want any of the women prying. And why should they? If we are careful, we shall outwit them. If you use my room, I shall remain in yours. If by any chance one of them should come to your chamber, I would be there and should be able to hold them off until I could reasonably bring you back to your chamber."

"Do you think that could be done satisfactorily?"

"Your Majesty, we will make it so. It is a good plan. I will take a message to Master Culpepper. I will tell him how he can come up the back stairs where I shall be waiting for him. I shall bring him to you and there shall be none to see him but ourselves."

We were excited by the plan. I was sure Thomas was too, and once it had been put to us, we would be ready to incur any risk, so anxious were we to be together.

Jane was such a ready conspirator, as anxious—or almost—to bring about the meetings as we were. It was the sort of adventure she loved to take part in.

I remember one occasion well. We were at Lincoln again, and the King was riding off to a nearby meeting at the house of one of his loyal friends some distance away, so that he would spend two nights there. For the first night the plan worked, but on the second, as I was going up to Jane Rochford's room, two of the ladies-in-waiting came unexpectedly to my room. They were Katherine Tylney and another, called Margaret Morton.

They looked surprised, and I felt it would be wise to give them some explanation. I told them I was going to Lady Rochford. I should have dismissed them, but I hesitated and they came with me to Jane's room.

Jane looked amazed to see them, but she could say nothing, and I knew that she was uneasy, for she was about to go and meet Thomas to bring him up to me.

She was flashing a signal to me to get rid of the women, so I told them that I should not need any of them as I was not quite ready to retire and just wished to have a little private conversation with Lady Rochford before doing so.

They immediately retired but probably thought it rather strange.

When they left, Jane laughed.

"I feared Your Majesty would keep them here to meet the gallant gentleman," she said.

It seemed rather amusing, although it had given me an uneasy moment. I am afraid I was not good at thinking quickly in such a dilemma. But when Thomas arrived, the little mishap was quickly forgotten.

The next night that the King was absent, I made sure the ladies were dismissed early.

Despair

It was October before we arrived at Windsor, and at the end of that month we were back at Hampton Court. Henry expressed his great pleasure in being in one of his favourite palaces.

"It was tiresome that His Majesty of Scotland should have seen fit to disappoint us," he said. "But, I promise, he shall be the one to feel that disappointment and learn that he should have given a little thought to the matter before behaving in such a fashion. The rest was well enough. I'll swear that there were many who were inclined to play the rebel who will think now very seriously before they attempt it. And here I am, back in Hampton Court with my sweet young wife. At least I am blessed in her."

It was at such moments that I experienced a twinge of conscience. But all would be well, I assured myself.

Thomas and I would be very careful, and in fact I made a special effort to be even more loving towards the King—if that were possible. It was no use being remorseful. I could not have resisted Thomas however much I had tried. I now felt that, from the first moment I had met him when we were children, we were meant for each other.

On the day of our arrival, the King and I received the sacrament together, and there was one moment when I was deeply moved. It was while the King knelt at the altar, and, folding his hands together as though in prayer, he lifted his eyes and said with great feeling: "I render thanks to Heaven and to Thee, oh Lord, that, after I have suffered so much tribulation in my marriages, Thou has seen fit to give me a wife so entirely conformed to my inclinations as her I have now."

There were tears in my eyes. I had made him happy. No one could blame me if I had stolen a little happiness for myself.

As we were leaving the chapel, Henry called to the Bishop of Lincoln, who was his confessor.

"You heard my words at the altar, Bishop," he said.

"I did, Sire," replied the Bishop. "You are indeed blessed in the Queen, and she in you."

"That is true, and the whole country should thank God with us. I would have a public service of thanksgiving, which the Queen and I shall attend."

"I am sure the people will rejoice in Your Majesty's good fortune. The happiness of the King is that of the entire country."

"Pray acquaint Archbishop Cranmer of my wishes."

"I will do so without delay, Your Majesty."

That service never took place, because on the morning following that when the King made his declaration at the altar the Archbishop handed him a piece of paper with the request that he would take it to his private closet and read it . . . alone.

I did not see the King once during the next day, which surprised me. I had expected to hear of the thanksgiving service that was to be arranged.

Another day passed. I heard he was not in the palace and I thought it strange that he had left without advising me of his going. I presumed it was some important business which had demanded immediate attention. It was, of course, but I did not know of what nature.

For the next few days the King did not return and I was surprised when Lady Margaret Douglas told me that a Council of the King's ministers had arrived at the palace and was demanding it should see me.

It was customary for people to request an audience, and I was surprised that they should express themselves in such an authoritative manner.

I was more than surprised, and decidedly startled, to be confronted by such important men as the Archbishop of Canterbury, Bishop Gardiner, the Duke of Sussex and, to my extreme discomfiture, my uncle, the Duke of Norfolk.

They showed none of the respect to which I had grown accustomed, but surveyed me with expressions of great severity.

Then the horror of the visit dawned on me when the Archbishop solemnly informed me that I was accused of having lived an immoral life before I had led the King, by word and gesture, to love me. I was guilty of treason.

I could only stare at them in blank dismay. I was numb with fear. I began to cry out: "No . . . no . . . I am innocent!"

They continued to regard me sombrely and I saw the contempt in my uncle's face. I was terribly afraid then. I could think only of my cousin, laying her head on the block, and that a similar fate awaited me.

I went on screaming: "No . . . no!"

The Archbishop was reading out the sins I had committed.

They knew about Derham. I was finished. It was the end. It had caught up with me. I had refused to see it coming until it was right upon me. They would cut off my head, as they had my cousin's.

I fell into a frenzy, crying, laughing until I fell down in a faint.

When I opened my eyes they had gone. It was not true, I told myself. It was a hideous dream. Jane Rochford told me afterwards that they thought I should lose my reason. She said I kept sobbing and calling out that it was not true. She sat with me all through that night, she said, although I was unaware of her. I kept shouting that the axe was not sharp enough. It would be with me as it had been with Lady Salisbury. I must have a sword from France, as my cousin had had. But I would not die yet, I was too young. I wanted to go away . . . right away . . . and never see the Court again. I had never wanted to be here.

"You were indeed near madness," said Jane.

On the morning of the next day, Archbishop Cranmer came to see me again. He seemed less terrifying than on the previous day. But perhaps that was because he came alone.

He made me be seated, and he said quietly, almost gently, with a show of pity: "You must calm yourself. You do no good with these frenzies. The King will be merciful to you if you confess your sins."

Of course he would be merciful. He loved me tenderly. The last time I had seen him, he had been going to arrange a thanksgiving to God for having given me to him. He was grateful for all the happiness I had brought him. It was those accusing men who had frightened me. The King would be kind, as he had always been. I would explain to him. I would tell him that I wanted to confess, and then all would be well. I was young and I was ignorant. I had been left to those wanton men and women. He would understand. I felt better.

The Archbishop said: "You must confess what you have done. If you insist on your innocence, it will go ill with you. We have proof of your behaviour. I must tell you that we know all. It is true, is it not, that you were not a virgin when you came to the King? You have behaved in a licentious manner with a certain Francis Derham and Henry Manox. Do not attempt to deny it if you would have the King's mercy."

I tried to make my voice steady.

"I was very young," I said. "I knew little of the ways of the world. I believed myself betrothed to Francis Derham and that that meant we could behave as husband and wife."

"So you admit this?"

"With Francis Derham, yes."

"And Henry Manox?"

"No."

"But you have behaved in a wanton manner with him."

"It was different. I was very young . . ."

"It is enough," said the Archbishop.

"What will happen to me?"

"You know the law."

I began to shiver. I saw myself there. Did they blindfold you that you might not see the block? Did they lead you there and help you lay your head on it? How long before the axe descended?

I began to cry and hardly recognized my own voice, shrill and uncontrollable.

"You must not go into another frenzy," advised the Archbishop. "You must tell me all. It is the only way to save yourself."

I thought: What will they do to Derham and Manox? And then, in horror, I thought of Thomas. They had not mentioned him yet. Oh, God, help me, I prayed. They must not know. I remembered those nights we had spent together such a short time ago. Derham was before my marriage. That might possibly be forgivable. But Thomas . . . oh, there was real danger there, from which we could never escape.

They must not know. Whatever happened, I must save Thomas.

I told them about Derham . . . all that I could remember. I had to stop them thinking of Thomas.

Cranmer seemed content to keep to Derham. I could see what it meant. It was that matter of divorce. My spirits rose. The King would divorce me so that he might marry again. It would be as it had been with my immediate predecessor. She was happy enough now. Why should I not get through to the same contentment . . . with Thomas?

"There was no contract with Derham," the Archbishop was saying.

"No," I replied. "There was no contract."

"But carnal knowledge," said the Archbishop.

~

I cannot recall exactly how everything happened. I had just been overwhelmed by a nightmare, from which there was no awakening. Events which followed now seem jumbled together. I had said this. I had done that. The brief calm which had come to me when the Archbishop had hinted that there was a possibility that I could receive mercy did not stay with me long, and it is only now, when I have moments of acceptance of my fate, that I can see how events fitted themselves together and brought me to where I am now.

If I had been a clever person, I should have seen it approaching long before it reached me. But I had never been shrewd and was particularly gullible. Simple myself, I judged others to be the same. I had not realized how I was watched and despised because I was unfit to fill the role which had been thrust upon me. People do not like to see those whom they consider below them raised above them; and they seek to bring the offender down. They were angry because of the King's besotted devotion to this foolish girl, just because she had a pretty face, a seductive body and a sensual nature. Power-hungry men felt she might have some influence, which her ambitious relations might use to their advantage. And carefree, ignorant and unworldly as I was, I did not know that they were watching me, waiting for an opportunity to destroy me.

The Protestant faction, comprised of men like Cranmer and the King's brother-in-law, Edward Seymour, Earl of Hertford, were suspicious of the

Catholic Howards. As for my uncle, he might have warned me, helped me, at least prepared me in some way, but he had abandoned me as being too foolish to be of any use, and so he had ignored me. And thus I was left to those who would destroy me.

In my very household were Joan Bulmer and Katherine Tylney, and both were fully aware of my relationship with Francis Derham. How foolish I had been to allow them in. When I had been confronted by those men, I had realized at once what would happen to me, and the shock was so great that, as Jane said, it had almost robbed me of my reason; and it is only at this stage, by piecing together what I have heard and experienced, that I can see how it was all brought to a head, to that terrifying moment when they had all come to tell me of my fate.

It had started through John Lassells, who was the brother of Mary Lassells, one of the women who was with me in my grandmother's house at Lambeth. She, like so many others, knew what had happened between Francis Derham and me.

John Lassells had some minor post at Court. He was a stern Protestant, a puritan, one of those men who are bent on preserving a place for themselves in Heaven and are certain that they are one of the few who know the way to achieve it. They are determined not to enjoy life and, even more so, that no one else shall.

His sister, Mary, needed to work, and he asked her why did she not try for a place at Court. Had she not once been acquainted with me when I was in a far less exalted position—just a young girl in the care of my grandmother?

Mary, in a state of great virtue, explained that nothing would induce her to take a place in my service. In fact, she was very sorry for me. Naturally her brother wished to know why.

"Because she is light in her behaviour," was Mary's reply.

Such an accusation needed explanation, and John demanded one. I felt sure that Mary gave it with relish. She told her brother that Francis Derham had declared we were as good as married and behaved accordingly. Moreover, she added, Henry Manox had boasted that he knew of a private mark on my body.

The righteous John Lassells would have immediately persuaded himself that this knowledge must not remain solely in the Lassells' household, and he went to his priest and told him what he had heard. The priest immediately communicated the information to Audley and Hertford. This must have seemed a heaven-sent opportunity to these men, who decided to lay the information before Archbishop Cranmer, with the suggestion that he should be the one to pass it on to the King.

As a result, John Lassells was brought to the Archbishop and a paper was produced and presented to the King for his private reading.

I tried to imagine what Henry would have said when he received this incriminating document. I believed it was true that he had been deeply shocked and refused to believe it, and that he had berated the Archbishop for daring to write such slander against his queen. I believed he would, in his love for me, have accused the Archbishop of listening to the evil slander of rogues.

But, of course, doubts would beset him. It was only natural that they should. He might recall that I was no shrinking bride. I had thought then that my ready responses had surprised him, even though he was delighted with them. He must have convinced himself that they were due to my admiration for the glorious personage who had become my husband. After all, I had been raised up from a very lowly position.

So, when he read that account of my past, brought to him through the courtesy of the Archbishop and John and Mary Lassells, he might not believe it, but he would have to make sure.

I could see clearly how it had happened. He had ordered that John and Mary Lassells be held in London, and Sir Thomas Wriothesley be sent to question me.

Almost immediately, Derham was arrested, not in connection with me, but on a charge of piracy committed in Ireland. I suppose there were grounds for this, and I wondered whether the fortune of which he had talked so much was to be acquired in this way.

At this time, I was in a sorry state. I was kept confined to my apartments where I alternated between fits of terror, anguish and moods of optimism. These last were very brief, for I could not really believe in them. I had been very indiscreet with Derham, but that was before my marriage. That was not really criminal, was it? I had deceived no one. Most of the women knew what was happening.

I tried to shut out of my mind all thoughts about Thomas. Thomas must never be mentioned. It must seem as though I knew him only as some vague figure in the King's household.

If only I could get to the King, talk to him! I promised myself that I would find some way of doing this. I would explain to him those misdemeanours of the days before I had married him. I would remind him how young I had been. I would explain how I had wanted to confess everything right from the beginning.

I saw very little of my ladies with the exception of Jane Rochford. She kept me from sinking into utter melancholy.

I was afraid to sleep, for sometimes dreams could be more frightening than reality. When I was awake I could persuade myself that the King would come to see me soon. I could imagine myself sitting on his knee, cajoling. I believed he must be hating this situation as much as I was. He would want to return to those comforting pleasures of the old days. I would force myself to picture the reconciliation. I would plan what I would say. I would delude myself into believing that it was real. And then I would see the utter absurdity of it and be plunged into despair.

Jane told me what had happened to my grandmother, which added to my misery.

"Poor lady! It all happened under her roof. They have visited her."

"Who?"

"Those who came to you—the Duke, her stepson, among them. She knew they would come. Derham had left some coffers in her house and she was afraid they might find in them something concerning you . . . letters or goods. She had the coffers opened. That is against her. And there was Damport. Do you remember Damport?"

"No."

"He was a close friend of Derham's."

"Was he the young man with the beautiful teeth?"

"That is he." Everyone knew Damport by his teeth. He was very proud of them and he smiled perpetually so that everyone could see them.

"Yes, I do remember now. I have seen him with Derham."

"The Duchess gave him money."

"Why?"

"Mayhap because she thought he might tell something which Derham had confided in him."

"Tell me what you know about my grandmother."

"It is only a rumour, but everyone is talking of it. They are amazed that the Duke should work against his own family. Some say he aims to show the King that he is his most loyal servant . . . even if it means working against his own flesh and blood."

"He does not care for any but himself, I believe."

Jane nodded. "Your uncle Lord William Howard has been arrested with his wife . . . and . . . I know how you will feel about this . . . and I hesitated before telling you . . . but the Duchess, she too has been arrested. She is in the Tower."

"Oh no! That cannot be. Not the Duchess . . . oh, my poor, poor grandmother. And why Lord William?"

"Mayhap because he was at the Duchess's house often when you were there. They are saying that he could not be unaware of what was going on . . . as the Duchess could not have been."

"I cannot bear this. It is too much."

"I can but tell you what I heard. It could be that it is only gossip."

"I fear this is true. And Norfolk does nothing to help them."

"All he does is hold up his hands in horror and distance himself from those who are in deep trouble."

"My poor grandmother. She is old . . . she will die."

"They say she is frantic with fear. She talked of the old Countess of Salisbury. She believes that what happened to the Countess will happen to her."

"Oh, Jane, what will happen to us all?"

Jane could not answer that. There was fear in her own eyes. How far was she involved? They had arrested my grandmother and Damport. What of Jane Rochford?

There were some matters of which even she could not trust herself to speak. Thomas! That had happened after the marriage. That was the greatest sin of all. For that there could be no excuses.

We were both caught up in a terrible fear.

∾

Derham was brave. They put him to the torture. They would be ruthless, I knew. The torture would not stop until they had the answers they wanted.

He had told the truth. He had admitted that he and I had regarded ourselves as husband and wife, and that we had lived as such. What they wanted him to admit also was that our relationship had been continued after the marriage.

Derham was indeed a brave man. He had lived an adventurous life. He would be fully aware that these men were bent on destroying me and wanted to bring a charge of treason against me.

Treason! I thought. Little Katherine Howard, who knew nothing of such things—a traitor! If I had been unfaithful to the King and there was a child, that child could be heir to the throne. It was the first time this thought had occurred to me.

I was horrified. I thought of those meetings with Thomas. What had I done?

This was the unforgivable crime. This was indeed treason.

I had not thought of it in that connection before. When did I ever think before I acted? Thomas had not thought either. Our emotions were too strong for us.

Of one thing I was more certain than ever: No one must ever know what happened during those nights on that journey. And now they were trying to force Derham to confess.

The rack was one of the most excruciating instruments ever devised by man; and Derham was its victim. He was in the hands of ruthless men who cared nothing for human suffering, human dignity and human life. All they wanted was to gain their own ends. What were they doing to Derham? He was jaunty, carefree, a pirate who had loved me. He still loved me. But surely even he could not stand out against the torture of the rack.

But when they took his poor broken body from that cruel instrument, he had said no more than that he had already told them. He regarded me as his wife and had acted accordingly. After he had returned from Ireland and I was the King's wife, there had been no communication between us other than that which involved his work.

Damport was less brave. I saw him as a victim caught up with something with which he was not in any way concerned. He had merely had the misfortune to be a close friend of Derham. All they wanted him to do was betray some confidence which Derham had given him. I was sure there was nothing to betray, for Derham would only tell him what he had already confessed. Derham did not tell lies.

Damport thought he was safe. He had done nothing wrong. But they insisted that there must be something Derham had confided in him, and if he would not tell them willingly, they must force him to do so.

I wondered what the poor young man felt when he heard those sinister words. They had noticed his beautiful teeth, and he had betrayed his pride in them.

He had remarkable teeth, they told him. He was naturally very proud of them. It would be a pity if anything happened to spoil them. Now they must ask him what it was that Derham had confided in him.

There was nothing, he insisted.

Did not Derham say that the King was an old man and, when he died, he, Derham, would marry Katherine Howard?

No, Derham had said no such thing. Would he think again? It was very important. Derham *had* said that, had he not? No, no. I could imagine his voice—high-pitched, insistent—Damport would not lie on such a matter.

I could picture those cruel men admiring his teeth. Such a great pity. How often did one see such teeth?

I was horrified when I heard what they did to Damport. They took out those beautiful teeth with an ugly instrument and reduced his mouth to a bleeding mass.

I could imagine his agony.

"Yes, yes!" he cried. "He said that to me. When the King, who was an old man, died, he would marry Katherine Howard."

It was too late. He had lied to them for no purpose. And it had not saved his beautiful teeth—for they were already ruined.

They had taken Manox too. Merely a humble musician, he had not been seen in my presence since he arrived at Court. He immediately admitted to a certain intimacy a long time ago. There was no evidence that he had even spoken to me since.

He was not a man of good character. They questioned him and did not feel that it was necessary to apply the torture.

All their hopes were fixed on Derham.

~

My Uncle Norfolk came to see me. My hopes rose slightly. It was true I had known little kindness from the Duke, but I deluded myself into thinking that he might help me—for he was, after all, my uncle. I was of his blood. He must in all reasonableness do what he could to save me. He had some influence with the King. He was one of the foremost men in the land. I was in such an abject state of misery that I clung to any hope.

That was soon dispelled when he stood regarding me with scorn and obvious dislike. There was no trace of pity.

He began by upbraiding me.

"You wicked creature! Do you realize how the King is suffering because of your lewd conduct?"

I began to stammer that I knew he would be

grieved, and I was sorry for it. I had wanted to tell the King what had happened right at the beginning, but had been prevented from doing so.

He waved an impatient hand.

"Have done with your babbling. You have brought shame on your family. You have disgraced us all. A curse on the day you were born."

"Please . . . please," I cried, feeling the hysteria rising within me. "I am sorry . . . I am . . ."

"Sorry! You will be sorry, without doubt. The King is sunk deep in sorrow. He gave you much and how did you repay him?"

"I did all I could to please him."

"God help me to endure this," he murmured. "You graceless girl! The King wept . . . wept indeed . . . tears of anguish . . . when he heard the truth. He says he will never marry again. You are a wicked, lewd girl . . . to have brought him to this. You are a disgrace to your family."

I was feeling angry now. It helped soothe my wretchedness a little. I whipped it up, for I did not want to break into one of those fits of madness which had beset me since I had feared what my fate would be; and because I was as terrified of living as much as dying, I did not know which way to turn. I was like a trapped animal. I was a fool to have thought that Norfolk would have brought a spark of hope to my desperate plight. So I fanned my anger against him.

I cried: "Should you condemn the rest of us?"

He stared at me. "What mean you, insolent girl?"

"I am aware of your friendship with your laundress. Can you really be so very shocked by me?"

He stared at me, and I was pleased to see he was taken aback.

He stammered slightly: "I am not the wife of the King."

I laughed sardonically.

"Pray do not seek with insolence to excuse your loathsome faults."

"You can add hypocrisy to yours, my lord."

I thought he was going to strike me, for he came towards me, hand raised. But doubtless he thought I was a pitiful creature, not worth his venom.

"I'll have none of your insolence," he said. "Do not attempt to prattle of what is beyond your understanding."

"That is not beyond my understanding. It is, after all, a simple enough matter. I may be a foolish girl, but you, a man of rank and mature age, are an adulterer."

His face was suffused with purple colour. I did not care. I was too much afraid of death to be afraid of him; and I knew by now that he would have done nothing to help me. Indeed, he was on the side of those who would destroy me.

I said: "Then does it depend on who commits the act whether it is a sin or not? What of the King himself? The Duke of Richmond was his natural son."

"Be silent! Do not add idiocy to your immorality. If you talk thus, there will be short shrift for you. I told you that when the King heard of your conduct, he wept . . . yes, bitter tears. Think what a future you could have had. The King believed in you. You deceived him completely."

"I did not. I did not. I was myself . . . all the time."

"You . . . a low wanton, sporting with a servant!"

"A higher rank than a laundress, and he is a Howard."

He glared at me, ignoring the reference to his Bess Holland.

Then he said: "There are more than one claiming the name who are unworthy to do so. Your grandmother, the Dowager Duchess, has with her son behaved in a most unseemly manner. What a sad day for the family when they joined it. You have spurned my help, as has your grandmother. She is a foolish old woman. She is in the Tower now and this could cost her her head."

"Oh no. She has done nothing . . . nothing."

"She is a traitor. She knew of this . . . this intrigue between you and Derham and she accepted it. She allowed you to marry the King, when she knew full well that you were unworthy to do so."

I was silent. It was true, in a way. She had known what had taken place between Derham and me. She had not allowed me to mention it. Then she had shown her guilt by opening Derham's coffers, for fear something incriminating might be found there. She had given Damport money to persuade him not to reveal anything he might know against Derham. I could see that she had behaved in a very guilty manner. But she was old and tired and frightened. And the Duke would do nothing to help her—any more than he would for me. He would show himself to be against us more vehemently, in order to ingratiate himself with the King.

I could see that he was indeed our enemy.

There was only one who would help me, and that was the King himself.

I cried out: "I will speak to the King. I can explain to him. He will understand. He will listen to me. He will not be cruel . . . as you are."

"You talk like a fool. Do you think the King will see you now that he knows you for the slut you are?"

"He will . . . he will. I know he will."

"You have done enough harm already. Why am I plagued with such a family? And you are worse than any. To think that you are a niece of mine! There was that other niece. You know what happened to her, do you not? And here you are, proving to be such another. Your Uncle William and his wife! We have always been a great family . . . and these intruders!"

I wanted to tell him that the family had not always held high honours, even before his father married a second wife, who was his own stepmother. I felt wretched, thinking of her in that cold prison—she who had always felt the cold so keenly, and now she was old, infirm and very, very worried.

I wanted to shout at him, to tell him how heartless he was, how he cared only for himself, but what was the use? I was terrified that I would fall into one of my wild moods, when I became hysterical and in an even worse state than I was now.

I was greatly relieved when he went. He left me with a firm resolve. I had been right when I had said I must see the King.

I must. He was the only one who could save me. A word from him and everything would be well. I believed he would help me, if I could only talk to him.

～

I was obsessed with one thought. I had to find a way of seeing the King. I realized that no one would help me reach him. I had to find my own way to him. I would kneel to him. I would beg. Did I not know how to enchant him? I would appeal to him, remind him of what we had been to each other. Had he not said he had never had such pleasure in a woman as he had had in me?

I knew how to cajole and caress. I knew what pleased him. I would enchant him again, just as I had when we were first married.

I could do it. I knew it. The most difficult part was to reach him.

Although I did not see most of my ladies-in-waiting now, and Jane was the only one who talked with me, they were still in the household. They must not know what I intended to do.

Jane had said: "You know the King still loves you. They say he is very melancholy. He does not take pleasure in his food, as was his wont. They are saying he would have you back if it were not for his ministers. That is what he really wants."

"I'm sure . . . if I could only speak with him . . ."

"They have sent messengers to France informing King Francis of all that has happened, and Francis has sent his condolences and sympathy. If only they had not done that."

"What then?" I asked eagerly.

"The King would not want King Francis to think

that the King of England could keep a wife who behaved as they say you have and then mildly forgive her. That is why they sent those messages to France, before the King could make some excuse for having you back."

"Oh, no . . . no," I said.

"But yes. It would destroy the King's dignity . . . his standing. It would show him to be too dependent on you. Oh, they have made it difficult for him, but the fact that he wants you back should put heart into you."

"It does. It does indeed, for, if he wants to . . . surely he will."

"Well, you see, these people who are responsible for putting you where you are now . . . well, it would go ill with them if you were taken back to favour. They would think you would have your revenge."

"Oh, I would not. I would not. I would be only too happy to forget."

"Poor Derham. He will never be the same again. He is destroyed. Innocent Damport . . . you see, you could not forget."

"Oh yes, poor Derham. He was so handsome. Oh, Jane, what can he be like now?"

"It is for you to think of getting back. If the King

loves you enough . . . it could be so. They are saying he is more unhappy now than when he was ridding himself of Anne Boleyn, and that his feelings were no stronger for her than they were for you . . . in the beginning."

"Oh, Jane, if only I could speak to him."

"If the opportunity should come, you must be ready."

"I swear I will, Jane. I swear it."

I looked for it. I waited for it, and it came at length.

The King was at Hampton Court. My spirits rose at the thought of that. If it were going to happen, it would be now.

I realized that, although I was not in a cell, I was to a certain extent a prisoner.

My ladies were there, as they had been, although apart. They were, in a sense, my jailers. I had never attempted to break free from them, having no inclination to walk out. I could not face anyone at Court in my present situation. I was in no mood or any state to do so. All I wanted was to hide myself.

But now I must leave my apartments and get to that section of the palace where the King might be. I knew at what hour he would be attending mass in the chapel, where I had often been with him. If I could reach him while he was there, I could be certain of seeing him, and that was what I proposed to do. To reach the chapel, I must traverse the long gallery which led to it, and this entailed descending the back stairs from my apartment before I came to the gallery; then I could hurry along it to the chapel.

I had only a vague idea how I should act when I saw Henry. My hair was flowing about my shoulders in the style he most liked. I would throw myself at his knees and I would sob out my misery. I should tell him that I only wished to live if he and I could be happy again as we had been when we were first married.

I pictured him as I had seen him so many times, his face creasing into tenderness, the slackness of his mouth, which could look so cruel and yet be gentle for me; I could see the tears of sentiment in the little eyes. I knew exactly how to make him look like that, and all I needed was to be with him.

I left my bedchamber and went quietly to the

adjoining room. There was no one there. Cautiously I opened the door which led to the ladies' quarters. I paused and listened. I heard the sound of voices. Some of them were there.

I hesitated. Jane had said that they would try to prevent my leaving. I dared not wait too long or mass would be over and the King gone. I should have to chance being seen. In any case, who were they to prevent my going where I wished? I was not their prisoner . . . or was I?

I glanced into the room. A group of them were seated at the far end. I did not have to pass them—just slip quietly to a door and out to the stairs.

I was halfway to it when one of the ladies looked up. She exclaimed with surprise and stood up. I saw that it was Margaret Morton.

"Your Majesty . . ." she began, but I took no notice and sped towards the door.

They were all on their feet now.

"Your Majesty, what is it you require?"

I did not answer. I was through the door and starting down the stairs.

"Your Majesty! Your Majesty!" They were coming

after me. I knew they would try to stop my reaching the King, as Jane had warned me they would. I felt the hysteria rising in me. I must see him. I must. Everything depended on it. They were close to me now . . . not just one of them, but at least half a dozen.

"Where are you going?" I thought that was Katherine Tylney.

"Your Majesty! Come back. We are here to serve you."

I thought: You are here to prevent my reaching the King.

I was in the gallery now. I ran as fast as I could. I was breathless . . . and they were very close to me. One of them reached out and caught my gown. I snatched it away. I had reached the chapel, but they were surrounding me.

I saw Katherine Tylney, Margaret Morton and Joan Bulmer among them. There was fear on their faces. They were as determined not to allow me to see the King as I was to see him. But I was one and they were so many.

They were all round me. They laid their hands on me.

"Leave me," I commanded. "Leave me."

They did not answer. They looked sly and triumphant as they pulled me away from the chapel door.

"Take your hands from me," I cried.

"Your Majesty is unwell. We are going to look after you. Come . . . let us take you back to your apartment."

I kept crying out to them to leave me, to take their hands from me, but they dragged me away, nearer and nearer to the stairs. I was sobbing, cursing them, screaming with fury. Perhaps he would hear. But perhaps he did not *want* to hear. I must make him look at me. Only my presence could do that.

I could hear that wild hysterical voice, and realized it was my own. I was bereft of all hope as they dragged me up the stairs. I was back in my chamber . . . in prison. I could hear them talking of me.

The Queen had had another of her mad turns.

I lay still while the wildness passed away. I felt limp, exhausted, saying to myself, I can never escape. It is coming to me as surely as it came to my cousin.

I was sunk in utter melancholy and despair.

The Journey to the Tower

It was a few days later that I heard I was to leave
Hampton Court for Syon House.

Jane Rochford said that this might be a good
omen. It meant that there were people who would be
uneasy about my seeing the King. They had prevented
me on one occasion, but what if I should succeed?
What if he were to decide to take me back, as many
people thought he might be inclined to do? How
would all those who had worked against me fare then?

It was the sort of theory one welcomed when one
was feeling desperate. I forgot that Jane was one who
liked to build up a dramatic situation, to have a plan
and attempt to discover devious ways of putting it
into practice.

Common sense told me that, if the King really
wanted me back, he would soon find some means of

getting me. But in my present desperate state, it was comforting to grasp at any hope.

Jane was with me at Syon, a house on the north bank of the Thames near Richmond. It had been a nunnery suppressed by Henry in 1532, when the house had passed to the Crown.

How different it was from Hampton Court! Here indeed I felt a prisoner.

Perhaps I was thinking of poor Lady Margaret Douglas, who had recently been held here under restraint and had been sent away to Kenninghall to make way for me.

Margaret, too, seemed a person destined to fall in love with the wrong people. Perhaps she and I shared a weakness in that way. She had been in the Tower before on account of her attachment to my uncle, Lord Thomas Howard. She had been released from there to be sent to Syon House; then her lover had died and she was freed. Now she was in disgrace again, because of a liaison with another member of my family. This time it was my brother Charles, and she found herself a prisoner in Syon House until my coming, when she was moved to another place of confinement.

Poor Lady Margaret! She must often wish she had not been born royal. It seemed unfair that she should be imprisoned for falling in love and wanting to marry the brother of the woman the King had chosen for his queen. If Lady Margaret could not expect reasonable consideration, could I?

It was at Syon House that I heard the most alarming news of all. Jane brought it to me. It was the first time since the disaster that I had seen Jane so anxious.

She gasped: "Thomas Culpepper has been arrested."

I thought I was going to faint. This was indeed disaster. I had hoped by some means to get word to him, to beg him to slip out of the country—but I had been unable to do so.

"What does it mean?" I asked Jane.

"That someone has betrayed him."

"Who? Who?"

"It must be one of the women . . . those who were with us during the journey, the ladies of the bedchamber."

"So they knew!"

"They cannot be sure, but they will know that he came to your bedchamber by night, maybe."

I covered my face with my hands. I wanted to shut out everything . . . the memory of my cousin . . . the terrible fate which could befall us. We had been in acute danger before, but now there was no hope. If the King knew that I had been unfaithful to him, that would be the end . . . the end of Thomas and of me. He might forgive what had happened before our marriage, but never what had happened after.

A terrible understanding came to me. What if, during those nights, I had conceived a child? Yes, indeed, I was guilty of treason.

What had these women known? What had they seen? With all this talk about the lewd life I had led before my marriage, they would be ready to believe the worst.

Would they question Thomas? Without a doubt they would. Would they do to him what they had done to Derham . . . and Damport? No, I could not endure that. His beautiful body, to be broken on the rack . . . as Derham's had been.

I did not know what to do, which way to turn. This was the worst thing that had happened. I could not bear to think of Thomas in the hands of those cruel men. Oh, why had he not left the country? Why had he not seen what was coming? He should have been aware of what was coming . . . more so than I. Oh, why had he stayed to meet this cruel fate?

There was no comfort anywhere. Even Jane had changed. I had never seen her like this before. Gone was the plotter, the schemer, the one who revelled in drama. Whichever way she turned, she saw herself at the centre of the tragedy.

Who was it who had arranged the meeting with Thomas Culpepper, who had cleared the way, kept the women out of sight, as far as possible? Who had connived and contrived? Jane, of course.

She was caught up in this, guilty of making the way easy for the Queen, which was an act of treachery towards the King—one which might involve the future heir to the throne.

Jane was with me in this trouble.

I saw the terror in her eyes. She could not comfort me, because she could not comfort herself.

We sat side by side, staring ahead of us. If this were proved against us, it would be the end of me . . . and possibly Jane, too.

~

We waited for news.

They would put him on the rack, as they had poor Derham. Would he tell of those nights when the King had been absent and we had given ourselves up to our passion? Would they force the truth from him?

It would be the end.

Jane was by turns sunk in melancholy or almost demented. She feared death greatly. Did not we all?

She said: "I think perhaps this is what I expected would happen to me one day. Ever since those two went to the block, I have been haunted by them. I mean your cousins—Anne and George. I helped them there. She was destined for the block, but George . . . oh, not George. It was cruel. It was wicked. I did not believe they were guilty . . . either of them. A charge of *that* could never have been brought against them. There will be those who say that Elizabeth is a bastard. How could that be? You only have to look at her to see who her father is. Anne had to go because she was in the way. She had no son and the King was tired of her. He wanted Jane Seymour. I am not to blame for her death. It only hurt her reputation. But George . . . my husband. I loved him, Katherine. He was the most charming man I ever knew. And they chose him for my husband. How could he have cared for me? In a way he *was* in love with his brilliant sister. Not in love perhaps, but he loved her as he loved no one else. How could he be expected to feel anything but contempt for his far-from-exciting wife?"

"Jane, he loved you as a wife."

"He loved me not at all. I might not have been there, for all he knew. I was just an encumbrance. I would be there . . . they would all be together . . . they and their clever friends. People like Thomas Wyatt. He was in love with her, like all the rest. Lucky Wyatt. He managed to escape the axe. Norris . . . Weston . . . they were not so fortunate. They were all round her. Poetry . . . music . . . all with which I could not compete. And then I had my revenge, did I not? I was the only one who laughed in the end. I envied her so much, and it was all because of George."

"It is all over, Jane. You distress yourself unnecessarily. There is nothing you can do about it now."

"But it is there! It has been there ever since that

May Day of 1536. Five years . . . more than that. It has haunted me. And now, here it is, as I feared it would come. It was my evidence that set the case against George in motion. The King was jealous of that feeling between Anne and her brother. He was only too ready to believe anything against them." She laughed mirthlessly. "How reckless I am becoming, to say these things which I have kept hidden all these years! But what does it matter now? It was my evidence . . . false evidence . . . which cost George his life. My revenge on him for not loving me. I wanted revenge and by God's Holy Mother, when you think of their once-haughty heads rolling in the dust, you must agree, it was mine."

I tried to stop her, but she would not be silenced.

"Envy," she went on. "I envied her. There are seven deadly sins, and one of them is envy. It is the greatest of them all. I envied Anne—not her crown, but because my husband loved her far more than he ever loved me. I hated her. I wanted to see her brought low. I wanted her to be hurt in the way she had hurt me. I killed my husband. I deserve to die. And now . . . I am going to."

"No, no. Jane, they will do nothing to you."

She shook her head. "They have taken Culpepper. That means they know. They are questioning Katherine Tylney and Margaret Morton. They will know he came on those nights during the journey. They are bent on betraying us all."

"But not you, Jane!"

"I was there, was I not? I arranged it. Oh, what fools we have been! Why do we not think of these things before we do them?"

"Jane, Jane, be calm!"

"I am afraid of death. I have too many sins on my conscience. George comes to me in my dreams, and I see him laying his head on the block. He lifts his head then and he looks at me. He says: 'Jane, why did you do this to me? You knew it was false. I loved my sister, yes. She was the most interesting and exciting person I ever met, but there was no incest and you knew it. Why did you do this to me?' then I say to myself: 'Why did I? I did it to revenge myself because you could not love me as you loved your sister. You could not love me as I loved you.'"

Then she was sobbing wildly.

And the next day she was taken from Syon House for questioning.

～

I do not remember how I lived through those next days. I raged against the Almighty, and then I pleaded with him. How could this terrible fate have befallen me? They were going to cut off my head. It had happened to many before, and now it was my turn.

There were times when I cried out to Heaven to give me another chance. I would go into a nunnery. I would devote myself to God's work. I would do anything . . . suffer any hardship, if only I could keep my life. I longed for the hours when I could sleep, but then I was tormented by dreams. I longed for unconsciousness, that blissful unawareness into which, from sheer exhaustion, I would now and then sink. And all the time I was tortured by thoughts of what was happening to Thomas.

I missed Jane. I wondered what was happening to her. They would be questioning her. Cruel men would be watching her.

There were several women to attend me now. I was so weary; unaware of them, except to notice with relief that none of those who had betrayed me were there. They had the grace to keep Joan Bulmer, Katherine Tylney and Margaret Morton away. I was avid for news of Thomas and to hear how Jane was standing up to the questioning.

I begged them to tell me what they knew. They heard scraps of gossip, of course. I think they were sorry for me. I could see the glances they exchanged, which I guessed meant that they were wondering whether a little knowledge would help me or whether it would be better to leave me in ignorance.

I humbled myself and I implored them to tell me.

They had heard that there had been an enquiry into what had happened at certain of the places we had visited during our tour of the country. Margaret Morton and Katherine Tylney had told what they had seen, heard and conjectured.

I tried to remember those nights, and all I could think of was Thomas's arms about me, his words of love and how happy we had been.

They knew that Thomas had come to my apartment

and had been there late at night. Lady Rochford had brought him in and had tried to keep his presence secret. She had obviously not been completely successful. They knew that Thomas Culpepper had stayed well into the night. I had on occasions told them I should not need their services, and that they were not to come to my bedchamber until I sent for them.

It was all as damning as it could be. Those women had watched, whispered and drawn their own conclusions.

I was nearly mad with grief when I heard that Thomas had been put on the rack. They had treated him viciously when they had tried to make him admit that I had committed adultery with him. But he denied it, even under the extremity of torture. Dear Thomas, he knew well that to have confessed would have meant death for me.

Thomas would know that right up to the time of his arrest there had been a glimmer of hope for me. It had been different with my cousin. She was utterly doomed, for the King wished to be rid of her. But he did not want to lose me. He was not tired of me. Had he not been preparing a thanksgiving service because of his satisfaction with our marriage? And when the blow had come, he had been deeply unhappy. I heard that he had called for his horse and had ridden for miles alone, so distressed was he. He had lost his desire for food; he had wept because I was not what he had believed me to be. Yes, there was a hope. But if he knew that while I was married to him I had taken a lover, his fury would be great. It was possible that he would want revenge.

In spite of Thomas's refusal to admit that he had been my lover after my marriage, he had been condemned to death, and Derham was to die with him.

It was cold December. Christmas would be with us soon. I thought sadly of other Christmases and the excitement of planning festivities. There would be no more such Christmases. Even if I were to experience more, they would be haunted by memories of those two young men.

It was a long day and there was no sleep for me during the night which followed. I could think of nothing but those two young men, lying in their cells—guilty of no crime but of loving me.

They were taken to Tyburn, there to be hanged,

cut down alive, disembowelled and their inner organs burned before their heads were cut off . . . the most agonizing departure from this life which could have been devised.

I was frantic with grief. Let them have my head if they must. *I* had been careless. *I* had been wanton. I found loving too easy. I was clever at nothing but that. Oh, if only I had known . . . if only I had been able to see into the future . . . if only I had not been the one to bring those two to this!

I was greatly relieved to hear that the sentence on Thomas had been modified. Because he had noble connections, he had been given a more dignified manner of execution and had been beheaded. Not so poor Derham. He had undergone the entire cruel sentence.

So they had died—those two men whom I had loved.

Thomas did not betray me even in the face of death. God would forgive him the lie, I knew. It was done for love and surely that cannot be a great sin in the eyes of a God who is said to be love.

They told me that before he laid his head upon the

block Thomas made a speech to the waiting crowd.

"Gentlemen," he said. "Do not seek to know more than that the King deprived me of the thing I love best in the world and, though you may kill me for it, she loves me as well as I love her, though up to this hour no wrong has passed between us. Before the King married her, I thought to make her my wife, and when she was lost to me I was like unto death. The Queen saw my sorrow and spoke kindly to me. I was tempted to beg to see her. I did. That is all, my lords, on my honour as a gentleman."

To the end his one thought had been to protect me. So, nobly he died.

Poor Derham suffered the greater torture. I rejoice that he, too, is now at rest.

~

Christmas had come and gone. The heads of Thomas Culpepper and Francis Derham were rotting on London Bridge. I saw them in my nightmares. I was a little quieter at this time. Hope came and went, but life no longer seemed desirable.

I wondered why they did not kill me. I supposed it was because the King had not chosen a new bride. He would in time, I was sure. Poor lady! The fate of Henry's queens was not a happy one. I was sorry for her, whoever she should be, and there were times when I almost longed for the day when I should go to the block.

I wondered about the experience. What did it feel like, to walk out to the Green? First there would be the summons to the Tower, and then the waiting. But perhaps not for long. Sometimes the thought came to me that the King would not let me go. I had meant too much to him. I had been the wife whom he had been waiting for. I shall never forget him as he stood at the altar, thanking God for giving me to him.

Perhaps he was waiting for a time when he could forgive me. I believed he would have done so if Katherine Tylney and Margaret Morton had not told him of Thomas's visits.

And still there was no decision. No sentence had been passed on me, though the fact that Thomas Culpepper had been executed must have meant that the charge of adultery had been accepted. There were times when I felt indifferent. Whatever happened, I could never be happy again. Always with me would be the memory of Thomas on the rack . . . taken to Tyburn, the axe descending on his once proud head.

On the tenth of February, the deputation came to take me to the Tower, and I knew then that the end was near. My heart was sick and my fears had returned during the intervening weeks since the executions of Thomas and Francis Derham, and I had sunk into such deep melancholy that I could feel nothing but intense grief. I was at least relieved that Norfolk was not amongst those who had come to take me to the Tower.

A cold wind was blowing along the river. I thought, is this the last time I shall see it? How familiar it had been during those days at Lambeth. I kept thinking back to them, of Francis giving me the French fennel and my delight with it. I thought I had loved him then. I remembered my grandmother's wrath when she had discovered what had happened. My poor grand-mother! Still a prisoner, fearful of death, as I was.

London Bridge. I glanced up and wished I had not done so. It was all over in a matter of seconds, but I had seen those grisly relics . . . those decaying heads of the men I had once loved.

We had reached the grim fortress. It loomed up before us. What despair had beset those who had entered it, as I was doing, but there could be no more deep and bitter anguish than that which assailed me now.

~

The next day I was visited by Sir John Gages, the Constable of the Tower. He told me that the King had given his consent to the Bill of Attainder. The death sentence had been pronounced on me and my paramours Francis Derham and Thomas Culpepper. That sentence had already been carried out on the two men. Mine had yet to be.

So here I was—a prisoner in the Tower. This is how it had happened to my cousin. I thought of her so often, and now here I was, living out the story for myself.

It was uncanny. There were times when I could not believe it; but now the end was near, I felt calmer than

I ever had since I had first become aware of the terrible fate which was looming before me.

I was told that Thomas Cranmer, Archbishop of Canterbury, was at the Tower and would like to speak to me.

When he was brought to me, I thought he looked very sad.

"Your Majesty," he said. "I am very concerned. You know there is a Bill of Attainder against you, and you know what this means?"

"Yes, I know," I replied. "And I have been expecting it for a long time."

He nodded. "I have come to tell you that there may be an escape from your tragic situation."

An escape? Could I be hearing correctly? What escape could there be? Was he suggesting I could step out of the Tower to where a barge would be waiting to take me away—to France perhaps? It was to France most people usually escaped. I must be dreaming. The Archbishop could not be suggesting such a wild plan.

"If you would agree that there had been a precontract between you and Francis Derham, then it could be said that you were never married to the King."

I stared at him, trying to assess the meaning of this. So, if it were agreed that there were a precontract, it would be as in the case of Catherine of Aragon. I would never have been married to him. Henry could go ahead and marry someone else when he wished. I could see it might be a way of saving my life.

There was a kindness in this Archbishop. He was trying to show me a way of escaping the axe, for, if I would not agree, there was only one way for Henry to marry again. This was my death—as in the case of my cousin.

Betrothed to Derham! It was what we had said, but there had been no betrothal. Was I going to buy a possible reprieve in such a way?

I said slowly: "My lord Archbishop, I was never betrothed to Francis Derham. It was talked of, but there was no true betrothal."

He shook his head sadly. "'Tis a pity. If it were so, there might be a way."

He was looking at me almost appealingly. He wanted me to tell him I had been betrothed.

All kinds of thoughts were rushing through my head. Did the King want it? It must be so, or it would not have been suggested. Was it because he could not bear to think of the head he had so often caressed falling to the executioner's axe?

There was another thought. Two queens beheaded in a few short years! Two divorces . . . or as good as! And the other dead in childbirth! There had once been a rumour that, at the time of Jane's death, there had been a chance to save either her life or that of the newly born Prince, and when the King had been asked to decide, he had replied that, while it was hard for him to get a son, wives were easily come by. That may not have been true, but the fact that there had been a rumour meant that the thought must have been in someone's mind. People were already whispering about the unfortunate lives of Henry's queens. Was that the reason why he was not eager to behead another of them? Would some people call it murder?

But there had been no betrothal, and I had done with lies. I did not want to live . . . without Thomas. So I said: "It is not true. I was never betrothed to Francis Derham."

"My lady, Your Majesty, I am sure that if you agreed, there might be a way out of your trials."

"There may or may not. I do not know. But I cannot say there was a betrothal between myself and Francis Derham."

He looked at me mournfully and went away.

The Last Day

I had asked that my good friend, the scribe, might come to me and that I might be alone with her. Close by, Jane Rochford was sleeping. They had given her something to quieten her, for a wild mood was on her.

She came and we talked in the way we had done while I told her the story of my life and relived all that had led me to this room in the Tower.

I said to her: "My dear friend, you have listened and you have written it down, as I could not have done. Thus I have lived it all again. This is the last time we two shall be together, for tomorrow I shall be no more.

"They have sent Jane to me. She is in the cell nearby. Tomorrow she is to lead me to the scaffold, and when they have cut off my head, they will do the same to her.

"Poor Jane! She is in a sorry state. It is the guilt, you see. Perhaps I should feel guilty, but strangely enough, I cannot. I loved too readily. There are some of us who are like that. They call it sin. Yet it was love. I loved them both. Francis cared for me. We had beautiful moments together. He went to Ireland to make a fortune, and it was all that he might marry me. His face was soft and gentle when he gave me the French fennel and other gifts. But Thomas was my true love. We would have been happy together. I even thought Manox was handsome once, and he was a beguiling musician. And the King . . . he was old and not handsome when I knew him, but he was so powerful, and power is such that it can have an effect on a woman's senses. I loved them all. I wonder who decided that love was a sin?

"But enough of this. There is little time left. This will be my last day on earth, for tomorrow I shall be with my Maker. It is strange that I can say that with a certain calm. I could not have done so two months ago.

"It all changed when Thomas and Francis died."

~

Jane came to me during the day. There was a certain madness in her eyes. She was fearful of death; she thought it was retribution for what she had done. How terrible for Jane to have that on her conscience, but it had worried her very little until she was facing death. I suppose she was thinking that it might have been so different. If George Boleyn had been her devoted husband, he would not have ended his days on the scaffold. What she had implied about the relationship between brother and sister would not have affected Anne. The King had wanted Anne out of the way so that he might marry Jane Seymour—so she was doomed.

I wondered who would be the next wife when I had gone. But there was no time to waste in such speculation.

Jane said to me, as she had said twenty times before: "I have brought myself to this end because of what I did to my husband and his sister. This is God's punishment, the vengeance of the Lord."

I thought she was going off into one of her fits of

madness, and that was when I made them take her to her cell and give her something to quieten her.

Thus I was left alone for my last talk with my friend.

That morning I had them bring the block to me. I was not sure of the procedure, for I had never seen an execution. I wanted to be sure how I had to act. I wondered if they would blindfold me and if I should have to be led.

There would be people there to see me, and I did not wish to do something unseemly. And there was something else. I wanted to be brave. I wanted to be calm. I wondered if my uncle would be there. I felt more angry against my uncle than any other. The only time he ever spoke kindly to me was when the King wanted to marry me and when I became Queen. My poor grandmother was in that fearsome place . . . sick with pain and fear. She was his stepmother. How could he care so little? His father must have loved her, and he did nothing but revile her.

I hated him. I should not do so. One must not hate people when one is about to die.

I put my hands on the block. This was where my cousin had lain her head in the last minutes of her life.

She had been brave. She would be. I hoped I could be as she had been. They told me the same block was used for the Countess of Salisbury. And now . . . it is for me.

Goodbye, my friend. Do not grieve for me when I am gone. I believe that God will judge me less harshly than my fellow men have done. He will understand that I meant no harm to any. He gave me the gift to love and it was love that destroyed me. Perhaps I shall be with Thomas, and I should be happier there, no matter where, than in any other place that could be found for me on earth.

The Scribe

The following day Katherine was taken out to the scaffold, which had been set up on Tower Green before the church of St. Peter ad Vincula.

She was calm and dignified and there was an air of resignation about her. She looked very beautiful. A small crowd of people had come to watch her die. I noticed that the Duke of Norfolk had the grace not to be among them.

She stood by the block on which, the previous day, she had lain her head in practice, and she turned to the headsman, who looked most disconcerted.

She said to him firmly: "Pray hasten in what you must do."

He knelt before her and begged her pardon.

She repeated: "It is what you must do." Then she

faced the crowd and said firmly: "I die a queen, but I would rather die the wife of Thomas Culpepper. God have mercy on my soul. Good people all, will you pray for me?"

Then she knelt and laid her lovely head upon the block and the axe descended.

~

There was a strange preoccupation throughout the country. People could not forget that this was the second queen who had been killed at the King's command, for, try as he might to hide behind the verdict of his Parliament, it was he who had signed the assent. There would be pity for the one who was chosen to be the next Queen of England.

The King might give a banquet to his Council the day after Katherine's death, and a few days later make good cheer with the ladies of the Court, but it was easy to detect that his heart was not engaged.

He looked older. He was indeed fifty years of age. It was true that during his brief marriage he had seemed younger. He had been in high spirits then; he had ridden a great deal, and his temper did not fray as easily as before. It was different now. He looked every year of his age. He was sad and deeply depressed. Katherine had given him back his youth, and now she was gone. He was listless; he had lost his desire for revenge.

The Duchess of Norfolk was released, and, with her, her son and daughter-in-law.

Perhaps the King only wanted to forget the beautiful girl who had delighted his life so briefly. Many had seen his distress on hearing of her lack of chastity; they had seen the tears he could not restrain; they suspected that, if it had been possible, he would have kept her. But he could not have sly Francis jeering at him as a cuckolded husband. There are some humiliations a king cannot endure. So it was done; she was gone; and he was a most unhappy man.

Lady Rochford was executed immediately after the Queen. She made an announcement on the scaffold to the effect that she deserved her fate because she had given false evidence against her husband and her sister-in-law. That was past history and nobody cared very much.

The question which was being asked throughout the Court was: "Who next?"

There were a number of ladies who might have been considered. A furtiveness crept into their manner. Some of them found excuses to leave Court. Few wanted to be chosen as the King's sixth wife.

The Prince of Wales was very delicate. He was surrounded by tutors and was said to be more interested in his books than in the outdoor life. His poor health caused great disquiet and there was alarm throughout the royal nurseries if he so much as caught a chill. The Lady Mary, for whom several matches were being suggested, was an unhappy lady. The Princess Elizabeth was at Hatfield and often in the company of the little Prince. She was now nine years old, with the learning of a person twice her age; she bore a striking resemblance to the King in her looks.

It was obvious that the need for a son still existed. That was why the ladies of the Court walked in fear.

And at last she appeared—this lady who was destined to be the next victim. She was gracious, elegant, intellectual, and twice widowed, having been married to men many years older than herself. She was well acquainted with all the royal children and a favourite with everyone. She was the perfect stepmother, sober, good-looking in a quiet way—in fact, everything that Katherine had not been. She was, in fact, ten years older than the late Queen.

Poor woman! I wondered what her feelings could have been? She must have been in a state of shock, for she remarked to the King when he told her she had been chosen: "It would be better to be your mistress than your wife." This, from one of the most sober and chaste of ladies, betrays the state of her fear.

Alas for her! It was not a case of choosing, but being chosen, and on the twelfth of July of the year 1543, one year and five months after Queen Katherine Howard had lost her head, the King was married to Catherine Parr.

Bibliography

Aubrey, William Hickman Smith, *The National and Domestic History of England*

Bagley, J.J., *Henry VIII*

Bigland, Eileen (ed.), *Henry VIII*

Bowle, John, *Henry VIII*

Chamberlin, Frederick, *The Private Character of Henry VIII*

Fisher, H.A.L., *Political History of England*

Froude, James Anthony, *History of England*

Hackett, Francis, *Henry VIII*

Hume, Martin, *The Wives of Henry VIII*

Lingard, John, *History of England*

Pollard, A.F., *Henry VIII*

Salzman, F., *England in Tudor Times*

Scarisbrick, J.J., *Henry VIII*

Stephen, Sir Leslie, and Lee, Sir Sidney (eds), *The Dictionary of National Biography*

Strickland, Agnes, *Lives of the Queens of England*

Trevelyan, G.M., *History of England*

Wade, John, *British History*

Passion, politics, and drama—
more great Tudor-era novels from Jean Plaidy,
also available from HarperWeekend

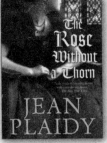
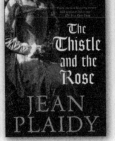